Grounding Griffin

Alicia
Happy reading!
Lucy lennox

Lucy Lennox

ISBN-13: 978-1542700030

Cover Designer: Angstyg—www.AngstyG.com
Editor: Hollie Westring—www.HollieTheEditor.com
Professional Beta Reading: Leslie Copeland
Formatting: Champagne Formats

Sign up for Lucy's newsletter for exclusive content and to learn more about her latest books at www.LucyLennox.com!

Grounding Griffin is dedicated to
my husband
who thinks my novels are menus he can order off of.
Bless his heart.

About *Grounding Griffin*

Griff: I learned early on that the easiest way to avoid a broken heart is to always be the first out the door. Caring about anyone or anything is asking to be disappointed, which is why I avoid relationships and chase freelance gigs—ghost writing restaurant reviews and penning articles about the efficacy of cheesy pickup lines—instead of chasing my dreams.

Besides, dreams don't come true for people like me. And no one, not even the sexy-as-hell bartender at the club can convince me otherwise. Because I'm never risking my heart again.

Sam: As a bartender I've watched a million pickup artists work their magic, but none as talented as Griffin Marian. He's a flirt, a good time. Hooking up with him was supposed to be just a fling. I wasn't supposed to care about his fractured past or his buried dreams. I have my own future to worry about, especially after that stupid food critic scuttled my hopes of finally opening my own restaurant.

But, the more time I spend with Griff, the more I'm beginning to realize that my plans mean nothing without him. If only I can convince him to give us a chance to follow our dreams together.

The Marian Family

Thomas and Rebecca Marian

Their children (oldest to youngest):

Pete, married to **Ginger**—they have twin girls

Jamie (meets **Teddy** in *Taming Teddy*)

Blue (meets **Tristan** in *Borrowing Blue*)

Thad (dating Tristan's cousin **Sarah**)

Jude (meets **Derek** in *Jumping Jude*)

Simone (hmm….)

Maverick (Book 5)

Griff (*Grounding Griffin* is his story)

Dante (Book 6)

Aunt Tilly—Thomas Marian's aunt
Granny—Tristan's grandmother
Irene—Granny's wife

Prologue

Griff

WHEN THE ENTREE CAME, IT LOOKED MORE LIKE A PILE OF empty scrotums (scrota?) stacked one on top of the other. I blinked and looked again. Yup. Still a big ole stack of sac.

"Remind me again what I ordered, if you don't mind?" I asked the server.

"Deconstructed aubergine nestled amongst tousled morels paired with a sugared sunchoke soufflé accompanied by foraged youngling sprouts and teased with a lemon foam."

I blinked again. What the ever-loving fuck did he just say?

"In English, please?" I asked.

"Eggplant, mushrooms, some Jerusalem root thingy, sprouts, and yellow puffy stuff," the man whispered next to my ear. "Good luck with that."

I sighed before lifting my fork to take a bite. A promise was a promise and I couldn't very well write a review of the restaurant without tasting the food. Monte Mancini owed me big time for this one.

The day before, I'd gotten a message from a friend of mine who was the regular food reviewer for a magazine called *San Francisco Nights*. Monte had called in a panic, begging me to take his place writing the review so he could fly to Italy to visit his ailing mother. I got the feeling his ailing mother was really a nude beach on the east coast of his native country. Lucky bastard.

But I had agreed to write the review in his stead and submit it in his name, taking his reservation and showing up at the appointed time that night. As a freelancer, I had been assigned a few restaurant reviews before, but I was certainly no expert on gourmet fare.

In order to fool the readers into believing the half-assed attempts of Griffin Marian were really the choice words of vaunted Monte Mancini, I would have to pay attention and take copious notes as soon as I returned home.

The meal tasted like… how did I say this politely?

A gargantuan mountain of testes.

The resulting review wasn't pretty, and I made Monte swear never to throw me to the wolves like that again.

Prologue

Sam

"GODDAMNED MOTHERFUCKING JACKASS," I SCREAMED AT the laptop screen. "That pretentious poser couldn't have picked a different night for his review? Jesus Christ."

My roommate, Jason, tutted some unintelligible words of reassurance I knew were bullshit. It wouldn't be fine. The owner of the restaurant was looking for an excuse to fire me and replace me with a less expensive head chef. He and I had never seen eye to eye on what kind of entrees to feature anyway, and I'd been less successful at holding my tongue with him lately.

I knew this review would be the straw that broke the camel's back.

"Listen to this. 'Pretentious, unaffordable farce' and 'gelatinous mousse-type substance.' Is he joking? Does he have any idea how much gourmet ingredients cost and what soufflé is even supposed to taste like? I've never made anything gelatinous in my life. He probably wouldn't know a delicate mousse if one landed airily on his upturned nose. And if he wanted affordable, he should have gone to McDonald's, for god's sake."

I kept reading. The only consolation was the fact the night he'd apparently come in had been that insane day where anything that could go wrong did go wrong. Franklin was going to have to listen to reason when I explained the bad timing.

No such luck. It turned out Franklin didn't give a shit that the day the reviewer came in was the same day all hell broke loose with our fresh food supplier and two cooks called out at the same time. What should have been choice poultry hand-selected for coq au vin was actually a crate of live chicks. The thirteen pounds of Kobe beef filet had been replaced by thirteen cases of giant eggplants for some reason, and we also received Jerusalem artichoke roots instead of globe artichokes. Not at all the same thing.

But I had adapted like a fucking boss and put out an amazing spread, even patting myself on the back for being so creative. Was it up to my usual standard? No, but it still tasted good.

The reviewer was entitled to call a spade a spade, I guessed. And, well, I couldn't disagree with him on it looking like testes (testii?).

By the end of the day I was out of a job, and by the end of the week the highest-paying job I could get was tending bar at a gay club called Harold and Richard's.

And it was all Monte fucking Mancini's fault.

1

Sam

Three Months Later

Fucking flirt; there he was again. That beautiful jackass pulling the same exact lines on yet another man at the bar. This was the fifth night in a row I'd watched him lay it on thick with some unsuspecting dude.

It was Saturday night at Harold and Richard's, or as the locals called it, Harry Dick's. I was manning the bar as usual and was knee deep in pouring blow-job shots for one of the servers when I noticed the man at the bar. I had begun to refer to him as "Foxy" in my head and couldn't argue the appropriateness of the moniker.

He was seriously gorgeous. Probably a couple of inches shorter than my six feet, with a slender but fit build and an adorable boyish look to his face topped by a head full of thick curly brown hair begging to be tousled by my pillows. I couldn't tell the color of his eyes in the alternately dim and flashing lights of the dance club, but he had a scar that bisected his left eyebrow and a smile that punched in dimples when he really turned on the charm.

Apparently turning on the charm was his schtick. Every night for five nights he'd sat on the same stool at the bar, dropping cheesy-ass pickup lines on anyone and everyone who sat on a stool next to him. Tonight one of his unsuspecting victims was a big grizzly bear. Probably six four and a million pounds of monster truck muscles covered in hair. Just the thought of the beautiful slender guy with that big hairy dude set my teeth on edge.

I quirked a brow at Foxy, but he didn't seem to notice. He began with his usual pickup line, "Hey, foxy. Can I buy you a drink?"

My eyes rolled like Pavlov's dog after having heard this shit so much. I let out an annoyed sigh, which apparently got his attention. The man narrowed his eyes at me, shooting me a look that said, *Mind your own business, asshole.*

I rolled my eyes again at him for good measure. He huffed and turned his charm back on the bear.

"What would you like, cutie?" Foxy asked the bear sweetly.

The bear growled something unintelligible.

Fox looked back at me and said, "Did you get that?"

"Uh, no. All I heard was a grunt. Try asking him again, and this time we'll see if he speaks English," I suggested with a smirk. Clearly the guy didn't speak bear any more than I did. Luckily, the man didn't seem to hear our exchange. He was busy eye-stripping Foxy and licking his lips in anticipation. I shuddered with revulsion.

"I'm guessing he wants whatever you have on tap," he said with a shrug.

"Sure thing, Foxy." I winked, grabbing a glass to pull the beer. "And what would you like? Another Shirley Temple?" I teased.

"Yes, actually. That sounds divine. I'll take a Shirley Temple with vodka. But eighty-six the Temple and double up on the Shirley."

What the fuck did that mean? I handed the beer to the Neanderthal and made a drink with vodka and extra ginger ale with just a splash of grenadine. I added a plastic sword full to the hilt with maraschino cherries, a hot-pink paper parasol, and a flamingo swizzle stick for good measure.

"Here you go, princess," I said, putting down a napkin before setting the concoction in front of him. He took one look at the girly drink and couldn't hold back a laugh.

"Thanks, Theo." He smiled at me. *Who the hell was Theo? I wondered.*

I went down the bar, helping fill orders and gathering empty glasses. By the time I made it back to check on them, Foxy had gotten to phase two of his usual routine.

"That's amazing. Tell me more about yourself, buttercup," he said, batting his eyelashes. I snorted and got another death glare from him.

"Ready for another round?" I asked the two men. Foxy nodded and I began to pull the tap for the bear's beer. While I waited for the foam to settle, I noticed the bear begin to paw at the man buying him drinks. My hackles rose, and I suppressed a grumble.

Why the hell was this lovely person picking up random dudes in a gay club? He could have anyone he wanted. Why quick fucks with whoever happened to sit on the stool next to him? He never shopped around on the dance floor or flirted with someone who drew his attention. It was always whoever happened to sit on the stool next to him. Was he really that lazy?

I handed over the beer and made the Foxy Temple. By the time I slid it in front of him, the bear was nuzzling Foxy's neck and I caught a brief moment of unease in Foxy's eyes. He wasn't enjoying this. *What the hell?* Then why was he doing it night after night?

I couldn't help but say something to him.

As he reached out to take the glass from me, I clamped my hand around his and pulled him toward me. "Can I have a quick word with you at the end of the bar?" I said in a low voice. He pulled back and looked at me quizzically.

3

"Why?" he asked.

"Humor me," I said.

"Sorry, sweetie, I'm busy chatting with my friend here. No, thanks."

He went back to flirting with the beast as if I'd never spoken.

Fuck that.

Ten minutes later, I made and "accidentally" spilled another Foxy Temple on him.

"Oh no," I cried. "I'm so sorry! Let me help you clean that up. I think we have some stain remover in the employee lounge if you want to follow me back there."

He sighed and turned his fake charm back on the giant. "I'll be right back. Keep my spot warm, baby doll, m'kay?"

Foxy followed me to the end of the bar where the doors to the bathrooms and employee lounge were. I grabbed his elbow and pulled him into the break room.

"Hey," he said, yanking his elbow out of my reach. "Get your hands off me."

"Oh, do you mean to tell me you don't like it when a stranger paws at you? Could have fooled me," I growled. "What the hell do you think you're doing?"

His nostrils flared and his jaw set. "None of your damned business."

"It's my business when I'm the one watching you throw yourself at strangers."

Foxy laughed. "What, you're keeping tabs on me? I can't go out and have some flirty fun with people in a club? What are you, my mother?"

"That's not it. I just don't get it. Unless you were, like, picking up johns or something," I suggested after having a horrible thought.

His jaw set. Clearly I offended him, which wasn't my intent. "It's really none of your business, asshole. Your concern is neither necessary nor appreciated. Certainly not enough to warrant ruining my favorite shirt." Fox pulled the hem of his shirt, frowning at the pink stain from the grenadine in the drink.

"Sorry," I muttered.

"It was a gift," he said.

I grabbed the stain remover and squatted down in front of him, using some wet paper towels to blot the stain gel onto the spot. I reached my other hand under his shirt so I would have something to press against. "I'm really sorry about this. And I'm sorry I implied you were a prostitute. It just didn't seem like you wanted to be there. I thought you might want an excuse to escape the big oaf."

He sighed. "Whatever. I need to go home anyway. I shouldn't have ordered another drink. More than one and I get a splitting headache," he said in a gentle voice above me. I tried not to shiver at the sound.

"You have to let this stuff set in for, like, fifteen minutes before washing it off, but it should work since we caught it quickly," I rambled.

He looked down at me. God, he was adorable. "Okay."

As I removed my hand from under his shirt, the backs of my knuckles brushed against the skin of his abdomen, and I heard his breath hitch at the same time all the blood in my body shot down to my groin. My brain went a little fuzzy and my words got mixed around on my tongue.

The guy was sex on a stick.

"Thanks," Fox breathed, pulling at the hem of the shirt to keep the wet spot away from his skin. As the shirttail flapped, I caught a glimpse of a tattoo peeking out from the waistband over his hip.

The only word I could make out was *Chaos*.

I wanted to follow that script down into his pants with my tongue.

My mouth opened and dumped out any pride I may have had before entering the break room. "I got you. I mean, I don't *have* you. What I meant was, I *got* you. You know, the stain. It's on. Not like, *it's on*, but the stain stuff is *on*. The stain," I stammered, going for gold in the shut-the-fuck-up Olympics.

"Jesus Christ," I exhaled. "My mouth isn't working right. I need to get back out there. To the bar. To tend bar. At the bar. But you can stay in here while I wait. While *you* wait, I mean."

"Are you drunk?" he asked, trying hard not to laugh. And failing.

"No," I told him with a glare. "My mouth just went through a thing. That's all. It's fine now."

"You sure?" he asked. This time he wasn't even trying to hold back a laugh. Ugh, he was so pretty. It was like I wanted to pet him on the head or something. Who was I kidding? I wanted to pet him everywhere. I might have stared at him for a few long beats without realizing I was making even more of a spectacle of myself.

"Theo?" Foxy asked.

"Huh?" I asked, trying to shake off my hormonal haze.

"You should probably go back to the bar. To tend bar. At the bar."

Then that fucker winked at me.

As I walked out the door I heard him call out, "Thanks again for the help."

I bumped into the doorframe before hurrying back to the bar and apologizing to the two other bartenders for leaving them hanging. We were slammed. It was thirty minutes before I could make my way back to check on Foxy, but when I did, he was gone. It was probably just as well. My face was still beet red from embarrassment.

2

Griff

I DIDN'T KNOW WHICH I WAS FEELING MORE STRONGLY ABOUT: amusement over how his mouth got the better of him or absolute pants-dropping lust at the guy being so damned hot.

The sexy bartender looked like that guy from the Divergent movies. The actor's name was Theo something, otherwise known as Hottie Mc-Hot-As-Fuck. I wasn't sure I'd ever had such an immediate attraction to anyone in my life. I wanted to lick him all over, from his short brown hair down past his moody eyebrows and dark stubble to his Adam's apple and the few chest hairs I could see sneaking out of the top of his Harry Dick's T-shirt.

Mmm-hmm.

I'd noticed him every night I'd been there. My eyes hadn't been able to ignore his biceps moving as he poured drinks and his perfect round ass wrapped snugly in worn denim. Sometimes when he reached to grab a liquor bottle, his shirt rode up and exposed some of that delicious skin above his low-hanging jeans.

Fuck.

Okay, so maybe that answered which one I felt more strongly about. Clearly it was the lust more than the amusement. But they were related. I didn't want this hot guy thinking I was a slut, or worse—someone picking up guys for money. While I'd never actually slept with anyone for cash, even when I was homeless, I'd done some seriously shady shit for food and a warm place to sleep.

But that's not what this was about, and I wasn't that boy any longer. This was about a story I was doing for a magazine. I was a freelance journalist and had been tasked by an editor to put together a piece on using pet names to pick up guys at the clubs.

Before I could go back out there and try to explain things to the sexy bartender, I got a text from my brother Dante asking where I was. He was downtown and wanted to crash at my place. I told him I'd meet him there as soon as I could.

After a quick bathroom visit to wash the stain remover stuff off, I shouldered my way through the crowd toward the exit. One glance toward the bar confirmed Theo was slammed with drink orders. I sent up a silent prayer of thanks that he'd make plenty of tips despite the break he'd taken to help me. I threw some cash under my empty drink glass and made my way to the door.

Dante waited for me on the front stoop of my building. He had his ratty old gray backpack as usual, and his earbuds hung from his ears.

"Hey," I called out to him as I approached. When he looked up, pulling one earbud out, his face opened up into a genuine smile.

"Hey, Griff. Thanks for letting me crash. I stayed late at the library and didn't want to bother Mom and Dad."

"Did you at least text them to let them know not to worry?" I asked as I opened the door for him. My head was killing me from the alcohol; I couldn't wait to take some ibuprofen.

"Of course. You're the one who gives them gray hair, not me." He laughed.

"True enough. What were you working on so late at the library?"

"Research paper about Vincent van Gogh. It's not due until Wednesday, but I wanted to knock it out tonight so I can enjoy family dinner tomorrow without stressing about it," Dante said.

"Good idea. I heard a rumor Thad is bringing a friend to introduce to Simone. Should make for some good entertainment," I told him as we finally made it through the front door of my apartment.

Dante snorted. "Oh shit. She's going to kick his ass. Doesn't he remember what happened when Blue and Tristan tried setting her up with that guy they met on their honeymoon?"

"Thad is an eternal optimist. He won't let one failed attempt stop him," I said with a laugh.

I turned on some lights and offered him a drink. He grabbed some water out of the fridge and took off his jacket before sitting on the couch.

"So, where were you tonight?" Dante asked.

"Harry Dick's again. I'm still working on that piece for the magazine," I explained.

"Pick up anyone yummy?" he asked.

I shook my head. "No. A giant beast put the moves on me but then I got harassed by the bartender until he ended up staining my shirt. And then he got all sweet and goofy."

Dante looked at me skeptically. "You got hit on by a big guy. The bartender harassed you. Then you turned him into a blob of quivering goo. Okay. Was the beast cute?"

"Uh, only if you like large prehistoric mammals."

Dante smiled. "Well, was the bartender cute?"

"*So fucking hot.* Like… how do I describe him? Let me put it this way: I'd have his babies. Even if I had to shove them out of my dick with no anesthesia. That's how hot he is," I explained, wiping the back of my hand over my forehead dramatically. "He looks like that guy from Divergent who plays Four."

Dante smirked at me. "Yes, Griff, but is he *attractive*?"

"Shut up." I moaned, falling back against the sofa cushions. "It doesn't matter because he thought I was a whore."

"Rewind, brother," Dante requested.

"You heard me. He thought I was propositioning a john when I started sweet-talking the guy on the stool next to me."

"That's why Mr. Harry Dick harassed you?" He laughed. "Oh god. Did you punch him?"

"Hell no. Are you crazy? Then I would have been kicked out for sure. And can we please not call him that? Yuck."

"Griff, you have a crazy life. No matter how steady and normal I start to think you've become, you pull out a story like this. Please tell me you're going to share this over family dinner tomorrow. It might take Simone's mind off the fact she's still the current Marian pity party queen."

"Even if I didn't want to tell it, you know Pete will find a way to weasel it out of me. He always knows when there's embarrassing shit I don't want anyone to find out about," I complained.

"Yup. Might as well rest up. Tomorrow there will be a house full of Marians waiting to hear the story of how Griff Fox decided to have Harry Dick's baby."

I threw a pillow at him and left him to fend for himself on the sofa. "It's Griff Marian, you asshole. It's been years since the adoption, and you still think of me as that scrawny kid from the shelter," I called back over my shoulder.

"That's because Griff Fox saved my life. I love Griff Marian plenty. But Griff Fox will always be my hero," he called after me with a smile in his voice. The words were no less meaningful despite hearing them a thousand times.

The next day Dante and I slept late and had coffee and toast before taking turns in the shower. I loaned him some clean clothes before we made our way down to our family home in Hillsborough.

* * *

The two of us were the youngest of nine children. There were five biological brothers, a biological sister, then came the three of us who'd been adopted through the LGBTQ youth program. The nine Marian kids ranged in age from Dante's twenty-one to Pete's thirty-eight. We were a crazy crew, make no mistake.

Our parents, Thomas and Rebecca Marian, were two of the sweetest, most generous people you'd ever meet. When two of their sons came out of the closet in their teens, Thomas and Rebecca began volunteering at the youth program to show their support.

Becoming a part of this family felt like winning the lottery. Not only were they comfortably wealthy, but they were loving, accepting, and down to earth. Sunday family dinner was practically sacrosanct, but even if it hadn't been, I wouldn't miss it for the world.

We got to Mom and Dad's and made our way toward the kitchen. As soon as we got close, Dante started asking about the sexy bartender again. Jerk. I should have known he'd bring it up the first chance he got. Pete wasn't the only brother who loved embarrassing me.

"What are you two arguing about?" Jude interrupted us as I reached out to give Simone a hug.

"Remember that piece I was writing about using terms of endearments when picking up guys in the clubs?" I asked.

"Yeah," Jude said.

"Well, the whole thing got shelved when I took that ghostwriting job in February. Now that I'm done, I decided to take it up again."

"Tell them about the bartender," Dante interjected.

I glared at my brother.

"So I've done the pickup thing at several clubs already and only need a few more nights of experimenting before starting the article. The bartender at Harry Dick's keeps eying me like I'm doing something wrong, and last night he finally pulled me aside to accuse me of—"

Dante interrupted again. "Who gives a shit? Tell them about wanting to have his babies."

I felt my face heat up. "Anyway, long story short, now I want to see him naked."

Aunt Tilly sighed, resting her chin in her hand. "Tell us more about this studmuffin. Does he have a tight ass?"

Granny chimed in. "More to the point, when are you gonna fuck him?"

I loved my family, but they were not subtle. I felt my face heat up with all the attention.

Desperate to change the subject, I turned to Blue and his husband, Tristan.

"I didn't know you were driving in this week." They lived a couple of hours away in Napa where Tristan owned a vineyard.

"We came in last night actually," Tristan said. "Blue missed his mommy."

Mom came walking into the kitchen in time to hear that and smiled. "Awww, I missed you too, honey."

Blue blushed. "Shut up, Tris. I didn't say I missed my mommy. I said it had been a while since we'd been able to make family dinner. We missed those weekends we were in France, and I just didn't want to miss another one if we could help it."

Tristan leaned over and kissed Blue tenderly on the temple. "I'm kidding, babe. I missed everyone too. And obviously Piper missed your dad. I haven't seen her since we got here."

Mom laughed. "She slept in our bed last night, and Thomas was in heaven. He's enjoying her so much he mentioned wanting to get a puppy. I had to smack him. The puppies outside are for Jude and Derek only. None for us."

Mom was a vet and had her fill of animals at her clinic all week. She said that adopting an animal who needed a home was like pulling a stone out of a dam. The only thing keeping her from crazy animal lady status was her ban on adopting any.

I offered to help fix the salad and joined Blue at the sink cutting veggies. Pete and Ginger's twin girls dashed through the room with

Piper on their heels.

Jamie and his husband, Teddy, showed up looking exhausted but happy. "Where have you two been?" Blue asked. "I thought you were starting classes soon, Jamie."

"Classes start tomorrow. We flew in this morning from Greenland. Teddy was doing a spread on the Arctic fox for *National Geographic*. It was amazing, but I'm beat," Jamie admitted.

Dad finished hugging the guys. "You didn't need to come all the way here this weekend. You could have had the day at home to recover."

This time it was Teddy who spoke. "Actually, we haven't been home yet. We flew into SFO instead of Sacramento and came straight here. If we don't fall asleep in our food, we'll head home to Davis. If we do, we'll crash here if that's okay."

"Of course, hon," Mom said.

Finally Thad showed up with a new friend named Dillon. Simone had gone to the backyard to call the girls in to wash their hands. We all made our way outside with the dishes to the two large tables by the pool. The twins rushed past on their way to the kitchen, and Simone caught sight of Thad and Dillon.

"What the *fuck?*" Simone snapped in recognition of the new guy as she stepped backward and almost fell into the pool. Dillon lurched forward to steady her, but he overshot and tumbled them both into the deep end.

The rest of us stood there in complete shock while they came spluttering to the surface, Simone screaming, "You *jackass*. Get your hands off me," as Dillon tried helping her to the shallow end.

She kept yelling at him until they could both stand. Dillon let go of her and threw up his hands to yell right back.

"You're so goddamned stubborn. Why the hell can't you ever accept help, you crazy—?" Anddd, that was when he remembered her entire family, including her father and at least ten other Marian men, were standing there watching everything.

Dillon froze on the pool stairs, water dripping and clothes sodden. His mouth hung open as he saw the audience he had.

"I am so sorry," he began, holding out his hands in a defensive gesture. "I am so sorry for everything." He tried to retain his soggy dignity as he apologized over again and told Thad he'd see him later before disappearing through the side gate.

Like in a tennis match, our collective heads swiveled to my drenched sister.

"What?" she snapped. "You've never seen someone fall into a pool before?"

Thad finally regained his tongue. "I take it you two have met?"

"Who, Dillon? Nope. Never seen him before."

Then she stalked off to her bedroom to find dry clothes, not realizing no one had mentioned his name.

Just then, Granny and Irene walked out onto the patio.

"There's a soaking wet beefcake hitchhiking in your driveway. Tilly offered him a ride and told us not to wait up," Granny said, looking around at the gaping faces surrounding her. "Shit, what'd we miss?"

3

Sam

SUNDAY WAS USUALLY THE DAY I COOKED BRUNCH FOR MY roommates. They loved living with a professional chef because it meant they ate like kings. This Sunday was no exception. After the late-night shift at the club, I slept in until around 10 a.m. before getting up and prepping the groceries I'd purchased the day before.

Today I was making crêpes with sautéed pears, gouda, and thyme. I put together a fresh fruit bowl as well as a melted chocolate sauce dip in case anyone felt particularly indulgent.

Jason came out of his room first, scratching his bare chest with one hand and his scruffy beard with another. "Coffee?" he mumbled.

"Yup. Sit, I'll get it."

After handing him a cup, I gave him a few minutes to doctor it and get the first sips down before talking to him.

"Where did you guys end up last night?" I asked. Jason and Robbie had been hoping to spy on my ex. They knew he'd be drunk and dancing in a club anywhere other than Harry Dick's.

"Are you kidding? Everywhere, man. That guy's a slut. No offense."

Tell me something I don't know, I thought. "No shit," I said.

"We followed him to four different clubs before we saw him settle on one target. He was draped all over Neil if you can believe it." Jason laughed. "We think they went home together."

We'd gone to college with Neil, and he was like the gay male equivalent of a tiny scared mouse baby. "Neil Hooper?" I asked just to be sure.

He snorted. "Yeah, little timid Neil. Poor kid. Johnny probably ate him alive when he got him alone."

My ex was gargantuan. He'd been a linebacker in college and then became a meatheaded gym rat. Don't ask how we ended up together for almost a year and a half. Pure stupid lust on my part. The guy was very shallow. I'd gone through this experimental phase where I wanted to get manhandled and tossed around a bit. Luckily, the phase ended just before Johnny decided to sleep with every little guy he came across. It was anyone's guess as to why he was attracted to my six-foot self in the first place.

Jason and Robbie loved following Johnny to gay clubs because he looked like a skinhead NFL homophobe. He lumbered through gay clubs leaving a wake of people behind him who were either terrified of him or intimidated but turned on by the idea of sex with the beast. It was pretty funny. When we'd been together, I had gotten a kick out of seeing people's reactions to him.

I finished putting the fruit in the bowl when Robbie came through the front door. "Sorry I'm late. I went for a run since you told me there was going to be chocolate."

I poured another coffee for Robbie as he headed to his room for a quick shower.

When we all sat down to breakfast, Robbie raved about the crêpes. "These are fucking amazing," he said around a mouthful.

"Hey, Jason, did you tell him about Neil last night?"

"Yeah. Total trip. Wonder if he ended up in traction. No way could a guy that little take a dick that big," Jason said.

"Spoiler alert: the dick isn't that big," I informed them. "And he probably wasn't taking it as much as giving it."

"Aw shit, man. Don't make me lose my appetite now of all times." Robbie groaned. "How was work last night?"

"Slammed. Made some good money," I said before taking another sip of coffee and remembering the other part of the night that was good.

"Oh-ho." Jason chuckled. "What have we here? A shit-eating grin on our boy Sam's face? Do tell, Chef Coxwell."

"It's nothing. Just saw a cute guy, that's all."

"A cute guy? At a dance club? That can't be right." Robbie feigned shock.

"Shut up." I laughed. "You know I don't usually notice or give a shit. This was different. This guy was fucking adorable. Like, I wanted to steal him and snuggle the hell out of him."

Robbie choked on his crêpe. "I'm sorry, you mispronounced 'fuck his brains out.'" Jason laughed and pounded Robbie on the back.

"I know. It's crazy. I wanted to fuck his brains out too, but something about him just… I don't know. I couldn't stop thinking about just grabbing him and holding on to him. Maybe I'm feeling maternal and protective for some reason. I need someone to look out for now that Lacey's away at school."

Jason put his hand on my shoulder. "Aww, someone's having their period. It's okay, Sam. Robbie and I will feed you chocolate and play you *Terms of Endearment* later. Robbie, what did we do with that antique VCR we found in the time capsule?"

Robbie laughed and reached out a fist bump to Jason. "So, did you ask him out?"

"No," I said with a huff. "He left before I could."

"Did you get his name?" Jason asked.

"No, but I think he'll be back at some point. He's been in every night this week." I didn't tell them about spewing out humiliating nonsense at the guy. They'd never let me live it down.

We finished eating, and Jason offered to clean up. I changed and headed for the YMCA to swim laps. When I swam, I was able to completely relax. I wore earplugs not to protect my ears from the water but to keep noise out. I'd been on a recreational swim team while at UC Berkeley and had fallen in love with the meditative feeling of pulling myself through the water.

By the time I got to work at the club that night, I was relaxed and happy. Having cooked, spent time with friends, and swum, it was turning out to be a great day. Sundays were like Fridays for me since I had Monday and Tuesday nights off.

I spent all night trying not to put Foxy's face on every man who sat at the bar. Finally, I gave up and resigned myself to getting through my shift as quickly and profitably as I could. There was a rich-looking older man making eyeballs at me on one end of the bar, and I spent the rest of the night flirting with him to max out the tips coming my way.

After last call, he asked me to come home with him, and I declined with as big a smile as I could. When he suggested a quick suck behind the club, I wanted to roll my eyes. Instead I said politely, "Maybe next time."

It wasn't the first time someone had hoped to get me out back, and it wouldn't be the last. What surprised me most was how many people actually thought that was how I liked to get off after being on my feet in the club for eight hours.

As I left that night, the same man was waiting for me outside. This time his pleas for a quickie were more aggressive and rude, almost to the point of making me nervous for my safety. As I began to walk, trying to ignore him, I noticed him follow me. Luckily, one of the other bartenders ran to join me for part of the way. We only lived a block away from each other, and I'd never been more grateful.

The older man gave up and walked away, leaving me with a deep sense of relief that I didn't have to confront him.

* * *

The following day I agreed to help an old classmate from culinary school make ten dozen gourmet cupcakes and deliver them to a youth shelter for some kind of celebration they were having. I met Julio at the bakery where he worked, and we enjoyed several hours of conversation while we worked. After baking and frosting fifteen dozen just to be safe, we carefully set the boxes into the back of a van Julio had borrowed.

After we pulled up to the front door of the shelter, I began unloading boxes two at a time. Julio teased me for being too cautious and stacked two more on top of the two I was already carrying, making it impossible to see where I was going. I carefully made my way and tried to reach for the handle just as the door banged open, mashing the top two boxes against my face and chest before they tipped onto the pavement.

"Ow, fuck," I cried, bobbling the remaining two boxes. Two hands came out to help me steady them and before I knew it, the top of the stack had been lifted out of my hands. Someone apologized while Julio complained and tried to recover the two fallen boxes.

I looked up to see who had caused the caketastrophe and stared right into the eyes of my fox.

4

Griff

"OH SHIT! I'M SO SORRY," I SAID, HOLDING ONE OF THE boxes. It was him. Theo from the bar. My stomach did nervous somersaults while my heart threw up jazz hands. The man was even more beautiful in the light of day.

"What are you doing here?" he asked me with wide eyes of surprise. A deep blush bloomed over the skin of his neck and face; I couldn't help but grin.

"I volunteer here. When I saw Julio, I came out to help unload the van. Sorry, I wasn't looking where I was going. I feel terrible." I held the door open for him and then followed him to the reception counter where we set down the boxes.

Theo's face finally relaxed into a smile, and it felt like the sun had come out and shone its warmth on my skin. "It's okay. We made plenty of extras in case we ran into trouble. I'd ask you your name, but I think I'll just call you Trouble instead." Then he fucking winked at me, and my heart melted into a pool of lava that slowly made its way to my dick.

"Griffin Marian, Griff," I said, holding out my hand.

"Sam Coxwell, it's nice to meet you, Griff." His hand was big and warm. I wanted to hold it forever; instead, I dropped it like a hot potato and quickly stuck my hands in my pockets to keep from grabbing it again.

"Sam *Cox*well, huh? Sounds like the name of a *prostitute*," I said with a grin before turning to help finish unloading the cupcake boxes. I heard Sam mutter a curse softly behind me.

Once the truck was unloaded and Julio wished us a happy shelter anniversary, Sam hesitated before following him.

"Hang on, Julio," he called out to his friend before turning to me. "Do you guys need any extra volunteers today? It's my day off, and I'm happy to help."

We totally didn't, but I wasn't about to give up a chance to spend some time staring at his beautiful self. Especially since the club was closed that night and I wouldn't be able to see him later.

"That would be great, if you don't mind."

Sam said goodbye to Julio, and then I showed him around the shelter, explaining the program in greater detail.

"How did you get involved here?" he asked.

"I was homeless as a teen. A cop found me and gave me an ultimatum: the shelter or the foster system. I chose the shelter," I explained.

His eyes widened and he put his hand on my arm to stop my progress down the rows between bunk beds. I looked over at him and was blinded by his intense gaze. "I'm sorry, Griff. That's awful. How did you end up homeless?"

"When I came out, I was kicked out. A pretty common story around here."

I was pulled into a massive hug. Sam squeezed me for all I was worth, and I stood there frozen for a minute before relaxing against his warm, solid body and returning the embrace. God, he smelled good. As though whatever scent he used was made specifically to attract the Griffin Marians of the world. I silently sucked it in like nectar from a flower. I could live in those arms forever.

"I'm so sorry. That sucks." His whispered words came out of his mouth and straight into my ear, tweaking all my nerves and leaving me unsteady. I pulled back before I lost my shit and started crying or begged him to throw me down on a nearby bunk and have his sexy way with me.

"Yeah, well, it was a long time ago. So… ah, this is the dorm," I said in my tour guide voice while looking down at the floor. "It can house up to sixty kids at a time."

I sensed him looking at me out of the corner of my eye, but I ignored it and continued my tour.

When I finished showing him around, we ended up in the cafeteria where the party was starting. Music played from speakers in a corner and streamers and balloons hung around the walls and ceiling. At least fifty teenagers congregated in clusters around the room. Empty pizza boxes lay strewn around the tables and soda cans tumbled out of the recycling cans. It seemed like the party was a big hit.

My parents were there volunteering as well as a couple of my brothers and my sister. Dante probably had classes otherwise I was sure he wouldn't have missed it.

I introduced Sam to everyone we came across, explaining that Thomas and Rebecca Marian were my adopted parents. When my mom found out Sam had helped make the cupcakes, she gushed.

"They're amazing, Sam. So beautiful. How did you learn to make something so fancy?" she asked.

"Culinary school. Actually, my friend Julio was the one who volunteered to provide the cupcakes. I just pitched in to help him get it all done today so they'd be fresh. Otherwise he would have had to make some of them over the weekend," Sam explained.

"Julio is a doll. We've known him for years. We can't thank you boys enough for providing them. They almost look too good to eat," Mom said.

"I'm still feeling too guilty about the ones I crushed to try them," I admitted. "Maybe I can take the smashed ones home with me and eat them later. With a spoon. Alone. In the dark... Where no one can see me hugging and kissing the box," I joked.

Sam smiled. "That sounds like something I would do, but with pizza."

My brother Mav heard that one and joined in. "Oh, believe me, Griff would do it with pizza too. The jerk can eat anything and not get fat. If I eat any of the candy our receptionist at the vet clinic brings in, I feel like ass for the rest of the day."

"Oh, honey," Mom said. "You know better than to eat that junk."

Mav laughed. "I do, but sometimes it's too tempting to resist. Especially if it's a crazy day and I don't have time for a meal break. But then I have to run several miles to burn it off, whereas Griff can just go splash in the pool for a few minutes to stay fit."

Sam turned his head toward me. "You swim?" he asked.

Before I could answer, Mom started bragging. "He swam for USC."

Sam's eyes bugged out of his head. "No kidding?"

I smiled. "No kidding."

"What did you swim?" he asked, meaning my stroke specialty.

"Mostly fly, but I tried to swim backstroke whenever I could," I said. "You swim too?"

"I just swam on the rec team at Berkeley, and now I'm stuck with laps at the Y," he said. We grinned goofily at each other after finding a shared passion.

"I'm not sure I've ever randomly met another swimmer before outside of a pool," I admitted.

"Me neither. It's a little strange."

Simone walked up and gave me a shot to the shoulder and the evil eye. "What?" I asked her. "Why are you glaring at me?"

"You knew Thad was bringing someone yesterday to set me up with, and you didn't warn me? Thanks for that, jackass."

"How did you know that guy anyway?" I asked. Mom had moved off to help one of the boys find a drink, and Maverick cocked an eyebrow. I'd forgotten he'd had to work the day before.

"I didn't. I don't. Never mind," she said before walking off.

I laughed and told Maverick and Sam the story of Simone's big pool adventure.

"So who's the guy?" Mav asked. "How does Thad know him?"

"His name is Dillon Fisher, and all I know is that the guy isn't waterproof."

Sam put his hand on my arm, and I felt a tingle at his touch. "Wait. I know a Dillon Fisher from culinary school. Does he have kind of wavy blond hair in need of a cut?"

"Yes," I said. "Looks like he'd play Surfer Dude #3 in any cheesy teen beach movie?"

Sam laughed. "That's him. He's a good guy. I can't wait to give him hell about it when I see him."

"Good guy or not, no way is he getting anywhere near my sister again. She went ballistic," I said. "It's too bad though; he's kinda cute. I wouldn't mind having him around the Thanksgiving table."

Sam's face clouded. "He's straight though."

Maverick laughed. "Griff's never let that stop him before."

"Fuck you, Mav. That's a lie. Plus, crushing on a sibling's love interest is more Tristan's family's thing, not ours. It's kind of weird though, if you think about it. Six gay brothers yet none of us have ever had a problem come up between boyfriends and brothers," I said.

"Six gay brothers?" Sam asked. "You're one of six gay brothers? You're pulling my leg."

I shook my head. "Three of six biological kids in our family are gay and the other three were adopted through this shelter. So we were already gay. Then there's the black sheep. Simone. She's the only girl.

And one of the straight Marians."

"Did someone say my name?" Simone asked, walking up and handing me a cupcake.

Sam shook his head. "Now you're just messing with me."

Mav smirked. "Nope. Just ask Mom or Dad. They'll be happy to tell you all about it because they get that comment all the time. Simone's ex-boyfriend used to call us the Gaydy Bunch."

"Asshole," Simone and I muttered under our breaths at the same time. It was just what you did when John Alexander's name came up.

I looked down at the treat in my hand. The cupcake was chocolate with white frosting and some kind of cookie crumbs sprinkled on top. I looked at Sam, feeling guilty.

"Just do it, Griff. Even destroyers of children's cupcake dreams deserve to eat." He winked. "Besides, that's one of my favorites. Mint Milano, like the cookie," he said.

I took a bite and moaned. "Mmpf, mm-hmm," I said with the cupcake still in my mouth. "So good."

Sam's face lit up. "Glad you like it. If there are any Nutella ones left, you might want to try one of those too. They're the ones with little rolled up cookie things sticking out of the top of them."

After I finished the cupcake, Sam and I helped clean up and take the trash out to the dumpster with two of the boys who lived at the shelter.

"Frankie, how's your backside heelflip coming?" I asked one of the kids.

"Dude, I totally nailed it yesterday. One perfect trick but then I couldn't reproduce it for shit," Frankie said. "I need you to show me again some time."

"Just takes practice. Keep going for it, and it'll get more consistent. If you get your skateboard we can work on it for a few minutes before I have to head out."

I bumped fists with Frankie and chatted for a few minutes with a kid named Demarcus while Frankie got his board. After playing around on and helping him with his trick for a few minutes, I led Sam back into the building.

When we returned to the cafeteria, Sam thanked Londa, the shelter manager, and told her he'd love to volunteer the next time they needed help. She told him to leave his contact information by her computer at the reception desk, and she'd add him to the volunteer rolls.

He made a point of finding each of my family members to say his goodbyes, and then came up to me with a big smile on his face.

"Thanks for letting me be a part of this today, Griff. I can tell how special this place is, and your family is terrific."

"I'm glad you joined us, and thanks again for the cupcakes." For the first time in my life, I felt shy and unsure. "Uh… I guess I'll see you at the club later this week then?"

Sam tilted his head to study me before responding with a grin. "Sounds good. Take care of yourself, Foxy." The sweet man walked away, taking a little bit of the sunshine with him.

5

Sam

I DIDN'T MAKE IT TO WORK AT THE CLUB AGAIN UNTIL THURSDAY night. Monday and Tuesday were my days off, and then a coworker begged me for my Wednesday night shift to make up for one of his I'd covered the week before.

When I finally got settled behind the bar on Thursday night, I realized my body vibrated with a mixture of nerves and excitement. Hope that Griff would come in that night and dread that he'd hit on some strange man right in front of me if he did.

I couldn't get him out of my mind. Since seeing him interacting with the kids at the shelter that day, I had begun to realize he wasn't the arrogant pickup artist I'd seen at the club. I still didn't know what he did for a living, but I could tell he was kind and well loved by his family.

Seeing Griff surrounded by people who clearly adored him made me feel grateful. When he'd told me about being kicked out by his family, my heart had broken for him. Being abandoned by the people who were supposed to take care of you was a horrible feeling.

What would have happened to him if he hadn't found the shelter when he did? I couldn't bear to think about it.

"Why the long face, Theo?"

My heart sped up when I saw his cute face looking back at me from a bar stool. "Hey," I said, feeling my whole face light up like an idiot. "Why do you call me Theo?"

"Because you look like an actor named Theo. Ugly guy. Big hairy nose and warts all over. He usually plays the hunchback or ogre role. You'd recognize him if you saw him." He smiled.

I began making a Foxy Temple without thinking, adding a second sword full of cherries. I'd noticed the last time he liked them.

"Watch yourself, Foxy. That's my dad you're talking about. And I'll have you know he was just cast as Beast in the new Disney film," I said with a straight face as I carefully wiped down the glass before sliding the drink toward him.

Griff threw back his head and laughed, eyes crinkling and dimples popping. Damn, he was something to look at.

He took a sip of his drink and followed it by sticking a plastic sword into his mouth and sliding off a cherry. I hoped to god he didn't notice me drooling or, worse, filling out the front of my blue jeans as I watched those full lips fondle the wet cherries.

The club started to fill up and the drink orders came in one after the other. At one point Griff gestured to his glass, asking for another. I made another Foxy Temple, this time leaving out the vodka as I remembered what he'd said about the headaches.

After catching up on refills, clearing dirty glasses, and asking the barback to switch out a keg for me, I glanced back to where Griff was just in time to see him put his fake flirty smile on and point it at an attractive Nordic-looking man.

God-fucking-dammit.

I wanted to go over there and ask him what the hell he was doing, but it was none of my business. Dread coiled in my gut as I pictured the man wanting to take Griff home with him. Because of course the man would want to take Griff home with him. They all did. I was just one of many people who had fallen under his spell.

After several minutes of trying to ignore him and concentrate on my job, one of the other bartenders tapped me on the shoulder and pointed to Griff and his companion. "Those guys need refills."

Ugh.

I made my way back down there in time to hear it.

"That's amazing. Tell me more about yourself, cupcake," Griff cooed. I gritted my teeth.

"What are you having?" I asked the blond man. He took his horndog gaze off Griff long enough to glance my way. He looked at Griff's empty cocktail glass and back up at me.

"I'll have whatever he's having," he said, returning his full attention to Griff. His hand rubbed Griff's shoulder, and I wanted to smack it off.

Instead I grinned through clenched teeth. "Coming right up."

I made the Foxy Temple with vodka and slutted it up with fucking umbrellas and shit before sliding it to him. He took one look at it and raised an eyebrow at me.

"Foxy Temple," I said as if it was a thing. I made the virgin version again and set it down in front of Griff, trying not to look at him.

I heard him chuckle and tell the guy, "Try it and tell me what you think, hot stuff."

"You've got to be fucking kidding me," I said under my breath.

Griff must have heard me because he looked at me funny. I walked away and busied myself clearing dirty glasses and wiping up sweat rings from the surface of the long bar.

I pretended not to notice when the Nordic man leaned over and started nibbling on Griff's neck. And I also pretended not to notice when Griff looked uncomfortable about it. I put my head down and kept working. None of my business.

None. Of. My. Business.

It wasn't until they got up to dance that I started to lose my self-control. I slammed liquor bottles down too hard, I over-poured beer glasses, and almost cut myself with a corkscrew. I tried so hard not to watch the blond man grind his dick into Griff's ass, but I finally couldn't stand it. Why the hell was he letting this guy touch him when he clearly wasn't into it?

When they returned to their spots at the bar, Griff asked me for an ice water while the other man asked for two vodka shots. I caught Griff's eye and saw the slightest shake of his head. I poured one with vodka, filling the other with water without Nordic seeing me.

They clinked glasses and threw down the shots. The blond man smacked his lips and then leaned over to kiss Griff. I saw Griff pull back a hair but allow the kiss.

The blond guy said, "Come home with me." He threw some money down on the bar and reached to pull Griff's hand. As Griff put his hand down on the bar to climb off the stool, I put my hand over his and leaned in.

"Don't do this," I begged in a low voice.

Griff looked at me with eyebrows raised. "I have to," he said.

"You don't want to sleep with that guy, Griff. I know you don't. Why are you doing this?"

"I don't have time to explain myself right now," he said. My heart pounded out of my chest. "I have to go, but I'll be back."

He pulled his hand out from under mine and walked out, leaving me with a crushing pressure in my chest.

I tried hard to focus on my job for the rest of the night and not think about my fox in the arms of some stranger. The feeling of possession was strange. I wasn't sure I'd ever felt that way about anyone, and I sure as hell hadn't felt that way about someone I didn't even really know. Someone who must be insanely insecure if he made a habit out of picking up any random guy who sat next to him in a club.

After what seemed like fifteen hours, it was finally last call. Griff hadn't returned. Not that I thought he would. The Nordic man had been attractive and interested.

I began hauling trash out back and didn't see Griff come up behind me as I walked back toward the door.

"Sam?" he said softly. I whipped around and saw him standing there, eyes unsure and hands shoved in pockets.

Before I even knew what I was doing, I grabbed him, throwing my arms around him in a big hug. It was almost a kind of relief. Like seeing him there was proof of life, and I wanted to hold him to make sure he wasn't really in some seedy motel with a stranger.

Griff's arms came around me just as tightly and we held each other for a moment until things turned awkward. I pulled back and avoided looking in his eyes, terrified at what his reaction would be.

After a quick glance up to see his surprised face, I made another spontaneous move. Only this time it was a kiss instead of a hug. I cupped his cheeks and leaned in for a kiss.

Time seemed to slow down and every sensation was amplified. The softness of his lips. The prickle of his scruff beneath my palms. The sound of our breathing speeding up and the slight movement of the night air on my skin. Our tongues met in a light, testing touch and I was lost.

He tasted like… I didn't even know how to describe it. He tasted like *mine*.

Griff's hands clutched my hips as a moan escaped. I deepened the kiss and tried to crawl inside him to stay. I'd never wanted anyone more.

Finally, he pulled back, panting. "That was unexpected." Griff's mouth curled up in a sweet smile.

I staggered back as the reality of how forward I'd been him hit me full force. "I… uh… I'm sorry. I shouldn't have done that. To your face, I mean. I shouldn't have done that to your face."

Griff grinned. "No, don't you dare. Absolutely no take-backs in kissing. Especially that kind of kissing."

"What kind of kissing do you mean?" I asked, still feeling a bit dazed.

He studied me with a smirk. "Mm, my recollection is a little fuzzy. Let me refresh my memory." Griff strode forward and reversed our roles. He grabbed the sides of my face and brought his lips to mine. They were warm and wet and full, searching and teasing and so very delicious. My tongue joined his as I drank him in, unable to get my fill.

We kissed for what seemed like hours. My hands roamed down his muscular back and cupped his ass through his jeans. His fingers explored my scalp, bringing goosebumps to my skin with each pass.

My mouth traveled across his stubbled jaw to his earlobe and sucked it in. I fucking loved his earlobe—plump and silky soft. My teeth grabbed it gently and I hummed my approval, closing my eyes tighter trying to hold off the inevitable moment where we would no longer be physically glued together.

6

Griff

THE MAN WAS SIX FEET OF STRAIGHT-UP SEX APPEAL. WITH his arms wrapped around me, his scent in my nose, and his lips on my earlobe, I could have come right there without anyone touching my cock. A deep vibration moved through his chest.

"Green," Sam rumbled between breaths.

"Hmm?" I drawled as I preened under his attentions to my ear.

"Your eyes. Lime green. Fucking gorgeous," he murmured, still nibbling on my ear.

Something warm swirled in my stomach, and I turned my head to brush my lips over his temple. "Mmm, feels so good, Sam. It's been too long." I talked without thinking, but something I said made him freeze up.

Sam pulled back with furrowed brows. "What, like twenty minutes?" he asked, stepping away and crossing his arms. He might as well have turned a cold hose on me.

"What?" I asked.

"You went home with that blond guy two hours ago, and now you're saying it's been too long? Just how needy are you? Never mind. I have to go close up." Sam turned back toward the back door of the club.

"What the hell? Wait, Sam. Let me explain about that guy," I called out to his back. He held up his hand in a *don't bother* gesture as he grabbed the handle of the door. I called out to him one last time. "I haven't hooked up with anyone in months, *jackass*."

The door slammed as I turned and walked away. The sting of his rejection tamped down any confidence I may have had. If he didn't want me because he thought I was easy, then so be it. I didn't need to justify myself to anyone. I was fine on my own. And if he couldn't handle the idea of me picking up a few men in a club, then he sure as hell would never understand some of the things I did when I was younger. Fuck him.

He must have stopped and turned back around. "Griff, wait. I'm sorry," Sam called back to me. "Please explain."

I shot him the bird over my shoulder as I continued walking. I knew he couldn't come after me because he was still on the clock. I made it all the way back to my apartment before I let myself feel the raw sting of his words. One word in particular. If there was one thing I vowed to never be again as long as I lived, it was *needy*.

I didn't need shit from anyone. For more than fourteen years I'd tried to be reliant on only myself. Never would I let someone think I needed them. *Never.* Needing someone meant handing them the power to hurt you when they walked away. Forget it. No, thanks.

After my parents, the only people I'd ever let in were the Marians, and it took years before I'd allowed them into my heart. I even fought the adoption at first because I'd be damned if I'd allow another family to disappoint me like my own had. But after three solid years of Mom and Dad Marian showing up and loving on me despite my prickly outer shell, I finally caved. Once I became a part of their family, I realized my very definition of family had been perverted by my biological family. True family was there for you whether or not you needed them.

And, yes, I would go so far as to say I needed them now. I needed the Marians in my life. But there were almost twenty of them, so I had all the love I needed. Sure, I could use a regular partner for sex and fun, but loving and making myself vulnerable for someone new? Nope. Forget it. Never mind.

After I returned to my apartment, I stepped in the shower and wallowed in my hurt feelings as the hot water pounded my shoulders. Sam thought I was pretty much a whore, which hurt worse than it should have. I had busted my ass when I lived on the streets to make sure I'd never have to suck some stranger off for money. I did shitty stuff when I needed to, but I never, not once, had sex with someone for cash.

I scrubbed myself clean and dried off with a thick towel before falling into bed. I didn't think I was going to be able to show up at the club again the following night. Even though I needed more subjects for my article, I just couldn't bear the thought of trying to pick up another stranger in front of Sam, knowing what he thought of me.

I fell asleep with the stress of the article on my mind, the sting of rejection on my heart, and the memory of Sam's soft lips on my own.

7

Sam

HOW COULD I HAVE BEEN SO STUPID? DIDN'T I KNOW BETTER than to rush to judgement? Maybe there was some explanation as to why Griff picked these guys up if he didn't plan on sleeping with them. I couldn't think of one that made sense, but I wanted to give him the benefit of the doubt.

It was too late. I couldn't chase him while I was supposed to be at work helping close the club. Had I known exactly where he lived or even had his damned phone number, I would have tried to contact him to apologize and ask for a second chance.

I hadn't minded he'd been picking up guys at the club. Well, that was a lie, I definitely minded. But I was willing to get over it in order to be with him. It was the implication it had been a while I couldn't seem to get past.

By the time I got home that night, it was almost three in the morning, and I was exhausted. Jason was asleep on the sofa so I shook his shoulder and told him to go to bed. I showered and got into bed myself, but I couldn't shut my brain down.

After another hour, I finally gave up and found myself in the kitchen making large homemade macaroni-and-cheese casseroles before going for a swim. After swimming my ass off for forty minutes, I showered and headed to the youth shelter in hopes of finding a way to track down Griff.

When I got there I found Londa trying to move some stacks of chairs around. I offered to help her and we spent the next fifteen minutes moving all the chairs from the lobby back to the cafeteria.

"Thanks, Sam. What can I help you with?" she asked.

"I brought some mac and cheese for the kids, but I was also looking for Griff," I said. "Is he coming by today, or do you know how I can reach him?"

"You know, that's a good question." She smiled, taking the two big trays of macaroni from the bag I had set on the reception counter. "This smells amazing. The kids will love it. Thank you. As for Griff, let's ask Rebecca. She's doing some laundry in the back."

I wandered back to the big laundry room and found Mrs. Marian folding towels. "Need some help?" I asked.

"Oh, hi, Sam. Sure, that would be great. How are you doing, honey?" she said. Her smile was so sweet and genuine it plunged a dagger into my heart. Obviously she didn't know how rude I'd been to her son the night before.

"I'm okay. I was hoping to run into Griff though. Have you seen him?"

"Not since the other day, no. I think he's busy working on that article he's writing. No telling what library or coffee shop he's holed up in right now," she said.

"He's a writer?" I asked, feeling silly for not having known what he did for a living.

She looked at me with furrowed brows. "Well, yes. You didn't know? He's a freelance journalist. I thought that's how you two met since he's writing that article about using pickup lines in clubs."

Oh hell.

Well, that explained a few things. I couldn't help but bark out a laugh after letting out an enormous sigh of relief. No wonder he was so pissed at me.

"Oh my god," I said. "That makes complete sense. Thank you for telling me that. You have no idea how much I needed to hear it."

"Do you want me to tell him you're looking for him?" she asked.

"No, ma'am. I'll probably run into him eventually. I don't want to bother him."

"I'm sure it's no bother, but it's your choice." She went back to folding towels next to me for a few minutes before speaking again. "Listen, Sam. I was wondering if you'd come to dinner at our house on Sunday. We're so grateful that you've decided to help us out at the shelter and we'd love to have you over as a thank-you. Would you consider joining us, please? I hate thinking of you single boys never having someone cook for you."

She was so nice, and it had been a long time since I'd been mothered. It was impossible to say no. "Well, I'm supposed to work, but I can try to find someone to cover my shift."

"That would be great. Let me write down the address for you, and you can come around 4 p.m. if that works." She wandered off somewhere for a pen and piece of paper, returning to write down her address and phone number before handing it to me.

"What can I bring?" I asked, slipping the paper into my pocket.

"You don't need to bring anything, honey. You're our guest."

"Rebecca, I'm a chef. That's like asking a doctor not to do CPR when someone has a heart attack," I joked.

"Are you saying my cooking requires professional resuscitation?" she teased.

"No, ma'am. Forget I said anything," I replied. "I'll surprise you. Maybe I'll bring a meal for you to freeze for another night. Then I'll be far away before you taste it and realize I'm a fraud."

She nudged me playfully on the shoulder. "I'm sure anything you want to contribute will be appreciated, but it's not required. Oh, and the kids will be there."

"What kids? The shelter kids?" I asked.

"No, our kids. Simone, Maverick, Pete—" she said.

"Is Griff going to be there?" I asked nervously, dreading her answer. I could only imagine how he'd feel walking in his parents' house and seeing me there.

She hesitated. "I think he's going rock climbing on Sunday," she said without looking at me.

"Still, I'm not sure I should—" I began.

"Not taking no for an answer Sam, so just drop it, hon."

We finished the towels and moved on to folding sheets. Working together saved time and we finished quickly. On my way through the boys' lounge, I saw Demarcus from the other day.

"Hey, Sam. We were going to shoot some hoops out back. Wanna join us?" he asked.

"Sure. Just promise to go easy on me, because it's been a while."

I played basketball with a handful of teenage boys for about a half hour before they were called in to do homework.

That night at work, I tried again not to notice Griff's glaring absence at the bar. It was excruciating. I wanted a chance to apologize to him for the misunderstanding, but part of me was also worried he had moved his article research to another club. One where I couldn't watch his back.

The next night I saw him. It was almost midnight on Saturday when he came up to the bar. He looked amazing, dressed in a tight white T-shirt and dark low-slung jeans. The shirt showed the outline of what I could only assume were nipple piercings, and just the thought of them made me hard.

Sometimes when he moved a certain way, I could see a hint of a tattoo I hadn't noticed before peeking out from under his short sleeve. It reminded me of the one I'd seen on his hip. I wondered if he had others I hadn't seen.

He sat down at the bar and ignored me.

I walked up to him and smiled. "Hey, good lookin', whatcha got cookin'?" I asked.

He looked at me sideways like I was crazy, so I tried again.

"You tired? 'Cause you've been runnin' through my mind all day," I said, trying to jolly him out of his bad mood.

He narrowed his eyes at me in a death glare. "What are you doing?"

I dropped the smile. "I ran into your mom."

"And she hit you in the head?" he asked.

"No. She described the article you're writing about pickup lines at the clubs. I'm sorry, Fox. You have no idea how sorry I am that I misjudged you," I said, watching him.

"Whatever, it's fine," he said, looking down at the bar. I leaned across the bar and put a finger under his chin, tilting his face up to look at me.

"No, it's not fine. It wasn't fair, and I feel terrible. Can I please make it up to you, Griff? Maybe I can take you out to lunch tomorrow or something?" I asked.

For a microsecond, his eyes looked so vulnerable. Then they shuttered again, and I lost him. "Nah, I can't. I have plans already."

Oh right, the rock climbing. I had to let it go for now. Something told me pushing him would be a big mistake. But before I let it go, I wanted one thing.

"Then may I please get your number?" I asked.

He glared at me. Clearly I wasn't forgiven that easily. "Maybe another time," he said before a man sat down on the stool next to him, attracting his attention.

It was the same older man who'd propositioned me at last call a few nights before, and Griff began his usual routine. The man caught me staring at him and mistook it for interest. Throughout the rest of his time talking to Griff, he stared lasciviously at me. It was creepy.

Eventually, I decided to take a break to get away from watching

Griff put the moves on the man. Even though I now knew he probably wasn't planning on actually hooking up with him, it was still hard to watch. I took one look back at the pair, inadvertently locking eyes with Griff. I felt my chest tighten before looking away and continuing to the break room.

I escaped into the lounge and dropped down onto the sofa, leaning my head back and covering my eyes with my arms. After a short doze, I awoke to the sound of the lounge door closing.

8

Griff

I COULDN'T STOP MYSELF FROM WANTING SAM COXWELL. HE WAS all I could think about regardless of what had happened between the two of us when we argued in the parking lot.

After the older man propositioned me, and we walked out of the club together, I did my usual closing conversation where I asked him if it bothered him when people used terms of endearment. He looked at me like I was crazy.

"Fuck, man. I don't care what comes out of your mouth as long as my dick goes into it," he said with a laugh. I realized he was drunker than I'd originally thought.

"Thanks for the feedback." I smiled. "I'm going to have to take a pass tonight though."

"What? Why? Let's go have some fun," he said with a smirk.

"No, thanks. I'm still a virgin, and I'm having cold feet," I joked.

His face lit up at the fake news. "Oh. Well then, gorgeous, let me take you home and make your first time extra special. I'll take good care of you," he promised with a gleam in his eye that gave me the shivers.

"Umm, no. G'night," I said before returning into the club and making my way to the back corridor. That poor man outside probably wouldn't be able to follow through on his promise of sex anyway, if his whiskey breath was any indication of his intoxication level.

I poked my head into the employee lounge and found Sam leaning back on the sofa with his arms crossed over his face. I couldn't tell if he was sleeping or not, but I could see a tantalizing strip of his abs and happy trail where his shirt rode up. My tongue ached to explore it.

Part of me wanted so badly to approach him. Just sneak up and straddle his lap. But I still couldn't quite get past the sting of his words the night before. It was almost like he'd dangled this wonderful carrot in front of me and when I reached for it, snatched it away. The last thing I needed was someone who toyed with me.

I snuck back out and turned to leave, so caught up in my own inner conflict over Sam I didn't see the older man from the bar follow me out. As I turned the last corner to my apartment I heard him approach.

"What were you doing back there in the employee lounge?" he accused with a drunken grin on his face.

"What?" I said, turning around to stare at him. "None of your damned business. Why are you following me?"

"You promised me some fun tonight and I'm here to play. Surely you didn't think you could dangle your virginity in front of my face without tempting me a little past self-control, did you? That ass has been begging for me all night."

"No, it definitely hasn't. I'm sorry to disappoint you, but I'm not a virgin nor am I interested."

"Oh sure you are. If you want to play a little hard to get, that's fine by me." He grinned.

As he spoke, he came closer to me and I backed away, holding one arm out in front of me while reaching for my phone with the other. I would have laughed at the drunken threat if the man hadn't been taller than I was and packed with dense muscle.

He was on me before I could get my phone free of my pocket. The device fell to the pavement, and my other hand got caught between us as the man went for my mouth. His lips descended on mine, all probing tongue and scratching cheeks. He reeked and tasted of alcohol. Recoiling in disgust, I tried pushing him off me.

We scuffled on the pavement as he laughed shoved his hard-on against my crotch before thrusting one of his legs between mine.

"This your place?" he mumbled against my neck. Luckily, we were in front of a building three doors down from my own. I didn't answer him.

His hand reached down and started fumbling for my belt.

"Get the hell off me!" I yelled. "What the fuck, man? You seriously think I want some drunk stranger fucking me in the street?" My voice was a little hysterical, but I didn't think I was in as much danger as I could have been if he hadn't been so drunk.

He stumbled and almost knocked me down, accidentally elbowing me hard in the rib cage. I lost my balance, but he grabbed for me to keep me from falling. While I steadied myself, he pushed me face-first into the brick of the building next to us. He laughed in my ear. "Come on, kid, it'll be fun, I promise. Where's your place?" He reached around and fumbled for my belt again, managing to get it undone and pop open the top button of my fly.

His words kept coming out as if this was seriously going to be a fun hookup. He seemed to think I was into it.

I elbowed him and spun around, kneeing him in the nuts and then kicking out, only landing a partial blow to his thigh. He grabbed at the hem of my shirt before his leg buckled under him, my T-shirt ripping as he fell. I jumped away from him and started jogging farther along the street, reaching down to grab my phone from where it had fallen.

I didn't want to go to my building and show him where I lived, so I dialed 911 with shaky hands. After I explained what was happening to the operator, the man took off, stumbling and cursing. When he was out of sight, I told the operator he was gone and I didn't have any information on him other than the first name of Jeff he'd given me at the club.

When she offered to send a patrol car to take my statement, I told her not to bother.

I trudged up to the front door of my apartment building and tried to fit the right key into the lock. It took me a few tries before I got it. Just as I pushed open the door I heard a familiar voice calling from a few doors down.

"Griff, wait up," Sam said, jogging the last bit and bouncing up the few stairs to where I stood. As he took in the sight of me his smile fell and his face paled.

"Fox, what the hell happened?" The term of endearment spoken in his sweet voice almost caused my knees to buckle. I lurched toward him and felt his arms come up around me. After a minute of holding me tightly, he said, "Let's get you inside. Your face is all scratched up, and you're bleeding."

I handed him my keys and pulled off the rest of my ripped T-shirt, using it to hold against my cheek to try and stop the bleeding. I noticed blood on the shoulder of his Harry Dick's T-shirt and the skin of his neck.

"For what it's worth," I mumbled under the balled-up fabric, "I'm negative. Sorry I'm bleeding on you."

"I'm not worried about the blood, Griff. I'm worried about what happened to you."

Sam kissed my temple and slipped an arm around me while we walked up to my apartment door. I pointed out which key to use and he let us in.

After I lay down on the sofa and told him to help himself to whatever, I explained what happened. He found a clean dishcloth and wet it in the sink before coming to kneel on the floor next to me.

"That jackass followed you home?" he snapped, pulling the bloody shirt out of my hands and wiping my face gently with the damp towel. He wiped the cloth down my neck and followed the blood smears down my chest. That must have been when he realized my belt was undone. I thought he was going to faint. His face went white, and he snapped his eyes to mine.

"Griff..." he whispered, concern etched in his forehead. "Did he...? What else did he do?"

9

Sam

A RINGING NOISE SOUNDED IN MY EARS AND I WONDERED briefly if it was a harbinger of a stroke. I was so angry I was going numb. If that man—

"No," Griff said emphatically, reaching for my hand. "Nothing like that. He elbowed me and shoved me against a wall. He tried… that… but I spun out and kicked him before calling 911. He was really drunk. He probably wouldn't have even been able to keep it up."

The relief dropped my shoulders like a rag doll. I brushed Griff's curls off his forehead and dropped a kiss there before resting my own forehead on his. "Thank god."

We sat there like that for a moment. Just breathing and resting our heads together in grateful safety. I pulled back and kissed his forehead again before checking the scrapes on his face.

"What are you doing here?" Griff asked.

"I saw that man follow you out and had a bad feeling. He was a total creep to me the other night after my shift, and I wanted to make sure he didn't do the same to you. I told my coworkers I was leaving and headed here to make sure you were okay."

"How did you know where I lived?"

"I didn't. But I remembered Lusk Street from when I checked your ID last week," I admitted. "At first I thought it said Lust so it stuck out in my mind."

Griff laughed. "Is that right?"

"When I saw you at your door alone, I thought maybe I'd overreacted. Do you have a first-aid kit?" I asked, trying to change the subject from how much I sounded like a stalker. He pointed me in the direction of the bathroom sink and I returned with the kit I found in the cabinet.

I laughed after opening the kit. "Why do you have tampons in here?"

"Nosebleeds. They rock for that." Griff smirked. "But don't even think about putting one in my nose right now. My nose isn't bleeding."

"Damn," I said. "I was hoping to snap a photo and post it on Instagram."

I found the supplies I needed to tend to his face. "It looks like you have war paint on. These two scrapes here especially." I brushed a cleansing wipe lightly across his upper cheek and followed it with a smear of antibiotic ointment.

"Where else are you hurt?" I asked, raking my eyes over Griff's bare chest and trying not to succumb to arousal when my eyes landed on the barbells in his nipples. Fuck, I wanted those things in my mouth. I forced myself to look elsewhere.

"Here?" I asked, running my hand beneath his rib cage where an angry red mark remained.

He shivered under my touch, and I met his eyes. His pupils enlarged, and I couldn't look away.

"It doesn't hurt that badly," Griff said softly.

I realized my hand rested on his stomach, my thumb stroking the skin over his tattoo. I stood up. "Why don't I get you some ibuprofen?"

I wandered around in a circle until I came back to where he lay. I grinned sheepishly. "Where do you keep it?"

He laughed and sat up, breaking the spell. "I'll get it. Do you want something to drink? There's stuff in the fridge." Griff headed toward the bathroom and I watched the muscles of his back move as he walked. A large dragon tattoo covered his right shoulder blade and curled a scaly tail around his left bicep. It was unlike anything I'd seen and was sexy as hell. I wondered what had made him choose it.

I pulled out a couple of Gatorades and cracked one open for myself before wandering back over toward the living area where some framed photographs sat on overflowing bookshelves. The photos seemed to be mostly of Marian family members and Griff. There were a few I assumed were college friends and there were some that were taken at swim meets.

His book collection was fascinating due to the variety. Everything from classics to modern biographies, art, sci-fi, and self-help. I ran my hands over the spines of some of my favorites. *The Martian* by Andy Weir, *Ender's Game* by Orson Scott Card, and *Old Man's War* by John Scalzi. All favorites.

"You like sci-fi?" Griff asked from behind me.

"Love it. What's your favorite genre?" I asked.

"Right now I'm into creative nonfiction, like funny memoirs. My undergrad degree was journalism, but my master's was in creative nonfiction writing. Hence, the article about using pet names at the club."

"Your mom said it was pickup lines, not pet names," I said, turning to face him. "Tell me more about it."

"I basically use a pet name in everything I say to them and see how long it takes them to leave with me. Once they leave with me, I ask them how they feel about pet names. Then I come back in and do it all over again. It's not a scientific experiment or anything like that. It's a humor piece about my observations and the guys' feedback."

"Have you gone home with any of them?" I couldn't help but ask.

"Nope," he admitted. "I wasn't even tempted to come home and enjoy some one-on-one time with myself afterward." His eyes began to twinkle. "Well, until I started coming to Harry Dick's and saw you."

I looked at him. "Really?"

He nodded as his face and neck flushed deeper red.

I felt my own face heat up so I tried changing the subject. "So what other kinds of things do you like to write?"

Griff thought for a minute. "Most of what I write is humor. I do freelance work, so I dabble in a little of everything, but it usually reverts to humor in the end."

"What's your dream project?"

His eyes closed for a brief moment before he shrugged. "I don't know."

"Bullshit. Every writer has a dream. What's yours?" I pressed.

He blew out a breath and turned his lips up in a grin. "Why don't we skip the innermost thoughts part and go straight to the fact that I want to suck on your face a little bit?"

Griff's hand came up to run through my hair, sending warmth from my scalp to my dick. I leaned in and smelled his neck.

"If you insist," I said, lips against the skin of his neck. I kissed my way up to his mouth and stayed as gentle as I could. "Are you sure? You're injured. Maybe we should take it easy," I said between kisses.

"Hell no. You've been driving me crazy tonight. Every time you touch me I feel like electric sparks are skating across my skin. I want you naked in my bed, and I want your hands all over me."

I swallowed as the image of my hands all over a naked Fox made me want to throw him down right there on the floor. Instead, I turned him around and frog-marched him toward what I assumed was his bedroom.

My hands were on his bare skin just above the low waistband of his jeans. His dragon tattoo was right in front of me, and I had a chance to notice some of the intricate details. Sharp teeth, claws, jagged spikes across its back and tail. Fire licked from its mouth and smoke trailed out of its ears and nose. All defensive imagery, but right in the middle over the dragon's exposed chest was a rusty old cage covering a tiny glowing heart.

When Griff got to the bed he turned around to face me and reached his hands down to the hem of my shirt to lift it off. I leaned in to kiss him and felt his hands run up and down my chest and over my shoulders to my shoulder blades and down to my lower back.

I rested one hand on Griff's hip and the other on the side of his neck. My thumb found the tender skin behind his ear and stroked it as I licked deeper into his mouth. I moved my mouth down to his bare chest and found a nipple. I licked and sucked, tugging the barbell with my teeth and feeling my cock swell even more.

"Jesus, Griff, I could stay here all night and just play with these things," I breathed. His hands ran through my hair and my fingers dipped down inside the back of his jeans.

"Not complaining," he hissed as I tugged his nipple again. I moved one hand to the front of his jeans to stroke his erection through the denim. His cock was thick and long through the fabric, and I couldn't wait to get my mouth on it.

Moving my lips down his abdomen, I traced wet kisses lightly over his developing bruise and down to his hip, sliding his jeans down farther to suck harder the at the light skin over his sharp hipbone. I was able to see the entire quote inked onto his hip.

We live in a rainbow of chaos.

"Tell me about this," I murmured through shaky breaths, tracing the letters with a finger.

Griff sucked in a breath and tried to focus his green eyes on me. "It's a quote from the artist Cezanne. It basically means life is nuts, but there's beauty in it," he said, stomach muscles rippling under my touch.

My thumb kept rubbing pressure up and down his shaft

through the fabric until I finally opened his jeans and slid them all the way down. I took a minute to appreciate how well he filled out his dark blue briefs before I slid those off too.

Once he was bare, I gently pushed him to sit on the bed. He leaned back on his hands just as I lowered my mouth on him.

10

Griff

"JESUS *FUCK*," I GASPED AS SAM'S HOT, WET MOUTH TOOK ME all the way down on the very first pass. "God, Sam."

His mouth was all over my cock, sucking, swirling, and teasing until my nuts ran to hide and trembled with the need to spill all over every fucking thing.

I moaned and cursed, torn between the need to come and the desire to hold off and come with him. Sitting up, I reached for his fly, but his mouth felt too good and I fell back on my hands again.

"Don't stop," I begged. I saw Sam's mouth curl into a smile around my cock as his fingers teased me. That's all it took. I came shouting his name, unable to warn him ahead of time. He swallowed through it all and then spent extra time gently licking while I collapsed backward on the bed.

"Sunshine, I'm a little embarrassed by how quickly I came," I confessed. "Maybe that'll prove to you how long it's been for me."

He laughed and rubbed his cheeks with his hands. "I'll take it as a compliment."

Sam crawled up my body and dropped some kisses on my face, both cheeks and forehead.

"Your neck has some blood on it from my face. Want to take a shower?" I asked.

"That depends. Will there be naked entertainers in the shower?" He grinned.

"Do you have any money for tips?" I teased.

He smiled and stood, pulling me up by the hand and leading me toward the bathroom. I started the water while Sam stripped out of the rest of his clothes.

"Ooooh," I said before clapping a hand to my mouth in mortification.

His head snapped up with a questioning glance. "What was that for?"

"Nothing. Never mind," I said.

"Try again, pumpkin," he said with a laugh.

"I just… you're uncut. I like that," I admitted, feeling my face light on fire and incinerate right there in the bathroom.

His laugh was warm and easy, putting me at ease more than I would have expected. "Good to know, Foxy. I'll let you get a closer look later."

"Shut up." I laughed and pinched his ass. It was an incredible ass—all bubble butt and squeezable. I wanted to gnaw on it. I followed him into the shower, doing my best to maul that gorgeous ass with my greedy hands.

"An ass man, too, huh?" Sam asked over his shoulder. "Glad I could be of service."

"Your ass is stellar. But your cock is pretty wonderful too. Don't make me choose," I said, running my hands around to grab his shaft and pull gently. I turned him around and made sure he was under the warm spray when I knelt down.

"Mmm," I said, gently mouthing and tugging his foreskin with soft lips before licking the tip underneath. Sam sucked in a breath and grabbed for the tile walls. I loved to tease and take my time when I gave head. It was like a game: try to see how absolutely desperate you could make someone before you pushed them over the edge into oblivion.

So I toyed with him. I alternated from slow to fast and gentle to aggressive. I let him fuck my mouth and then I pulled off to tongue his balls and kiss his inner thighs. By the time I was ready to pull the trigger and push him over the edge, his dick leaked and his thighs trembled. He was crying out and cursing, begging me to make him come. I sucked him down and then backed off, looking up to make eye contact with him before sucking him as deep as I could possibly go, trying to wrap my throat around his hard length.

He came in a hot rush down my throat. His voice was muffled as he bit down on his fist and screamed. When Sam's other arm shot out to brace himself again on the tile wall, I wrapped my arm around his waist and held him. "Hold up, s-sunshine. Let me wash you off before you collapse."

I'd almost called him sweetheart instead of sunshine. It was one thing to joke around with corny terms of endearment, but it was another to use an endearment that actually meant something. I felt my body stiffen into self-protection mode, and I carefully let go of Sam.

I didn't make eye contact as I washed him with soap—clinical, efficient movements rather than caressing ones—finishing with a quick shampoo before handing him a towel. I walked out, leaving him to fend for himself as I dried off and got in bed.

Sam walked away from my bedroom, and I was afraid he was going to leave. My heart began to pound and every cell in my body screamed, *Stay, please, god, stay.*

It occurred to me I was running hot and cold, but I justified it with the thought that maybe he didn't notice.

When he came back in carrying two glasses of water, I let out a sigh of relief. I held the covers open and saw his face break into a grateful smile as he slid into the bed and held out a glass to me.

"Thanks," I said, taking a drink.

"If you don't want me to stay, speak up. Otherwise, I'm about ten seconds away from snuggling the shit out of you and serenading you with some jazzy snores." He grinned.

"Can I get one without the other?" I asked. "I do love a good snoring concert."

"Nope. They're a package deal." He finished his drink and set the empty glass on the bedside table before turning off the lamp.

When I leaned over him to set mine down too, he ran a warm hand up my back. "It's late," Sam said in a sleepy voice. "But at some point I want you to tell me about your amazing tattoo. I've never seen anything like it."

"Thanks," I said before leaning down and kissing his lips. They were wet and cool from the water.

I lay back on the pillow and felt Sam shift beside me. He turned me on my side and spooned in behind me. God, that felt good. It had been way too long since I'd had someone hold me like that in bed.

His stubble grazed my ear and I felt his breath before I heard his whisper.

"Stop overthinking things, Fox, and just be happy in the moment. I know your gears are turning in there, and you don't have to talk to me about it. I just want you to know it's okay. When you tell me to go, I'll go. But I really hope you won't."

I didn't know what to say. Normally I would have just lain there frozen and pretended like it had never happened. But I really liked him. And he was unusually sweet.

Rolling over within the circle of his arms, I reached my hands up to cup his face. "Thank you," I said before kissing him again. The rest of what I wanted to say refused to pass my lips.

I don't want you to go, and if I ever say I do, please stay anyway.

11

Sam

WE SLEPT LATE BECAUSE WE'D STAYED UP UNTIL FOUR IN the morning. By the time I opened my eyes, it was almost noon and I remembered Griff was supposed to go rock climbing. I wondered if I should wake him.

I leaned forward and placed my lips between his shoulder blades, kissing softly and inhaling his sleepy scent. The man's body was like a sensual buffet. The ways he looked, tasted, smelled, and felt were so very enticing.

My index finger traced the dragon, looking for tiny details the artist obviously enjoyed including in his or her work.

"You're tickling me," he mumbled into the pillow.

"No way you're ticklish if you can remain that still while I do this," I accused with a laugh.

"I'm a ninja. I've learned to control my physical response to external stimulation," he replied.

I reached around and tweaked one of his barbells. He yelped and curled up, making me laugh.

"The ninja master must be so proud of his star apprentice," I said. "Aren't you supposed to be rock climbing today?"

Griff turned to look at me. His curly hair was insane from having gone to sleep with it wet. His eyes were still half asleep and he had a pillowcase wrinkle on his cheek. Never had I ever seen anyone look sexier.

"That's a very random question, Sam. I don't rock climb. Why?"

"Your mom said you were going rock climbing."

He ran a hand through his hair, making it crazier. "My brother Jude climbs. You sure she didn't say it was him? But even then, he wouldn't go on a Sunday. We have a big family dinner every Sunday at Mom and Dad's house."

My stomach dropped and I groaned, leaning back against the pillow and putting my arm over my face. "Oh god. Your mom totally played me."

Griff propped himself up on an elbow and put a hand on my chest. "What do you mean?"

"She invited me to come eat at her house today and told me you weren't going to be there. She definitely didn't say it was a big family dinner. Your mom is up to something."

Griff laughed. "Did you tell her you'd come?"

"Yes. She wasn't taking no for an answer," I said in my defense.

"Not surprised. Well, payback is hell. I think we should figure out how to turn this back around on her," Griff said.

His fingertips traced circles on my chest and abs while he thought. My thinking juice drained southward, however, and I flipped him onto his back to take those damned barbells into my mouth again. After several minutes of the sensual torture, he couldn't stay quiet.

"Want you to fuck me," Griff gasped.

I sucked on his nipples while I palmed his dick and tickled the skin below. Griff whimpered as I licked a finger and snaked it under his balls to tease his hole. His body arched toward me and I could see his green eyes glassy with desire.

My mouth came up to twist together with his before I asked if he had condoms and lube. When he grabbed them from a drawer, I dropped them on the bed next to me and flipped him over onto his stomach. I remembered him telling me it had been a while since he'd been with anyone, and I sure as hell didn't want to hurt him.

I pushed his knees up under him until his ass was in front of me, completely exposed and fucking gorgeous. My mouth dropped kisses on each perfect cheek, teeth nipping here and there and fingers grabbing at the firm roundness. Damn, I was going to enjoy this.

My lips moved in a wet trail to the top of his crease where I licked down until my tongue found the right spot. He gasped as he felt my mouth on him, lapping and sucking and probing. I spread him open with my hands and dove in. His responsiveness made the whole experience even hotter. He whimpered and moaned and shuddered.

He gripped the sheets in tight fists and kept repeating the word *fuck* like it was a prayer. I pulled back my mouth and slid a wet finger into him, feeling his muscles squeeze and relax around my finger. God, he was tight.

Alternating mouth, tongue, finger, thumb, I stretched him out as much as I could before opening the cap of the lube. He already quivered facedown on the bed. When I slid two lubed fingers inside him, he shoved back onto my hand and lost his patience.

"Get inside of me, goddammit, Sam," he begged.

I grinned as I grabbed the condom and slid it on quickly, drizzling lube out and then pressing the head of my cock against his tight ass.

My body went slow and steady while my heart raced wildly. As soon as I was all the way in, Griff's muscles relaxed and I was able to move. He propped himself up with his hands and shoved back against me, letting me know he was ready for it.

I grasped his hips and began to thrust in and out, relishing the feel of the firm muscles gripping my cock and the smooth warm skin under my hands.

The dragon rippled as Griff's shoulders moved. His hair stuck out everywhere, and I took a minute to appreciate a particular curl wrapped around the edge of one ear.

"You're gorgeous," I said, pressing my lips against his spine. "Feel so fucking good."

I pulled him up in front of me so we were both upright on our knees with my arms wrapped around his front for support. Griff's hand came back to grip the back of my head and hold me close.

He leaned his head back on my shoulder and I kissed his mouth hungrily as I continued to push up into him. I grabbed his cock and began to stroke, sliding my other hand up his chest and onto his collarbone.

I felt his cock jumping in my palm and I began to whisper into his ear. The words came out garbled: *want, need, please.*

Griff tensed, clutching the arm I had around his chest with both of his hands before coming in great shoots arching over the sheets in front of him.

"That's it," I gasped as his tight body began to squeeze my cock in earnest. Sheets of heat radiated from my balls to the outer reaches of my fingers and toes. The pleasure licked at my muscles, causing me to release in violent shudders.

We fell forward, and I pulled out, leaning sweaty and heavy against Griff's back as we took in deep breaths. My arms were wrapped around his front and my face was buried in the back of his neck.

He turned around to face me and bury his face in my shoulder, his arms wrapped around me. I had no idea what was behind this gesture, but I would gladly take it and return it. It didn't take a genius to determine that right now, I'd take whatever Griff Marian was willing to give me. I was falling quickly and falling hard.

12

Griff

I TRIED TO PLAY IT OFF LIKE IT WAS COMPLETELY NORMAL TO grab someone into a tight, never-let-you-go stranglehold right after super-hot sex. For all I knew, it was normal. For some kind of weirdo sex-hugging cult.

My heart hammered and sent out lots of stupid feelings I wasn't prepared to deal with. I needed to lighten the mood, pronto. Before pulling away, I snuck my tongue out to lick the salty sweat off his neck and felt him shiver.

"Do you have a phone number for Dillon?" I asked, pulling away and climbing off the bed.

Sam tilted his head and frowned at me, clearly taken aback by my abrupt mention of another man.

"Who's Dillon?" he asked.

"That guy from culinary school who had a weird thing with my sister, Simone."

"Oh, the surfer dude. Um, no… I don't think so. Why?" he asked,

61

following me to the bathroom.

"I just thought if we could convince him to come to family dinner again, it would be a good start to Mom's payback."

"Wouldn't be nice for Simone though. What about us staging the same scene and me tumbling you into the pool? That could be funny," Sam said, turning on the sink.

"Hmm, that's a good idea too." We kept brainstorming ideas while we cleaned up. At one point Sam got very distracted by my nipple piercings again, and I had to resist the urge to go for round two.

"I was going to cook something to bring, but the ingredients are at my place," Sam said as his mouth made its way back up to mine. His hands were all over my ass and my back, and our chests pressed together.

"You don't need to make anything. You're our guest—*ahhh...*" I said when he licked his tongue into my ear. "Stop, you're distracting me."

"Distracting you from what, sugar britches?" he teased, continuing to suck at my sensitive ear.

"You'll never win at that game, pookie-bear. I'll own you and we both know it." I grinned. "I get paid to drop the cheesy nicknames, remember? I'm like a pro."

"If you say so, Foxy."

"Fuck," I groaned, palming my swelling cock. That man had a way of getting to me with just one word. "You win. How did you learn about my name anyway? You called me Fox before we even met."

Sam stopped his attentions to my ear and pulled back to look at me. "What are you talking about? You always start off with the guys in the club by saying, 'Hey, foxy, can I buy you a drink?'"

I snorted. "Oh right, but Fox was my last name before I was adopted."

Sam's eyes widened. "No shit?"

I shrugged. "No shit."

"I've been calling you Fox and your name really was Fox?" He laughed. "Wait, does it bother you? Like, bad memories or anything?"

"Not at all. It's a part of me. And somehow you say it differently than anyone else does. Like… I don't know. Just different." I looked down at his happy trail and ran a finger through the hair there. "I like it when you say it."

Sam tilted my chin back up and started kissing my jaw and then my neck. If I hadn't felt so wrung out from earlier, I might have been up for more action.

"We should have had a threesome so there was someone to dress us while we kept kissing," I mumbled.

Sam barked out a laugh. "That's as good a reason as any, I guess. Next time?"

"Nah. I'm not very good at sharing, to be honest."

"Me neither," he growled before rousing himself enough to look for his clothes.

After dressing I agreed to go with Sam to his place so he could cook whatever it was he wanted to bring to my parents'. The idea of him coming to Marian family dinner was a little strange. It made my stomach twist, so I tried not to think about it. People brought friends to family dinner all the time. It was a casual affair. No big deal.

When Sam remembered the only shirt he had was dotted in blood, I realized exactly what I was going to do to poke fun at my mom. I grabbed a T-shirt from my dresser for him to put on. He looked at it skeptically. "You really want me to wear this?"

"Not only do I want you to wear it, but I want you to wear it to dinner."

"Oh hell no." He laughed. "That's not fair to your poor mother."

"She deserves it," I reminded him. "She'll get a kick out of it, I promise. My family has a thing about funny T-shirts. This was one of the ones made after my brothers' weddings earlier this year."

Sam shrugged and put the shirt on. "All right, let's do this. If anyone in your family keels over from a cardiac event, though, don't blame it on me."

I read the familiar pink print on the white shirt. *The Marian Type.*

Something inside me jangled. The man wore my clothes. And a shirt that implied we were getting married, no less. *Dear god.* I began to think the joke was on me.

But Sam was so laid back it was contagious. Being in his presence comforted and relaxed me to the point of letting go of worries more than usual.

When we got to his apartment, I met his roommates. He had told me on the way over they were named Robbie and Jason, but what he failed to mention was that Robbie was actually Robert Warren, son of the famous actor, Darren Warren.

I looked from Robbie to Sam with a laugh. "A little heads up would have been appreciated," I said under my breath.

Robbie laughed. "No way. Sam and I have a deal. We both vowed long ago to never mention our infamous fathers to others. I've kept up my end, so I expect Sam to keep up his."

I narrowed my eyes at Sam, but he looked away. *Who the hell was his father?*

"Well, it's nice to meet you, Robbie. You too, Jason. Is your dad someone I should know about as well?" I joked, trying to ease the tension in the room.

"Well, if you're in the market for a nice used pickup truck, then he sure is," he joked. "He owns Tri-City Auto in Cumberland, Kentucky. Surely you've heard of him."

"Is he the one who wears the big chicken costume and yells at the camera in those TV ads?" I winked.

"Nope. His is a donkey costume, because if you don't like his prices, you can kiss his ass."

We were all laughing when the doorbell rang. Robbie looked guilty and began to blush.

"Who are you expecting, Robbie?" Jason asked with a smirk.

"Don't say one fucking word, either of you. Understand?" He

glared before opening the door.

The man at the door was a petite, shy-looking guy. Robbie greeted him with a hug, but when the man saw Sam, he recoiled. I looked at Sam to try to figure out what was going on.

"Hi, Neil," Sam said. "It's okay. Come on in."

The man walked in and greeted Jason with a small smile and a wave. Jason introduced me to Neil and explained they'd all gone to college together.

Robbie said, "I invited Neil over for brunch, not realizing our chef wasn't going to make it home last night, *ahem*."

"I know, I'm sorry. I forgot to text you guys, but I can whip up some sandwiches if anyone's hungry," Sam said.

"I'd like one," I said, raising my hand. "Need any help?"

Sam smiled at me, sending rivulets of warmth through my chest. "Sure, buttercup, I'd love some help."

I rolled my eyes but didn't miss the crazy looks the other three men gave Sam. "Long story," I told them before following him to the kitchen.

Someone called out after us, "We have time!"

Once our lunch prep was underway and Sam started pulling out ingredients for the corn dip he wanted to make for my parents' dinner, I asked him the question.

"Who's your dad, Sam? Why did Robbie say he's infamous?" I asked.

Beautiful brown eyes turned to look at me. "He's a retired football player and complete jackass. We aren't really on speaking terms."

I squeezed his shoulder. "What about your mom?"

"She took off when I was fourteen and my sister was six. Got a big divorce settlement and began traveling the world looking for her next sugar daddy, I guess."

Whoa.

I stepped forward and slid my arms around him. "I'm sorry."

13

Sam

"THAT SUCKS, SAM," GRIFF SAID AS HIS WARM ARMS CAME around me.

I nodded and stepped in to get even closer.

"I had no idea," he said next to my ear.

I let out a breath and sank into him, enjoying the feeling of Griff's body pressed against mine and his scent enveloping me.

"She just couldn't handle the reality of being married to a cheating narcissist, so she left us with our grandmother. It's been over ten years, but it still hurts like a bitch," I admitted into his shoulder.

"Of course it does. But why didn't you stay with your dad?"

"I've always suspected it was because we cramped his style. He was enjoying his newfound singlehood."

We held each other for a while longer until Jason walked in. "Oh, uh, sorry. My bad," he said before turning to walk out.

I stepped back from Griff. "No, it's okay. The sandwiches are ready."

Griff took the plates out to the table while I finished putting the dip together and sticking it in the oven. We still had a little while before we needed to be at the Marians'.

I thought about my dad and the details I hadn't given Griff.

My father was Ray VanBuren, a famous retired quarterback and the current owner of the Oklahoma City NFL team. When I was only fourteen, my father had been caught having an affair with his coach's eighteen-year-old daughter. He'd been stupid enough to record video of one of their sessions and shared it with some friends, one of whom then sold it to the highest bidder in the press. The scandal had been brutal, and the resulting fallout between my parents had been a media spectacle.

How could I tell Griff the full truth about who my father was? If he found out I was raised by Ray VanBuren, he might wonder if I'd turn out the same way. And I could tell Griffin Marian wasn't the type who trusted easily to begin with.

I finished prepping my jalapeño corn dip and joined the others at the table in the other room.

During lunch, Neil must have hit a guilt-induced breaking point about hooking up with my ex-boyfriend because he suddenly blurted out, "I slept with Johnny."

Everyone else stopped talking and looked at the little guy. I could have sworn he was sweating.

"It's okay, Neil. I promise. No offense, but you're not the only one who's slept with him lately. I hope you were careful," I said.

"Who's Johnny?" Griff asked.

Jason shot a questioning glance at me before Robbie answered, "Sam's ex-boyfriend."

I shot my friend a look. *Thanks for that, asshole.*

"Sorry," Robbie said through a grin.

"It's fine. But seriously, Neil. You should find someone nicer. And more faithful," I said, trying not to notice Griff's eyes on me.

Neil shot a look at Robbie, and I realized what the deal was. Neil and Robbie. I could think of a worse pairing than these two. Robbie was a sweetheart and so was Neil. I grinned at Robbie and winked. *Yep, I see what you're doing, buddy.*

Robbie's face bloomed red before he looked away.

When it was time to head out to the Marians', I changed into a clean pair of khaki pants but kept on the shirt. I packed up the hot corn dip into an insulated bag and threw the bag of tortilla chips on top. It wasn't anything fancy, but it usually went over well with a crowd.

On the way over I was nervous for some reason, even though I'd already met many of the people I was going to see there. Griff must have noticed because he reached over to put a hand on my leg and squeeze. We were in his Jeep and the drive took a little less than an hour. When we pulled up in front of a multimillion-dollar mid-century modern home, I couldn't help but whistle when I saw it.

"I know. It really freaked me out at first. Thomas came from a wealthy family. His parents died before I had a chance to meet them, and Dad inherited everything. The only other person left from that side of the family is our crazy great-aunt. She'll probably be here, so be prepared. The woman curses like a sailor and will ask you if you pitch or catch as soon as she finds out you're gay. Oh, and her two best friends are lesbian grannies. They might be here too."

"Uh, what?" I laughed, assuming he was joking.

Griff shrugged. "Don't say I didn't warn you."

When we entered the house I heard several deep voices coming from somewhere in the back. I followed Griff to the kitchen where a group of people stood around the big island.

"There they are!" Rebecca Marian said. She met my eyes before giving me a quick hug and looking sheepishly at Griff. "I didn't know you were going to be here, Griff."

"Give it a rest, Mom," he said with a smile. "The gig is up."

"Uh-oh." She laughed, moving over to hug him too. When she pulled back, she realized his face was banged up. "Griff, honey, what happened?"

"Oh, uh, just a scrape. I tripped on the sidewalk in front of my building last night and rammed my face into the bricks," he said.

Fortunately, she got distracted from her concern when she noticed what I was wearing.

"Oh no you didn't." She giggled. "Boys, get in here," she yelled out to the backyard.

Two men walked in, one had strawberry-blond hair and the other was tall, dark, and handsome.

"This is Sam," Rebecca said proudly. "Griff's, uh, friend." Griff snorted at this and rolled his eyes at me.

The Italian-looking guy was Tristan and the lighter-haired one was Griff's brother Blue.

"No way." Blue laughed when he saw my shirt. "Babe, check it out." He looked at his husband with a knowing smirk.

Tristan took one look at it and burst out laughing. He reached out a hand to shake mine. "Welcome to the family, Sam. Buckle up, it's a wild ride."

Griff blushed an adorable shade of pink before mumbling, "He's just wearing the shirt as a joke to get back at Mom for conning him into coming. We're not dating or anything."

Disappointment shot through me like an unexpected zap from an electric outlet. It wasn't as though I thought we were life partners already, but I'd at least like a shot at dating the guy.

Blue pinched his husband in the side. "You're just as crazy as the rest of us, admit it."

"I am now, anyway." Tristan laughed as he snaked his arm around Blue's waist. Blue leaned against him, smiling, and it was so nice to see a couple clearly happy together and supported by their family.

After I greeted some of the family members I'd met at the shelter, including Simone, Maverick, and Thomas, I unpacked my hot dip and set it on the island. Rebecca swooned over it and found a bowl for the chips.

Other family members continued to arrive. Griff's brother Pete and his seemingly pregnant wife, Ginger. Apparently they had the only Marian grandchildren, but the girls were off at a friend's birthday party. Then came Dante, the youngest of the nine kids. He was a quiet sort of guy but seemed to be very close to Griff. I got the feeling Dante looked up to his older brother, and I was curious to hear more of their story. There was something about Dante's eyes that was either sad or just indicated an old soul.

A few minutes later, Jamie and his husband, Teddy, arrived. I had known several of the Marians were gay, but it was quite a different thing seeing it in person. Maybe part of it was my being so used to witnessing casual hookups at Harry Dick's. Whereas here, I was seeing loving, committed relationships in a family setting. It was nice. Reassuring and comforting in a way. Honestly, it surprised me how much it affected me.

Jamie was a wildlife veterinary professor at UC Davis and his husband was a photographer. I asked them how they met and heard the story of Teddy trying to convince Jamie to let him photograph him with animals in Denali.

"Sounds like one of those firemen calendars but with wild animals," I said.

Teddy threw back his head and laughed. "Don't give me any ideas. I am totally doing that for Rebecca and Thomas's Christmas present this year." He ran his hand through Jamie's wavy brown hair.

"Shut up." Jamie laughed. "Can you imagine? All Jamie, all the time."

"I'm always happy to photograph you," he said to Jamie before turning back to me. "He's amazing with animals, but he's also a natural in front of the camera."

Jamie blushed. "It's actually the skill of the photographer. What he didn't tell you was that one of the photos he took the week we met won the Gramling Prize."

"No kidding?" I said. "That's amazing. I'd love to see it."

Griff pulled my hand and led me out of the kitchen. "Mom and Dad have a print of it in the family room."

When we walked into the family room, I expected him to point to a framed print of the photo. Instead, he pushed me back against a wall and kissed me.

14

Griff

WATCHING SAM INTERACT WITH MY FAMILY WAS LIKE A drug. I'd never had a happy family as a child. No love, banter, or camaraderie. So when I became a Marian, I found so much I never even knew I'd been missing.

Standing in the kitchen was like having another one of those moments of glimpsing something I never thought I'd have. I saw Blue and Tristan teasing each other and sharing an inside joke. Teddy and Jamie bragged about each other. And all of them were able to reach out and touch the person they loved whenever they wanted to. No fear. No holding back.

I wondered if I'd ever get married. Would a marriage commitment somehow convince me to trust the other person not to leave? I didn't think it worked that way. You probably had to trust the other person first, then decide to marry them. The whole thing made my stomach turn sour.

Sam's tongue fiddled with mine and his arms wrapped around

my back.

"What was that for?" he said, smiling.

"You're a good sport, that's all. It's not easy putting up with this group."

"Mmm," he said as he claimed my mouth again. "So far, so good. Now show me that photo before I rip your clothes off and toss you onto your parents' sofa."

"Fuck," I mumbled before tearing my mouth off his and pointing to the wall across the room.

Sam wandered over to the framed photograph of Jamie sitting on a log with two baby beavers sitting on him. He studied it for several moments.

"Wow. Teddy is really good. Look at the light behind Jamie in the woods. That's amazing. Those animals just came right up to him and climbed on him?"

After we talked about it for a few minutes, we made our way back into the kitchen in time to see Aunt Tilly arrive with Granny in tow. After hugs all around and introducing Sam to the two ladies, I asked where Irene was.

"She's sick, honey," Mom said.

Granny snorted. "Yeah, sick of being around me. I think she just wanted some time to herself."

"Well, aren't you a handsome devil," Tilly said to Sam, raking her eyes up and down his six feet of drool-worthiness.

He blushed. "Thanks, ma'am."

"Call me Aunt Tilly, cutie." She smiled.

"Sure thing, doll," Sam said with a wink. Aunt Tilly might have actually giggled.

"Time to eat," Simone called out. "We're eating outside, but serve yourself in here first."

I noticed Sam's dip dish was scraped clean and the bowl of chips was empty. Score one for the new guy.

Dinner was a loud affair with Marians talking over each other and a total of at least fifteen of us sitting around two long tables.

Sam was able to hold his own, telling stories from the club and answering Tilly's questions about go-go boys. Every so often he'd reach over and rest his arm on the back of my chair, giving me just enough taste of his scent to make me crazy.

After a while, the dishes had been cleared and Maverick set out tubs of ice cream to go with some brownies he'd made for dessert.

I watched Sam as he spoke to Tristan on the other side of him. My hands itched to touch him but I'd be damned if I'd play boyfriends in front of my whole family.

They talked about Tristan's vineyard and the events he put on there.

"Right now we have a local caterer who comes in to provide most of our food for special events. We have a regular line cook at the restaurant attached to the bar, but Blue and I have been dreaming of expanding the vineyard to be more of a full-service resort with a spa and gourmet restaurant. The property that borders ours is considering selling us 200 acres. We would build some individual luxury cottages, a spa building, and a family home for the two of us with enough bedrooms for our own visitors," Tristan explained.

"Right now we have to put everyone up at the lodge, and it's just not as personal," Blue added, looking around at everyone's faces. "Plus, there's no room for the baby."

Silence fell until the only sound was ice clinking in someone's glass.

"I'm sorry, what did you say?" Mom asked in a restrained voice.

"Oh fuck." Aunt Tilly laughed. "Tristan's gone and knocked Blue up."

At the word *baby*, I grabbed for Sam's hand under the table without thinking and laced my fingers through his. He squeezed my hand without taking his other off the beer he sipped.

"About time," Granny added, holding up her wineglass for a toast.

74

"Wasn't for lack of trying, Granny," Tristan said with a laugh.

Sam choked on his beer and Simone squealed.

"Are you two having a baby?" Mom whispered reverently. "Really?"

Blue blushed fiercely but he nodded and smiled tearfully, turning his face into Tristan's neck.

Tristan laughed and kissed Blue's head before taking over. "We have a surrogate, and she just had her first ultrasound. Blue was too nervous to tell anyone until we knew everything was okay. We have pictures if you want to—" A cacophony of Marians interrupted him.

"OF COURSE WE WANT TO," Simone shrieked, jumping up to hug Blue and Tristan. Mom cried and Dad hugged her with a silly grin on his face.

I realized I gripped Sam's hand too tightly when he looked at me with a raised eyebrow. He leaned over to whisper in my ear.

"You okay?"

I nodded but didn't say anything, dropping his hand like it was on fire. He gave me one last look before turning back toward Tristan to offer him congratulations.

Pete and Ginger asked if they could snap photos with their phones of the ultrasound picture to show the girls. My nieces were going to flip out when they found out about the baby, and everyone got even more excited when they realized Pete and Ginger's child would grow up so close in age to Blue and Tristan's.

The rest of the evening passed in celebration and speculation. Everyone agreed it would be great if the baby could have Tristan's looks and Blue's artistic talent. Granny kept trying to explain that genetics didn't work that way because two men couldn't father the same baby. Finally Tilly snapped.

"Jesus, woman, let us daydream already. If I can't have Tristan's sexy ass in my daydream, then what the fuck is the point?"

Sam looked at me and I thought his eyeballs might fall out and roll across the patio. I shook my head and gave him a look that said,

I told you so.

After we said our goodbyes and Mom hugged Sam, making him promise to come again, we got into my Jeep to head back to the city.

"That woman is a piece of work," Sam said. I assumed he was talking about Tilly.

"I tried to warn you."

"Griff, she asked me to recommend some flavored lube. I might have stroked out a little bit."

"What did you tell her?" I laughed.

"I told her we hadn't covered that in culinary school. By the time she was done laughing, your brother Maverick had saved me."

"I tried to warn you. You handled the whole night remarkably well," I said, risking a glance over at him. He was striking. The glow from the sunset shone across his skin and it shot warm threads through his short dark hair.

"It was amazing, actually. I sometimes I forget I don't have that anymore. It's just my sister and me. Lacey went to college a few weeks ago on the East Coast, so this is the longest I've gone without seeing her. I loved being with your big family and seeing how close you all are. You're really lucky, Griff."

I was floored. For someone to tell me, Griffin Fox Marian, that I was lucky to have such a loving family? It was incomprehensible. My brain understood I was, indeed, lucky to have the Marian family. But my heart was used to being shuttered as a result of my first family. The one I hadn't been so lucky to have.

"You're right, Sam. I'm very lucky. How's your sister doing so far? Do you text her or talk on the phone?"

"We text every day but she's pretty busy. She rows for the University of Virginia, so she's juggling classes with sports and making new friends. She sounds happy though, so I'm not complaining."

"Does she still live with your grandmother?" I asked.

"With me, actually," Sam said. "She has a room in our apartment. Our grandmother, Hattie, died a few years ago when I was in culinary school. Lacey and I had a long talk about what to do and where to live. We decided to move downtown together and got the apartment. It put her closer to her school and several of her friends, and I was able to continue my courses and still be nearby in case she needed me."

"Do you ever see your dad?" I asked.

"Only once in the past ten years."

I reached over to hold his hand and kiss it. Heaviness fell between us.

"Fuck, Foxy. Let's change the subject before we both have to slit our wrists, okay?" he said with a smile. "A new baby, huh? That was some exciting news for your family."

"Nope, next topic please," I said quickly. Sam looked over at me, clearly surprised.

"Okay… what kind of flavored lube do *you* like?" he said, and we both started laughing.

By the time I pulled up to his apartment, we were back to easy flirting and joking around. Sam was so fun to be with, and I had to bite my tongue to keep from asking him to come home with me again. But I wasn't about to do anything that could be construed as needy.

I could tell he was a little unsure of how to say goodbye when it was time to get out of the car. The Jeep was double-parked, but I got out and came around to give him a proper goodbye.

The first thing that struck me as he stepped out of the car was the T-shirt he still wore. My heart stuttered and I almost tripped on the curb.

He gathered me into his arms and brought his face down to mine. Before our lips touched, he said, "Griffin Marian, I had an incredible twenty-four hours with you. You are smart and funny, not to mention gorgeous, and I am prepared to do just about anything to see you again." Then his lips were on mine with heartbreaking tenderness. The kiss started off light and worshipful, tasting and savoring before he probed deeper, and I let out a sigh into his mouth. His large hands held my face as mine grasped the waistband of his pants.

My heart slammed in my chest, and my head spun with words unsaid. If I didn't walk away then, I was going to beg him to let me stay.

I pulled away with a gasp, took one more taste of him with a quick kiss, and then pulled away again.

15

Sam

WHEN GRIFF PULLED AWAY, I SAW HIS HESITATION AND wondered, as usual, what was going on in his head. Obviously he was dealing with some internal conflict, and I assumed that was the cause of his vacillation between seemingly wanting to be with me and wanting to keep me at arm's length.

The only thing I could do was give him the space he wanted. We hadn't known each other long enough for anything else.

I gave him one last smile before turning and jogging up to my front door. When I got inside the apartment, I wasn't surprised to see Jason lounging on the sofa in front of some football on TV.

"Hey, where are the lovebirds?" I asked.

"They're in Robbie's bedroom fucking like bunnies. Didn't you wonder why I had the volume up so high on this thing?"

"What's Robbie's deal? Did he get jealous seeing Neil with Johnny the other night or what?"

"Dunno. But it's kinda cute, those two together. They came out of their sex cave long enough to share a pizza with me earlier. Neil's a nice guy. Must have been desperate to hook up with Johnny, no offense." Jason grinned.

"Stop saying 'no offense' every time time you mention him. God, I'm over it. Let's forget we were ever together, all right?"

"Good," Jason said, sitting up straighter. "Does that mean we can talk about Griff now?"

"Dammit." I chuckled. "What do you want to know?"

"First of all, is he the guy from the club you were talking about the other day?"

"Yes."

"And how, pray tell, was the… ah… *snuggling*." He snickered.

"Pretty fucking amazing actually," I admitted. "I really like this guy, Jason."

"I can tell. You were looking at him like you wanted to hand him the key to the kingdom."

"And I do," I said. "Too bad he's not ready for the key to my kingdom though. The guy is scared about something. Not sure what though. He's running a little hot and cold."

"All I saw was hot. He was looking at you the same way you were looking at him, and when the subject of Johnny came up, he looked bothered by it."

"Really?" I grinned. "That's good to know. Maybe a little jealousy will help him get his head out of his ass."

We spent the rest of the evening watching stupid shit on TV before I finally went to bed. I had to get up early the next morning and needed to get some sleep. Just as I was drifting off, I heard my phone ping. It was a text from Griff, and I couldn't help but smile.

Griff: *Hey sweet cheeks, you still up?*

Sam: *Barely. Whatcha doing, honey bun?*

Griff: *Just feeling like an idiot for not begging you to come home with me tonight.*

Sam: *You have no idea how happy I am to hear that.*

Griff: *I assume it's too late now?*

Sam: *I'm in bed and have to be at the culinary school in the morning.*

Griff: *Damn. Can I take you out tomorrow night?*

Sam: *Yes, please.*

Griff: *Okay. Text me tomorrow and we'll figure it out.*

Sam: *Sweet dreams Fox.*

Griff: *You too Sunshine.*

I fell asleep with a huge grin on my face.

* * *

The next day went by fast because I assisted a professor in an intense lab class on international cuisine. The professor spoke with a heavy Russian accent, and it was nearly impossible to understand him over the sounds of kitchen noises. The students kept pulling me aside to ask me to repeat his instructions.

The other class I assisted with reviewed wine fundamentals. After talking to Tristan about his vineyard, I was much more interested in learning about wine pairings and restaurant wine sales than I'd been before.

After 3 p.m. I texted Griff to let him know I was done for the day when I noticed Dillon leaning against the building. There was a woman plastered to his face and I recognized the petite frame topped with a curly brown mane from the day before. *Well, I'll be damned.*

Sam: *Guess who I'm watching play tonsil hockey with your sister?*

Griff: *WTF??*

Sam: *Simone is here at the Art Institute getting creative with a certain surfer dude.*

Griff: *OMFG she is so busted.*

Sam: *Should I go up to them?*

Griff: *Nah, it's too good. I don't want her to know we know.*

Sam: *Sneaky. I like it.*

Griff: *You done for the day?*

Sam: *Yes sir.*

Griff: *Want to meet me at my place?*

Sam: *I'm wearing chef whites.*

Griff: *And?*

Sam: *I don't want to wear them out somewhere on a date.*

Griff: *Then we'll just have to stay in. And if you're still not* *comfortable in them, I'll help you take them off.*

Sam: *Be there in fifteen minutes, snookums. Break out the flavored lube, I'm starving.*

I ducked into a market on the way there and bought some things on the off chance Griff would let me cook dinner for him. After grabbing a bottle of wine, I threw some condoms and lube into the basket too, just in case his supply was running low.

The young man at the cashier stand winked at me, and I silently groaned. Clearly I was planning a romantic dinner, and it made me wonder if I should have added some flowers to the basket. Too late. I couldn't wait any longer to get my hands on Griff.

When I got to his apartment building, I saw him jogging up the street with a bag in his hand and a big grin on his face.

"I hope that isn't dinner, because I just bought something to cook for you," I said.

"Nope." He smiled, leaning in to kiss me. "But it is edible."

"You did not just go shopping for lube." I laughed.

"I thought about it, just to make you laugh, but no. This is dessert."

When we got inside Griff's apartment, I carefully set down my bags to grab him and spin him around until his back was against the door. I grasped his neck and chin in my hand to hold him still while I kissed him.

"Mmpfh," he grunted. His hands landed in my hair and one of his legs wrapped around the back of mine. My mouth was all over him—lips, neck, ears. I pulled his shirt over his head and grabbed his nipple rings with my mouth. This time they were little hoops instead of the barbells. I groaned against his skin.

"*Fox*," I ground out. "Want you so badly."

His hands reached for the top buttons of my chef coat and I started with the bottom ones while still running my mouth all over his chest and neck. I stopped unbuttoning long enough to rub my hand over the front of his pants. I fumbled his fly open and reached inside to grasp his warm cock, running my thumb over the wet tip.

"Jesus, Sam, that feels so good," Griff said with a groan.

I finished shucking off the coat and pulled off my undershirt before kneeling down and pulling him closer with my palms on his ass. Not patient enough to wait any longer, I shoved his jeans down to his thighs.

"You dirty fucker." I laughed when I failed to encounter any underwear. Griff grinned and shrugged.

My nose went into the nest of his curls, inhaling that unique Griff musk that went straight to my throbbing cock. I rubbed my cheek against his shaft, feeling it jerk in response to my touch. My tongue came out searching for it, and I licked reverently up and down the length of him. God, it was perfect—cut and gloriously full with a fat head turned deep blush-colored. I mouthed it and teased the edges with the tip of my tongue.

Griff's hands were on my head, alternately gripping my hair and running fingers down the skin of my nape as I sucked up and down, taking him deep and then backing off.

"Oh *goddd*," he gasped. "*Sam*," he whimpered, trying to pull me up. As I stood, I saw green eyes with pupils wide and a face full of lust and longing. My fox at his most beautiful.

I kissed his lips, pulled his pants back up, and then turned him toward the bedroom, continuing to press kisses on the back of his neck, his shoulder, the dragon—all while we walked together to his bed. My hands wrapped around his front; one on his cock down the front of his pants, stroking, and the other at the base of his neck above his collarbone.

My tongue traced the dragon's heart. Griff's back muscles rippled in response to my teasing tongue. His hands clutched each of my arms as if to make sure they stayed wrapped around him.

"I want you on your back," I said into his ear before pushing him down onto the bed and grabbing for his jeans again.

16

Griff

AFTER READILY AGREEING TO HIS REQUEST, I WAS ON MY back being divested of my remaining clothing. My hand reached out to rub Sam through his pants when I had the most ridiculous thought. A laugh burbled out of me before I could stop it.

Sam's face split into a magnificent grin. "What's so funny, Foxy?"

"You know there is an Olympic diver named—" I began.

"Sam Cox," he finished for me. "Yes, I know."

"But they call him Steel Cox because he has nerves of steel. Don't know what made me think of it just now," I admitted. "But I remember Aunt Tilly thinking it was a joke and sending an email to the television network asking about it."

"Would it be possible to save the Aunt Tilly conversation until after the sex?" he teased.

"What, that's not turning you on? Hmm, I'll have to try something else," I pondered for a moment with a finger on my bottom lip.

"Don't hurt yourself there, princess." Sam laughed before poking out his tongue to mess with my nipple rings. I hissed and arched my head back.

"Jesus, that feels good," I breathed. I lay there enjoying the feel of his weight on me and the excitement that rippled through my belly with every tug of his mouth. My cock ached for him and I kept trying to thrust it up into him to find some friction. Finally, I'd had enough. I sat up and flipped him under me, catching him by surprise and enjoying the wide-eyed look that came over his face. He was a couple inches taller than I was and weighed more, but I was a competitive swimmer, no slouch in upper body strength.

I winked at him and stripped off his chef pants, enjoying the sight of his bright white briefs against the golden skin and dark happy trail above. My tongue went straight to that trail as my fingers found the shape of him through the cotton briefs. I squeezed and rubbed, feeling him swell underneath my hand until a wet spot appeared. My mouth found the wet spot and cupped it, the warmth of his body radiating through the fabric.

Sam's hips moved in anticipation, and I slid the briefs off him to release his erection. It stood away from his body, begging my mouth to devour it. I wasn't gentle or slow. My mouth laid into his hard cock like it was on a mission to suck the life right out of the man.

"Holy shit, oh fuck," he cried out. "God, that's... *mpfh*." His words became grunts and nonsense sounds as he writhed beneath the onslaught of my tongue and throat. When he said he was close to coming, I released him with a pop and climbed up his body to kiss his mouth. A whimper of complaint came out of him, and I tried reassuring him with my tongue in his mouth.

"Don't make me beg, Fox, *please*," he moaned when I pulled away to grab what I needed from the table.

"But what if I want you to beg?" I growled into his ear as I tore open the condom. A whimper came from his throat. I kissed his earlobe and his lips before sitting up and rolling the condom on him. I popped the cap of the lube, drizzling some on him and some on my fingers.

When I reached around to ready myself I thought Sam was going to come undone before I even had a chance to feel him inside me. He squeezed his eyes closed and put his arm over his face, biting his lip. "You're so fucking hot like that." He groaned.

I smiled as I pulled his arm away and leaned in for a kiss. "Don't you want to see me ride your Steel Cox?"

Sam rolled his eyes and hissed.

"Never call it that again, promise me," he growled. "I will kill you. I mean, after I'm done using your body for sex, obviously. Now mount up or I'm going to flip you over and pound you."

"He thinks he just threatened me," I muttered under my breath as I reached back to find his cock and guide myself onto it.

As I felt his hard length slide in, I let out a deep sigh of satisfaction. Sam cried out and squeezed his eyes closed again, tilting his head back to expose his Adam's apple. I leaned over to suck on it, moving my mouth up to his lips to kiss there as well.

When I began to slide up and down his cock, his eyebrows lifted, crinkling his forehead while his teeth caught his lips.

He felt amazing inside me and under my hands. I enjoyed pushing myself on and off him in long, slow movements. Sam wasn't having any of it though. I heard him mutter, "Fuck this," before pulling out and flipping me onto my back. He pushed my knees toward my ears and slammed back into me, bottoming out as deep as he could go.

"*Ahh*," I gasped.

He muttered something else, but I couldn't concentrate on what he was saying. All I knew in those moments was the extreme sense of all my switches being flipped and every nerve in my body zinging with need.

His hips pumped and our bodies joined, sweat beginning to pour off both of us as our hands clutched at each other. My orgasm hit like a monster wave that comes out of nowhere, tumbling you under and flipping you around until you can't remember which way to swim for air. Hot streams landed on my chest; Sam's voice was a hoarse cry above me. When his orgasm subsided, he looked down at me, still propped on his elbows above me.

The look on Sam's face was intense. His dark brown eyes smoldered at me and seemed to be searching for something in my own.

I reached my hands up to cup his face and bring it down to mine. Our eyes were still locked until my mouth touched his. As our kiss intensified, Sam's remaining pulses tapered off until the heat and passion was in our mouths and the light movements of his body into mine were a languid, liquid afterthought.

"Griffin," he whispered, pulling back to meet my eyes again. My name on his lips was a caress. His hips continued to roll, firing off nerves inside me I thought would have been overstimulated by now.

I reached a finger out to trace the lines of his face, down his nose and under his eye, along his jaw. "Do you have any idea how you make me feel?" I whispered.

Sam shook his head, never breaking eye contact. His lips were still red and raw from the kissing. My fingers brushed over them while I tried to gather up the nerve to open myself up to him a little bit.

"When you're near me, Sam, everything's brighter… Warmer, happier. Just… more." I shifted my eyes and swallowed. "And, well, that's something I've never really felt before."

His eyes warmed and his face softened, making me so damned glad I'd said what I did. I'd do anything to put that look on his face again.

He buried his face in my neck. "Thank you," he breathed against my skin.

I felt him slip out of my body, but we stayed there wrapped around each other for a little longer, not wanting to break the new connection.

17

Sam

MY HEART FELT AS THOUGH IT WAS GOING TO THUNDER right out of my chest. Griff's words were a gift I hadn't expected him to give. There were times when he seemed so closed off, afraid of revealing too much of himself. I didn't think he realized how much he'd already told me with his body, his lips, his eyes.

It seemed too soon for talk of feelings, but I was sure as shit having them.

After a quick trip to the bathroom to clean up, we lay there entwined on his bed, quietly enjoying the feel of each other. My fingers explored his curls, and I saw how many different shades of green were displayed in his eyes. Griff truly was gorgeous.

"This experiment of yours. Does anyone ever *not* want to go home with you?" I asked.

Griff's eyes twinkled with amusement. "You make it sound unbelievable."

"It *is* unbelievable. Who wouldn't want to take you to bed? I can't even comprehend that," I admitted, still twirling brown curls around my fingers.

"Honestly, everyone seems pretty willing if they're single, but there was this one guy who claimed to be straight," Griff said with a laugh. "He got so pissed."

"What? Where were you?" I asked.

"Harry Dick's. He must not have known it was a gay club, but come on. How can you not know it's a gay club the minute you step foot in there?"

"No shit," I agreed. "Was he blind?"

"No, but here's the funny part. He got so offended, all blustery about why I would assume he's into men, and then he went on to spend the next several hours at the bar even after I informed him it was a gay club."

Griff's dimples came out as he laughed harder. I leaned over to kiss them. "These fucking dimples," I muttered against his skin. "You're killing me, Fox."

I began to kiss him all over, nudging him onto his front so I could check out his tattoo again.

"Tell me about the tattoo," I said as I traced the textured tail around Griff's arm with my lips.

Goosebumps stood up on his skin where I kissed it.

"I got it a few years ago when I finally had some money," he said between heavy breaths.

"It's amazing. The detail is unlike anything I've seen. Who did it?" I asked, replacing my mouth with my index finger as I traced the scaled form back to his shoulder.

"Wha—? Oh, uh… my best friend, Nico. Used to do graffiti with me. I knew him on the streets."

"How did he go from being on the streets to becoming a tattoo artist?"

"Mmm, I can't think when you touch me," Griff purred until I pulled my hand away. "Shit, don't stop."

I laughed and returned to tracing the shapes of the image on his back.

"He, ah, let this tattoo artist practice on him in exchange for food. And then he ended up getting to know the guy well enough to become his apprentice. That was after the tattoo guy saw Nico's drawings. Once he was certified, his clientele boomed overnight. Now it's almost impossible to get in with him."

I studied the eyes of the dragon, lime green with hints of lighter and darker shades. "This dragon is you," I said.

"Yes."

"Your heart is in a cage," I said in a softer voice.

"Yes."

I turned him back over and placed a kiss on his chest where his actual heart lived. "Why?" I whispered.

His eyes squeezed closed and he shook his head. It was such a subtle movement I almost missed it.

"It's okay," I said, moving up to kiss his face. "Never mind. You don't have to answer that. Too soon. Sorry." Now I was rambling, so I clamped my mouth closed and snuggled into him.

Griff's arms tightened around me and I felt him begin to speak.

"It's okay. I'm just not used to talking about myself, that's all," he said. "I have a hard time with… that kind of thing."

I wanted to laugh at the understatement, but I didn't dare. "It can't be easy after being on your own as a teen."

"No. It isn't. And I was pretty much on my own before that too. I told you that my dad kicked me out because I was gay. That's only part of it. He wasn't a good person, kind of a loser, really. Always poor, always coming up with excuses why he couldn't work. I didn't realize that wasn't how all dads were until I got a little older.

"My mom died before I was eight, and my dad stopped even trying. Honestly, I don't think he ever really wanted me in the first place. He was always looking for someone else to take me. Any family members he had were too broke to help, so he ended up leaving me on my own most of the time. When I was thirteen, I approached a gay teacher at school to ask advice about whether or not I should come out to my dad, the teacher took it upon himself to call my dad in hopes of getting me into counseling. It was a huge mistake, but honestly, he didn't kick me out because of my sexuality. That was just the excuse he used to be done with me once and for all. It wasn't really about that."

"Really? That's terrible."

"What's worse is that I thought it was a joke. I kept trying to get back into the apartment. After two nights of sleeping on the floor in the hallway, a neighbor down the hall finally called the cops. The cops called family services, and I ended up in the system. It was really bad, Sam. The first foster family they put me with was so awful, I ran away and avoided any place that might send me back. Even a shelter."

My throat tightened at the image of a young Griffin alone and unprotected in San Francisco.

He continued, "A year later a cop gave me the choice between the system and the shelter, and that's when I met the Marians. It took six months before I would even trust them enough to go to Sunday dinner at their house. Finally, just before I turned sixteen, they adopted me. Even then, I'd run away periodically. I'd have these irrational moments of panic and just bolt. When you've been abandoned by everyone who's ever claimed to love you, it's almost impossible to trust that people will stick around. Or that you're even worthy of that."

I held him and wanted to take him inside me to protect him from ever feeling unloved again. "Griffin, you're worthy."

His head shook above mine in a "no" gesture. I lifted my head up from his chest and kissed him on the lips without making eye contact. I poured my feelings into his mouth because I couldn't bear to look into his eyes and see a trace of that unsure kid.

I felt helpless and wondered what I could do to make up for the pain he'd endured in his life. The answer was simple. I could be there for him and never let him down. I could be someone in his life who would adore him and help him discover how worthy he was. My eyes blinked open.

"Let me make you dinner. I brought groceries and wine," I said, pulling back from the kiss with a smile.

"I'm not sure that's what I had in mind when *I* asked *you* out to dinner," Griff said with a small laugh.

"But you're going to let me do it anyway because you're sweet like that," I prompted.

"I'm going to let you do it anyway because you're a trained chef, and I'm not stupid." He smiled.

"Fair enough." I laughed.

We pulled back on enough clothes to be decent and made our way out to the kitchen.

While I worked on dinner, Griff told me about his job as a writer. He'd spent a large amount of time that year ghostwriting a comedian's memoir.

"I can't tell you whose book it is, but it was so much fun to write. I spent some time down in LA with the comedian and her friends. Such a great group of people. They told me hours of stories about her so I could get a feel for her life."

"When does the book come out?" I asked as I searched through cabinets for olive oil.

"It should be out by Thanksgiving. They're fast-tracking it because she's so hot right now," Griff said.

"Is it Perri Knight?" I asked.

Griff's eyes widened and his lips pursed before curling up on the sides. "No," he said with his lips while nodding his head. *So fucking cute.*

"I see." I laughed. "Damn. I'll bet she'd be fun to hang out with."

"Totally. If I was friends with her, I'd want to introduce you to her. I'll bet she'd adore you."

"Maybe one day I'll be lucky enough to meet her," I said with a wink as I drizzled the olive oil in the pan on the stove.

"What about you, Sam? What do you want to do after you graduate from culinary school?"

"I've already graduated. I'm just helping teach classes there now while my mentor tries to bully me into applying to the CIA," I said.

"The CIA?" he asked in confusion.

"The Culinary Institute of America," I said. "Like the Central Intelligence Agency but with fewer spies and a shit ton more butter."

Griff laughed. "Ah, I see. And what would you do at this culinary spy school? Stroganoff surveillance? Eggplant espionage?"

The dimples. They were directly wired to my heart. And my groin.

"Do some more graduate work, try to get a job in one of the restaurants. I'm not sure. I think he just knows I'm waffling about what direction I want to go in since I lost my chef position a few months ago. He's afraid if I don't decide soon, I'm going to end up a deadbeat."

"Bullshit," Griff said. "I can't picture you as a deadbeat. Every time I see you at Harry Dick's you're busting your ass."

"He doesn't know that. He just knows I have money from my dad and can afford to put off the decision about what to do next. He doesn't realize I don't touch a cent of my father's money except to pay for Lacey's and my education. I work for everything else."

"Tell me more about being a chef. I wondered why you were tending bar instead of working in a restaurant."

I continued preparing the beef I was making. "I was the head chef for a high-end restaurant in town, but the owner was a jackass. He fired me a few months ago and a friend set me up with the Harry Dick's job."

"Have you ever thought about opening your own restaurant?" Griff asked.

"Yes. Actually, I was really close to signing a lease on some space when I lost my position at the restaurant."

My eyes stayed locked on the tenderloin I sliced. I wasn't sure how much of this I wanted to tell him. I was embarrassed about losing my job, and the resulting blow to my self-esteem had really thrown me off course.

Griff idly spun a basket of napkins around on the counter in front of him.

"So, what's the status of it now? Maybe you lost your job for a reason… so you can put your focus into the new place."

I blew out a breath. "No. I don't think so. The whole experience scared me off. The restaurant business can be fickle. Maybe I'm not ready for it yet. I need to find another head chef position to get some more experience first."

After the beef was sliced and seasoned, I began cutting up an onion and zucchini. Griff's green eyes were locked on the motion of my hands as I chopped the vegetables, and I forced myself to concentrate.

"You're distracting me with those green eyes of yours. Make yourself useful, kitten." I tossed him a bag of carrots. "Peel those."

Griff caught the bag of carrots and stood up. "I'm not sure I even own a peeler."

"I can do it with a knife if you don't have a peeler."

"Mr. Fancy Chef tries to impress his date with daring knife skills," he teased, rifling through a drawer. "I don't know whether to swoon or speed-dial 911."

Just as I was trying to think up a response, Griff's front door burst open and in stumbled two drunks.

18

Griff

I'D NEVER SEEN DANTE WASTED BEFORE. IT WAS ONLY SIX IN THE evening, but he was hammered. He burst through the front door like a cannonball and lurched straight to my sofa, falling onto the cushions with a deep groan.

"Ow, fuck, I'm gonna spin down," he mumbled.

I looked at the man accompanying him. His body was covered in familiar tattoos.

"Nico? What the hell?" I asked my old friend. "You and Dante were day drinking on a Monday?"

"Dude, sorry, dude," he slurred with a giggle. "It's his first time, so we celebrated. C'mere, gorgeous, and gimme some love. You know I wanna taste that sweet mouth of yours."

He stumbled toward me with his mouth open like he was going to kiss me. Before I had a chance to tell him he was dreaming, an arm shot out from behind me and stopped Nico's advance with a hand to the chest.

I turned to look at Sam with a raised eyebrow.

"Sorry," he muttered, lowering his arm.

I turned fully to snake my arms around him as I pressed my hips against his suggestively. "I don't mind. Thought it was kinda sweet, actually."

"Fuck you," he muttered while red creeped up his face. "Who's this?"

I turned back around and introduced them. "Sam Coxwell, this is Nico Salerno. Nico is the tattoo artist I was telling you about."

Nico leaned his head back in a melodramatic visual assessment of my sexy bartender.

"You're a damned fine specimen, Mr. Cox-Swell," he said, slipping his tongue all over the sibilant in the name, sounding like a snake.

Sam slid a hand under the back of my T-shirt to rest on my lower back, and the sensation of his warm hand against my bare skin made me shiver. As cheesy as it seemed, him touching me like that felt like reassurance he was mine, even if someone else was throwing out offers.

A giggle came from the sofa. "Cox. Cocks. *Cocksss*," Dante said.

"What's going on, Nico? Why did you bring him here, and where the hell have you guys been?" I asked.

"He's too drunk to go back to your parents' house, so he insisted I bring him here. He got inked and then we got drinked." He stopped and seemed to replay his own words in his mind before giggling again.

"Did you guys get high too? Jesus, Nico, did you seriously smoke up with my baby brother?" Now I was pissed. He knew better than to mess with drugs and my family.

"No, shit no. Griff, jeez. You know I don't do that stuff. No, man… What?" he asked, squinting in confusion.

"What, what?" I asked.

He burst out laughing again. "What were we talking about?"

I gave up and went to sit next to Dante on the sofa. "Hey, bud, how're you feeling?"

"Hey, Griffin Fox," he said with a silly grin. "I finally got my angel. Wanna see?"

"Sure. Let's see," I said with a smile. He'd been wanting to get a tattoo of an angel since before I'd met him, but Mom made him promise to wait until he was twenty-one. His birthday was months ago, but he'd spent time tweaking the design until he had exactly what he wanted. Blue and I had helped him create the artwork. Honestly, I was surprised he hadn't asked me to go with him when he finally decided to get it done.

He began to lift up his shirt but turned green before he got very far. Bolting for the bathroom, he stepped right out of one of his shoes. Nico laughed behind me.

"Oh shit. Mighta let him have a few too many," he said.

"You are so fucking dead," I warned him. "The kid doesn't drink, Nico. His tolerance would have had him shit-faced after one beer." I returned to where I'd been standing, and Sam's hand snuck back under my shirt, making me shudder again. I wanted Nico and Dante gone. *Now.*

"Dude, not my fault they over-served us. Blame the fucking bartenders," he whined.

I felt the hand on my back tense, and I wanted to elbow its owner for taking a drunk person so seriously.

"Where were you drinking?" Sam asked.

"Applebee's," Nico said before breaking out into laughter again. "Cheese sticks to die for."

I heard Sam snort-laugh behind me as I rolled my eyes.

"Applebee's? I can't even picture you in an Applebee's. Were you taken there with a gun to your head?" I asked.

"That's where Dante wanted to go, so we went. Apparently he likes their pork chops. And their piña coladas."

"Now you're just fucking with me," I muttered before going to check on Dante. He was leaning over the toilet dry-heaving. I wet a washcloth for him and squatted down next to him to hand it to him.

"Sorry, brother," I said. "This is the not-so-fun-part about drinking."

"It's okay," he said between waves. "Beats the throbbing I was feeling from the needle."

"Do you like the way it turned out?" I asked.

He turned his head and looked at me with the happiest face I'd seen on him in a long time. "Yeah, G. I really like it. Now I have him with me wherever I go."

Over the years he'd told me about having a guardian angel. Someone who'd saved his life before he came to California from wherever the hell he'd been before. He never said more than that or gave me details, but that guardian angel was like his touchstone. Someone to live for and something to believe in.

"I'll fix up the sofa for you. Come on."

"Nah. Can you just bring me a pillow and blanket in here? I don't think I'll be leaving the toilet for a while," he said miserably.

"Okay, bud. Be right back."

After collecting what he needed, including some loose gym shorts and a clean T-shirt in case he wanted something more comfortable to sleep in, I took it all to him. I set a glass of water on the counter by the sink and stuck a bottle of ibuprofen next to it.

Once he was settled in the bathroom, I returned to find Nico sitting in the kitchen watching Sam cook. Sam looked up at me with a smile. "Did you ever find a peeler, or do I need to get fancy with my blades of glory?"

"I found one," I told him, returning to my spot as sous chef. The carrot shavings fell away into the trash can as Nico alternated drinking a big glass of water and humming a familiar tune.

"Are you humming the tune of Jude's latest song?" I asked. "Quit that. Fucking earworm from hell."

"I'm going to tell him you said that," Nico warned me with a hiccup.

"Go ahead. No one is more tired of it than he is. Except maybe

Derek," I told him.

Nico laughed. "Can you imagine a megastar writing a song about being in love with you, that song going gajillion-platinum or whatever, and then getting sick of it because it's just played too damned much?"

"No. But I give them hell about it all the time. I told Derek he's going to be shopping at a mall one day with his kids and they're going to hear a song over the speakers. They'll ask if that's Daddy's song and Derek will roll his eyes. 'Yes, Daddy wrote it for me because he loved me—blah, blah, blah.' Then the kids will cry because they'll think Dad and Daddy don't love each other anymore. By the time I was done painting the scenario for him, Derek looked red-faced and guilty while Jude laughed his ass off," I said with a smirk.

"You're so mean." Nico giggled. "That poor guy is, like, the sweetest thing in the world. Don't tease him like that."

"Both of them are. Those two are sweet, like goddamned marshmallows dipped in chocolate and drizzled in honey. Makes my teeth fall out just thinking about them."

Sam looked up at me. "Are you talking about Jude-and-the-Saints Jude?"

"Yes," I told him, looking at him with confusion. "What other Jude would I be talking about?"

"How do you know him?" he asked.

Nico snorted. "Dude, you're fucking my best friend and you don't even know who his brother is?"

Sam shot a glare at Nico before comprehension dawned in his face.

"*That* Jude is your brother Jude?"

"Yes. Please don't make a big deal about it because then I'll have to kick you to the curb, and I really like your sweet ass," I admitted.

He grinned and then shrugged. "Meh, never heard of the guy. He's some kind of singer, you say?"

"And the sweet ass lives to fuck another day," Nico snickered.

I leaned over and kissed Sam on the mouth. "Thank you for not being weird about it. I forgot you hadn't met him yet. They couldn't make it to Sunday dinner. Probably because they were feeding starving war heroes or some shit."

Nico's lips pursed and his eyebrows narrowed as he saw me kiss Sam. I could see that was going to be a problem. Ever since we were kids living on the street together, Nico thought it was his job to look out for me. Now that we were both grown-ass adults, he still thought he had a right to have a say in what I did with my life. I gave him a look that said to calm the fuck down. He pointed his eyes at me and narrowed them even farther. *Make me.*

"So, Sam. What do you do for work?" Nico asked with a deceptively sweet voice.

"I tend bar at Harry Dick's," he said, sliding onions and garlic into the frying pan with the hot olive oil. The scents of heaven wafted toward me, and I bit back a moan of appreciation.

"Ah, ambitious, I see," Nico said sarcastically.

I felt my hand tighten around the peeler and wondered if I could stab him with it if I had to.

Sam looked at Nico with a smile. "It's hard to be ambitious when your family is worth a hundred million dollars. But I'm also a professionally trained chef, so I'm working on it."

The peeler went skittering across the floor, and Nico's ice water sloshed onto his shirt as his arm jerked mid-sip.

Sam went back to frying his onions as the phrase *hundred million dollars* bounced around my kitchen. Silence descended until Nico finally gathered his wits, sobering up a bit.

"Sam, I was wondering if you'd like a blow job right now. I give killer head, and I'd be willing to—"

I finally snapped back into the moment. "Fuck you, asshole. I found him first."

Sam's laughter rang out as he turned back to wink at me, and Nico pouted.

"But you don't need money; you have rich parents," he whined. "I'm just a poor orphan who could really use a sugar daddy."

"Poor orphan, my ass. You make over six figures doodling on people's bodies. Cry me a river," I said. "And you know I don't take money from my family, so shut the hell up."

"So sensitive," Nico grumbled.

"Nico, don't you need to go home?" I asked.

"I guess so. But think about what I said, Sam. Griff may have a tight little ass and a killer pair of lips, but I—"

"*Go*," I barked.

"All right, all right," he mumbled as he headed for the door. He turned around before walking out and put his thumb and pinky up to his face like a telephone. *Call me*, he mouthed in Sam's direction.

Sam smirked before going back to what he was doing on the stove. Beef slices slid into the hot onions with a mouthwatering sizzle.

I walked up behind him and slid my arms around his waist. God, he felt good.

"I'm sorry my best friend is an asshole."

"Nah, he just wishes he was the one sleeping with you," Sam said.

"Bullshit," I snorted.

"It's true, Griff. But he draws lovely dragons, so I'll give him that."

My chest puffed up with a smidge of pride. "Actually, I drew the dragon. He just inked it."

Sam turned around to look at me. "You designed that dragon? It's amazing. Holy shit. I didn't know you could draw."

"I don't do much of it anymore. Anyway, back to Nico," I began.

Sam's hand came to rest on my neck. "Have you slept with him, Griff?"

I leaned my forehead onto the top of his chest. "No, sunshine. Despite the way he makes it sound, I've never gone there. He's not my type." I felt him relax on an exhale, and I smiled, looking back up.

"What's your type?" he asked.

"Mm, let's see. Besides people who bullshit about having a

hundred million dollars? I'll pretty much blow anyone who cooks for me. And if the meal is really good, I'll let them—"

He leaned in and landed warm lips on mine.

After the kiss he mumbled, "Smart-ass," before returning to his pan on the stove.

I continued leaning against his back. "My type is smart, sweet, sexy, and fun-loving. I'm attracted to men who aren't dark and brooding. I have enough of my own dark and broody shit to deal with. I also like a guy who doesn't take everything too seriously but doesn't turn everything into a joke either."

My hands traveled under his shirt to lightly scratch his back. "What about you, Sam? What's your type?"

"Hm, let me think. Honestly, I'm not picky. As long as he has a big dick, I'm good."

I pinched his ass, hard. He laughed and reached an arm back over his shoulder to ruffle my hair.

"Fox, I don't know what my type was a week ago, but now it's curly-haired flirts."

I couldn't see his face, but I could hear the affection in his voice.

And fuck if that didn't draw me in and make me want something I'd never let myself have before.

19

Sam

AFTER WE ATE A LATE DINNER, WE FOOLED AROUND IN HIS bedroom until both of us felt like wet noodles and my balls were as empty as they'd ever been. I truly couldn't get enough of that man and wanted nothing more than to fall asleep wrapped around him. But his brother needed him more, and I didn't want to pull him in two directions.

I left him dozing and scribbled a note to tell him to call me after he got up and helped Dante the following morning. Thankful I didn't have work at the culinary school the next day, I fell into my bed and slept hard.

A loud knocking sound woke me up, and I shuffled to the apartment door still half asleep and dressed in nothing but boxer briefs.

When I opened the door and squinted out, I was attacked in a full-body rush. I stumbled back, struggling against my attacker until I realized he smelled familiar, and I clutched at Griff to keep from falling over.

"Jesus, you scared me, Fox. Thought you were an intruder or something," I said into his hair, breathing heavily from the adrenaline spike.

"Sorry. I woke up horny and had to come find you."

His voice sounded perky and happy. How the hell did he do that?

"You're awfully peppy for so early in the morning," I muttered.

"Sam, it's after ten." He laughed. "I didn't even know if you'd still be home. If you weren't, it was going to be pretty damned embarrassing to have to find you at work and jump you in front of your students. But don't worry, I was up for the challenge."

Griff pulled back from the embrace and smiled at me with those gorgeous green eyes dancing.

"God, you're adorable," I confessed before kissing the hell out of him, hands sliding down to squeeze his ass over his jeans. I felt his hands slide beneath my underwear to do the same until I heard a cough behind me.

"Fuck off, Jason," I said without taking my hands off Griff.

"Don't mind me; I'm enjoying the show." Jason laughed. "It's the closest I've been to getting some action in weeks."

"Why aren't you at work?" I asked, still nibbling on Griff's face as I walked him in the direction of my room.

"Flying out today to Denver for a business trip," he said. "Be back Friday."

"Mm-hm," I said before stepping Griff into my room. My cock throbbed and all I could think about was getting this man naked. "Stay cool. Dallas is a bitch in August."

I closed the door and turned to look at Griff. He laughed.

"What?" I asked. "Why are you laughing?"

"He said he's going to Denver, not Dallas," he said.

"Who gives a shit? Get naked."

* * *

Before we knew it, we'd spent half the day in my bed alternating between fooling around and talking. Griff was so easy to talk to that we never ran out of conversation. The time passed so quickly, I was surprised when Robbie knocked on the door asking if I wanted to order Chinese for dinner. The only food we'd had since Griff arrived was a hastily grabbed package of cookies during a bathroom break.

"Give me a second, Robbie," I called out. I looked at Griff with a raised eyebrow. "You want Chinese?"

He looked down, seeming unsure. "Maybe I should go."

"What? Why?"

He shrugged. "I don't know. I've been in your hair all day, and—"

"Do you hear me complaining?" I teased. "I'd like you to stay, but I understand if you want to go. It's up to you."

"Are you sure?" he asked.

"Griff, we've been naked together all day. It's pretty obvious I enjoy your company, isn't it?" I asked.

"Okay. Yeah, Chinese sounds good. Thanks," he said, returning my grin.

We threw on some clothes and joined Robbie in the living room. When he saw Griff, looking fairly well fucked, his eyes widened. "Oh, hi," he stammered. "Sorry, I didn't realize you had a visitor, Sam."

"It's fine. We're up for Chinese if you don't mind company," I said.

"Sounds good," Robbie replied as his surprise turned into a sly grin.

While we waited for the food, we gathered plates and silverware, fixing drinks and laying everything out on the table. Robbie told us about a student in his fourth-grade class who kept disrupting a math test that day with outbursts of laughter.

"It was weird because this boy is usually really shy and quiet. Nice kid but geeky and awkward. Every few minutes though, he snorts and breaks down into a fit of giggles again. I finally had to say something, so I asked him to share the joke with the class."

"Jeez, Robbie, you sound like every old fart who ever taught school in the 1950s," I teased.

"Tell me about it. You'd be surprised what comes out of your mouth around kids sometimes. Anyway, he looks up, braver than I've ever seen before, and proceeds to tell the joke to the class. 'What did the zero say to the eight?' he says."

We looked at him, waiting for the punch line.

"Well?" Griff asked. "What was it?"

"Nice belt," Robbie replied, deadpan. "And then the kid refocused on the math test and proceeded to ace it while the rest of the students just sat there with faces like, *What the fuck just happened*?"

We both sat there for a moment, staring at him. And then Griff began laughing so hard I couldn't help but join in. By the time the doorbell rang, we'd gotten Robbie to tell us several more stories about his students.

After we ate, we settled on the sofa in the living room and I grilled Robbie about Neil. He finally got so flustered at my questions that he began to fight back.

"So, Griff, how long have you and Sam been an item?" he asked with a smirk in my direction.

Griff's eyes widened and his entire body language shifted. "We're not an item," he corrected.

Robbie's brows furrowed, and he looked back at me. "Oh, uh. Sorry. I just thought since you guys have been together for like three days straight, that meant maybe something was going on. My bad."

I felt the blood rush to my face in embarrassment. Was this some kind of massive one-night stand on steroids? My jaw tightened and defensive words tumbled to the tip of my tongue. Before I would allow them to come out, I got up and went to the kitchen to get a drink and take a moment to get my reaction under control.

After fixing a glass of ice water, I leaned against the counter to sip it slowly. Griff's words still smarted, making me wonder what he was thinking. That led me to ponder how *I* was feeling about all this.

What did I think was happening between us? What did I *want* to happen?

Maybe this was the beginning of something pretty wonderful. I wasn't really the one-night-stand kind of guy, so if that was what he thought this was, I needed to put a stop to it. But I didn't *want* to. I wanted Griffin Marian in my arms, in my bed, and in my life.

Fuck.

The idea of putting a stop to anything with Griff made me feel wrong somehow. I wanted him so badly. He made me laugh and was a good listener. He seemed to care about the people around him. The man volunteered with homeless youth, for god's sake. He was a good person.

I let out a sigh, not realizing Griff had wandered in and watched me from the doorway.

"Hey," he said.

My eyes came up and took in his disheveled good looks. He was so damned pretty I wanted to scream.

"Hey," I replied in a quiet voice.

His head tilted as he studied me. "I should probably head out," he suggested.

"Probably," I agreed. Every cell in my body disagreed with the word my mouth uttered, but I couldn't let this extended fantasy fuck fest continue if that was all it was.

And if Griff wanted more, then he could ask for more.

"Okay then," he said, walking toward me.

My molars felt like they were going to break apart. "Thank you for today, Foxy. I'm so glad you came over," I said before stepping forward to wrap my arms him. It was one thing to let him leave, but it was quite another to do so without touching him again.

That hug in the kitchen was like heaven and hell swirled into one. It was the best damned feeling in the world to have Griffin Marian in my arms, and it was the worst thing in the world to let him go.

I ran my hands up from his ass to his back to his neck to his face before leaning in to kiss him deeply.

Want you. Please stay. Touch me, kiss me some more.

"See you later, sunshine," he said before walking away.

20

Griff

I WALKED OUT OF SAM'S APARTMENT FEELING DISAPPOINTED HE hadn't asked me to stay over. Was it crazy I'd wanted to stay? Obviously he was ready for me to go, so I went. And maybe it was for the best. I realized as I began walking home that I had a stomachache.

By the time I got to my apartment building, the pain was worse and I felt like vomiting. I pulled out my phone to text Sam.

Griff: *Bad stomach pain, what about you? The Chinese?*

Sam: *No, we're both good. You want me to come over?*

Griff: *Nah. Maybe just a bug. Sorry. Hope you didn't get it.*

Sam: *Text me later to let me know how you are. Ok?*

I didn't answer. When I got into my apartment, I raced straight to the bathroom and threw up. I rinsed out my mouth but decided to stay there in case it happened again. The tile floor was a nice cool surface on my hot skin, and I was glad Dante's blanket and pillow were still there. The pain became unbearable, and I wondered if it could be something more serious like my appendix or gallbladder.

My phone buzzed a few times with messages and calls, but I ignored it to focus on not vomiting again. I changed my mind. I wanted Sam there. Being in that much pain alone scared me, and he lived close by.

I picked up my phone to text him back.

Griff: *Please come over*

Just as I hit the send button, I heard footsteps in my apartment and realized I must have left the door unlocked.

"Griff?" I heard from the living room.

"Sam?" I croaked in surprise, looking down at my phone screen and wondering if I'd blacked out and lost time or something.

"I'm here," he said, walking into the bathroom and finding me curled up in a ball on the floor. "I got worried when you didn't answer your phone."

He reached an arm out to press a hand against my forehead, causing his eyebrows to furrow. "You're burning up. Should I call Rebecca?"

"No." I swallowed. "Call Maverick. He's dating a doctor in the emergency room. Number in my phone."

After getting Mav's voicemail, Sam left a message and then texted him to ask his advice. A few minutes later Mav called back and told him to take me to the emergency room where his boyfriend, Dave Lassiter, was on duty.

He half carried me to the Jeep and drove me to the hospital where Dr. Lassiter found us and got me into a bed. After acting like we were a huge imposition, he determined it was most likely my appendix. The diagnosis would obviously have to be confirmed via ultrasound before they could do surgery.

After he left, I turned to face Sam. "Is it just me or is that guy a douche? I've met him before but don't remember the ego."

"It's not just you. Hopefully he's just an ass at work," Sam said with furrowed brows.

While we waited, Sam held my hand and brushed my hair back from my forehead.

"That feels good," I whispered. "Thanks for bringing me."

He smiled the sweetest smile. "I'm glad you texted me for help."

"I was scared," I admitted.

He leaned forward and dropped a kiss on my forehead before carefully sitting down on the bed next to my hip. "You're in good hands now, don't worry."

I assumed he probably didn't want to stick around someone's hospital bed.

"Sam, you don't have to stay."

His eyes studied me before he answered. "Fox, do you want me to stay? Because if you're okay with it, I'd like to."

I let out a big breath. "Yeah. I'd really like your company. Thanks."

A nurse brought in a soft cotton hospital gown, telling me to change into it before the doctor came back in. Then he walked back out of the bay, sliding the curtains closed for privacy. I looked at Sam, who held the gown. There was a noticeable twinkle in his brown eyes.

I couldn't help but laugh, which caused me to double over in pain. "Ow, shit. Oh Jesus, Sam," I cried, reaching out my hand to squeeze his.

"Shhh, deep breath. Just give it a minute," he said in a calm voice.

I gritted my teeth until the pain eased off a little. Tears pooled in my eyes from the pain. Sam reached over and began undressing me, the tender intimacy of the moment making my eyes sting even more.

Was this what it was like to have a partner? Someone to look after you and take care of you when you needed help? The whole thing was too much. I let the tears come and was secretly grateful no one could differentiate tears of pain from tears of longing.

* * *

When I awoke from the surgery in a regular hospital room, I was surprised to see daylight coming through the cracks in the blinds. The light made me squint, but I could make out the empty visitor chair next to the bed. I was alone. The realization hit me harder than I'd expected. I closed my eyes again.

What the hell was wrong with me? I was used to being alone. Had, in some ways, always been alone. But I would have at least thought Maverick would've called Mom and Dad to come be with me.

I heard footsteps and opened my eyes. Sam walked in looking sleep tousled and wearing the same clothes from the night before. He carried a paper cup of coffee. My heart began to thunder, and the fucking heart monitor machine betrayed me.

At the sound of the beeps speeding up, Sam's eyes lifted and met mine. He broke out into a big smile.

"Hey, it's about time you woke up. I was starting to think you were faking," he said with a wink, setting the cup down on a table and cupping my jaw to place a kiss on my scruffy cheek.

"You're still here," I said, disbelieving.

"Of course I'm still here. Your parents are on their way. They were up in Napa at your brother's place, so Maverick waited until this morning to call them."

"Where's Mav?" I asked.

"He got here a little while ago. I just left him eating breakfast in the cafeteria because I didn't want to be gone too long. You thirsty?"

I nodded, and he went to find something cold for me to drink. Before he returned, Maverick walked in and checked all the medical things like the IV fluids, the heart and blood pressure monitor, and even the bandage over the incision, as if being a veterinarian made him some kind of medical expert. I was too dazed to fight him. I just stared at him in confusion until he laughed.

"You're on some pretty good pain meds, Griff. Just let them take you away if you want to, okay? Don't feel like you have to fight it to be social. Your body needs rest, and they're not going to let you out of here until tomorrow morning anyway. Might as well enjoy the free high."

He didn't need to tell me twice. I was out cold again before Sam returned with a drink.

* * *

The rest of the day went about the same. I dozed off and on while family members and Sam came and went. When I woke up the following morning, I felt more alert, and Mav arranged to take me home and stay with me for a few days. Sam visited each day to bring me a treat or just sit and watch a movie on the sofa. One night Maverick had an overnight shift at the emergency vet clinic, so when Sam fell asleep on the sofa during the movie, I asked him to stay over.

We got into bed together and kissed for a long time, just enjoying each other's roaming hands and lips, small moans, and whimpers. When I tried reaching into his boxer briefs, his hand came down to stop me.

"No way, Foxy. One more day. Doctor's orders," he said.

"That doctor obviously didn't notice how hot you were," I whined, trying again to slip my hand down his underwear. A laugh rumbled out of him as he grabbed my hand again, only this time he brought it up to his mouth to kiss it before stretching it gently above my head and finding my other one to join it.

With me on my back and both my arms held above my head, Sam took a moment to pull back and stare at me. The intensity in his eyes took my breath away.

"*Please*," I breathed. "I'm so hard for you it hurts. Please, Sam." I arched my hips up into him, pressing my cock into his and watching his eyes roll back.

"Fuck," he muttered before pinning his dark eyes back on me. "Stay still. You don't move. Only I move. Got it?"

I bobbed my head in enthusiastic agreement. Whatever Sam had planned was going to be good if his intense gaze was any indication. And the bossiness in his voice caused my pulse to skyrocket.

He reached into my bedside table drawer and pulled out the lube. Yes, oh *yes*. Good things happened with lube.

I pushed my pelvis up against him again in search of blissful friction, but he glared at me.

"If you move, I'll stop. Do you want me to stop, Foxy?"

I shook my head. "Nuh-un."

His frown morphed into a grin. "Thank god," he muttered, flipping open the cap on the bottle.

Sam stripped us both until we were bare before lubing us in a delicious frenzy of slick hands and cocks. I couldn't stop whimpering every time he gripped me or my shaft slid against his. If I moved at all, a growling sound started in his chest to warn me.

He lay over me, gloriously naked, and began to jack us together with one hand. His hips moved in time with his hand to slide against me, and I wasn't sure I would be able to hold out.

"Fuck, Sam," I gasped. "Won't last long."

"'S'okay, baby," he murmured, the endearment causing my stomach to flip and my breath to catch. He slid over me a few more times and I felt my toes curling against his calves. It felt so damned good.

He stiffened above me right as his climax hit.

Watching him come undone was spectacular. Tendons stood out on his neck, blood rushed to his face, and his mouth opened in a guttural noise.

It was enough to make me lose it. Sam held his weight off me for the most part, and my cum shot all over us, my cock jumping with each wave of pleasure rushing through me. "Ahhhhhhh," I cried out with a shudder.

At the sound of my cry, Sam's entire face lit up like the sun.

And fuck if that didn't turn me on all over again.

I knew he'd never agree to a second round even if my cock was up for it, which it wasn't, so after he cleaned us off, I contented my-self with more gentle kisses until we were both too drowsy to contin-ue. We fell asleep wrapped up together, and I realized sleeping in his arms was a thousand times better than sleeping alone.

21

Sam

ONCE HE FELT BETTER, GRIFF FINISHED HIS CLUB EXPERIMENT with no help from me. The last few nights he spent flirting with strangers were his most challenging because I wouldn't stop butting my nose in. It became a kind of game between us where I told him that every time a man touched him, I was going to touch him the same way the next time I got my hands on him. My favorite was when a very fem guy kept affectionately tweaking the tip of Griff's nose with an index finger and saying, "Well aren't you just the yummiest thing ever, cutie pie?"

I spent a good two weeks after that tweaking Griff's nose and calling him cutie pie. For some reason, every time I called him cutie pie, he called me jackass.

We slept together at either his place or mine almost every night, but deliberately avoided talking about anything remotely resembling the word "relationship." It was becoming comical, really.

One day we went to the Y for a swim and stopped at the front desk to check in. I told the woman I needed a guest pass. We were still holding hands, so the woman must have assumed we were dating.

Imagine that.

"I just need your boyfriend's name," she said.

At the word "boyfriend," Griff's entire body language changed, and he stiffened and dropped my hand like it was diseased. The sudden shift was becoming a familiar one. I couldn't decide if I wanted to laugh or scream.

Part of me thought it was funny that Griff actually thought sleeping together almost every night for two months didn't imply a relationship, but the other part of me was so pissed off, I just wanted to throw up my hands and storm out. In the end, I decided to let it go. I would allow him to have some more time to get used to the idea, before I put a label on whatever the hell we were doing.

After she let us through, we changed into our suits in the locker room without speaking before making our way out to the pool. Things still felt awkward between us and I wondered what he was thinking. We each swam at our own pace for several laps until I reached my hand out to stop him.

"Hey," I said softly.

He turned to look at me, pulling off his goggles. "Yeah?"

"We okay?" I asked.

"Of course. Why wouldn't we be?" Griff looked genuinely confused, and that was when I realized that he truly had no idea about the boyfriend thing.

"You seemed a little freaked when that woman called you my boyfriend," I explained.

He laughed, "No. Not at all. I can see why she would think that since we were holding hands."

I was relieved to hear him say that until he opened his mouth again.

"I mean, she'd have no way of knowing we weren't serious. We haven't even known each other for longer than, like, a month."

My head tilted him as I studied his eyes. *What the hell?*

"Actually, we've been sleeping together for two months, Griff," I said.

"Really?"

"Really."

"Oh. Huh. Lucky me then," then he winked and leaned across the ropes to smack a kiss on my lips. "Let's race. What stroke?"

Did I want to argue semantics, or did I want to play in the pool with someone who was quickly becoming my favorite person?

"Freestyle. Ready… set…," I said before blasting off from the wall. I heard him shout after me just as my hands broke the water in front of my head. We raced and flirted and teased for another hour and ended up having one of the most fun dates I'd ever been on.

The best part came after the swim, when we sat in the steam room, and each of us tried to pretend we weren't watching the other one heat up and turn pink. By the time we got back to the locker room, there was no doubt we were going to be taking a shower in a tiny stall together.

We waited until the coast was clear and then grabbed towels and snuck into a stall like randy teenagers. As soon as the water was turned on, the noise of the spray drowned out the small noises we were planning on making.

The first thing Griff did was complain.

"There's no bar of soap here, just these stupid pump dispensers. I was going to make a big production about dropping it," he whined softly.

I leaned in, running my hands down his slick ass cheeks and squeezing before sliding my lips along an ear to whisper, "Fox, if you want me to bend over, just ask."

His whole body shuddered and I felt his cock stiffen against the top of my thigh. "*Jesus,*" he muttered.

I leaned in to kiss him when I heard a deep grunt and rhythmic slapping sounds coming from another stall. Our eyes met and widened in surprise as we shared a look of amusement. Griff leaned his cheek against mine, his whisper blowing into my ear and lighting me up inside.

"Can't decide if that turns me on more or makes me want to rush you home to do this in private," he murmured. The word "home" was so intimate that it made me smile even wider.

"Home," I said, pinching his ass.

Boyfriend or not, I was the lucky bastard taking Griffin Marian home that night.

For the next few weeks, I followed his lead and went with the flow. We went out to dinners and movies, but I didn't call them dates. We introduced each other to friends, but I didn't call him a boyfriend. I watched his reactions carefully in an effort to be sensitive to his feelings, and in doing so, I discovered something interesting. Griff loved affection. He enjoyed going on dates with me, people knowing I was his, and any amount of PDA I was willing to give. His heart seemed to love it all. It was just his brain that was scared.

It was okay if I was his boyfriend as long as I didn't use the word. It was okay if we were dating as long as we didn't call it that. I knew his hang-up had to do with his past, but part of me wondered if maybe he would continue to let it go on like that forever if I never pushed for more.

By the time the end of October rolled around, I was a regular at Marian Sunday dinner. Everyone treated me like I was one of the family, and I'd finally had several opportunities to meet Jude and his partner, Derek. They were, in fact, ridiculously sweet men like Griff and Nico had described.

In addition to being kind and generous to others, they were also goofy about one another. It was fun to watch them interact because they still flirted with each other like they hadn't already been together for over a year. After hearing the story of how they got together, I began to realize that being so outwardly flirty with each other was new to them, and it seemed like maybe they were making up for lost time.

It was at a Sunday dinner on Halloween night when we finally got another sighting of Simone with Dillon.

Everyone except Blue and Tristan were at the Marians' house in Hillsborough and planned on staying through the trick-or-treat hours. Pete and Ginger's twin girls were busy preparing their costumes in the bedroom they used when at Rebecca and Thomas's house, and Thad was dumping bags of candy into large bowls on the dining room table.

I offered to take the kitchen trash outside for Rebecca and wasn't surprised to see Griff follow me out for some stolen sexy time. We couldn't keep our hands off each other, and by then, it had been at least an hour and a half since we'd felt each other up.

After dumping the bag into the large rolling bin, I turned around and latched on to my "just friend," kissing and licking and biting his lips. We stayed like that for a long time, sucking face like a couple of teenagers. Griff smiled and ran his hands through my hair as I pulled him closer to me, enjoying the familiar press of his body against mine.

Suddenly we heard a masculine groan and panting. "Oh god, Simone, *oh god*," the voice croaked.

Griff's eyes popped out of his head as his entire body went rigid, beginning to coil for attack.

"Oh hell no," I whispered, holding him against me. "Don't even think about it, Griffin Marian. She's an adult."

He struggled against me, shooting me evil eyes and tightening his jaw. I almost burst out laughing.

"Babe, stop and think for a second, okay?" I said. "Just hang on a minute before you do something rash."

"Sam, goddammit, let go of me," he growled in a low voice. "I swear to god I'll knee you in the nuts if I have to."

At that point a laugh finally bubbled out of me. "That's a bit counterproductive, isn't it? I happen to know you're pretty fond of these nuts."

We heard more sounds. This time Simone made a hissing sound before speaking. "Stop being a baby."

The man's voice sounded like the words were spat through clenched teeth. "I can do this, I promise. Just give me a second to get myself ready."

Simone sighed. "Whatever. You know, you really ought to be embarrassed. It's pretty small, to be quite honest. If it wasn't so miniscule, it'd be much easier for me to grab."

"Please, baby, just pull it. That's it," he cried. "Get it in there. Oh shit… argh!"

Griff's head shot up and his eyes got even wider if that was possible. The sound of a whimper was clear as day and Griff pounced, bursting out of my grip just as a scream split the air.

I let go of him, causing him to almost fall through dense shrubbery in search of where the voices came from.

"Oh hell," I muttered under my breath as I raced after him. "Whoever that is better run."

I caught up with him just as he made his big entrance. Simone and Dillon Fisher sat together on a stone bench in a secluded area of the Marians' garden. They were fully dressed and had their heads together looking down at something.

"*What the hell is going on here?*" Griff boomed. Simone and Dillon jumped, knocking heads in the process and almost tumbling off the bench.

Griff raced to grab Dillon by the shirt and haul him away from Simone. Dillon howled in disapproval. I knelt on the ground next to Simone and cautiously looked at the bump on her head.

"You okay?" I asked.

She looked past me to where Griff was playing superhero to Dillon's villain. "Get your hands off him, you asshole."

Griff shot daggers at his sister. "Make me."

I laughed again. "Nice, Griff. Way to model maturity for the woman."

Smoke coiled out of his nostrils as the green daggers landed on me.

"Simone, honey, what's going on? We thought we heard someone, ah, upset," I said.

"I was trying to pull a splinter out of Dillon's foot with some tweezers. I almost had it until your fucking boyfriend burst through here like some kind of psychopath. Griff, what the hell?"

Griff looked from Simone to Dillon and back to Simone. I saw a blush rise up his throat and felt a little sorry for him. He turned to Dillon. "First of all, he's not my boyfriend. Second of all, is that true about the splinter?"

Seriously? That asshole was going to take a moment to clarify a little tidbit about our non-relationship status? I forced myself to put the issue on the back burner for now and focus on Simone and Dillon. But it was getting harder and harder to give Griff that space.

"Yeah, man. Wanna see? There's a huge-ass sliver in the bottom of my foot and it hurts like a bitch."

We noticed Dillon was barefoot, and I realized the howling earlier was because Griff had forced him back onto his hurt foot.

"Fox, you made him stand up on the splinter. Let the poor guy sit back down," I suggested.

Griff looked sheepishly at me before letting go of Dillon.

"Ah, sorry about that. Misunderstanding, I guess. Honest mistake," Griff mumbled as he made his way over to where I stood.

Simone shot him the bird before she went back to digging into Dillon's foot with her torture tool.

I put my arm around Griff and pulled him in for a kiss on the cheek. "My hero," I teased, pulling him away toward the house.

"Shut up," he said before turning his face into my neck. "God, I'm so embarrassed."

We were well out of earshot when I turned to kiss his forehead. "Don't be. Everyone likes being defended from a helpless victim every now and then." I laughed. "Plus, now we know there's still something going on between those two. What's Dillon doing here?"

"Good question. You should grill her when she comes inside."

"Me? Why me? You're her brother," I said, running my fingers into his curls.

"Because I can't trust myself not to say something stupid, obviously. I'm an idiot who doesn't have even the basic social skills."

I looked at him with a smile, intending to tease him some more. But what I saw there was genuine self-doubt.

"Griff, you were being a brother. Period. What you did back there is exactly what I would have done had it been Lacey. Why are you doubting yourself?"

His blush was even deeper by now and I wondered why he was embarrassed now that it was just the two of us.

"I just don't want you to think I'm irrational or a hothead. My dad was that way, and I never want to be like him," Griff confessed.

I held his cheeks with both hands and made eye contact with him. "I don't think that about you at all. I loved seeing you rush to defend your family, Fox. Your heart is enormous, even if it is locked behind a cage." I smiled gently at him. "You know how you always describe Jude as being super sweet?"

He nodded.

"Well, you're not. You're the perfect blend of sweet and spicy, and that's my favorite combination. When I came here to your parents' house for the first time, I made a huge batch of that jalapeño corn dip, and it was gone before we even sat down. Know why people love it so much? Because the sweetness of the corn mixed with the spice of the jalapeños is the perfect taste pairing. Don't ever think you're not good enough or you're not what I want. You are exactly what I want, Griffin Marian."

His eyes were shiny emeralds as I leaned in to kiss him. After a few minutes of thoroughly inspecting my mouth, Griff turned the dimples on me. "You sweet-talking motherfucker."

22

Griff

WHEN WE ENTERED MY PARENTS' HOUSE, THE USUAL crew was gathered around, preparing for the Halloween festivities. The dinner itself was a sandwich buffet set out on the kitchen counter, and Sam had brought two kinds of pasta salads to go with it. As Sam and I made plates for ourselves, we saw Simone enter the house alone.

Sam caught my eye and quirked a brow. *Where's Dillon?*

I shrugged and tilted my head at Thad. *Ask him.*

Sam narrowed his eyes at me and shook his head, so I let out a sigh and turned to my brother Thad.

"Hey, what's up with Simone and Dillon?" I asked.

"Beats me," he said. "Why do you ask?"

We made our way to the dining room to take a seat around the table with everyone else.

"Dillon was here earlier. Didn't you see him?" I asked.

"What? No. You're kidding." Thad laughed. "Well, he didn't

come with me."

"Hmm," I mused. "Then he had to have come with Simone. And since she lives *here*, that's interesting. Wonder when they started dating?"

I heard Sam snicker beside me and shot him a look. Out of the corner of my eye I saw Simone standing in the kitchen doorway with a suspicious look on her face.

"For your information, Captain Overreaction, we aren't dating. We've just been fucking around since the summer," she snapped.

I whipped my head around, incredulous. Thank god our parents were still in the kitchen. "What do you mean just fucking around? You've been sleeping with someone for months and think it's still just fucking around? Simone, you're dating the guy. Admit it."

"What, like, are you asking if he's my boyfriend or something?" she teased. I noticed my parents enter and take their seats.

"No. I'm telling you that if you've been sleeping together all this time, that poor kid thinks he's your boyfriend. The whole world thinks he's your boyfriend. Hell, he *deserves* to be your boyfriend for putting up with you for that long," I spouted.

The entire room went quiet. I looked up to find almost everyone staring at me.

"What?" I asked. Heads swiveled to look at Sam who was standing up to gather his plate. My chest hurt as I watched him walk into the kitchen. What was I missing? I felt like I'd said something awful but didn't know what it was.

"What's going on?" I asked in a low voice.

"Oh, honey," my mom said. "That poor man is goofy for you."

I looked back toward the kitchen door he'd disappeared through and then back at Mom. "Yeah, I like him too. What does that have to do with Simone?"

Simone rolled her eyes and looked away. It was Derek who stood up and invited me to step into the other room for a moment.

When we were in the family room with the door closed, Derek

looked at me.

"Don't be an idiot, Griff," he began.

My brain whirred with thoughts of all the different ways I was an idiot, but I couldn't pinpoint the specific one he meant.

"You've been painted on Sam's skin since mid-August. It's the end of October and you still won't even acknowledge you two are in a relationship," Derek said in his gentle way. "You spend every night together, you volunteer at the shelter together all the time, you can't keep your hands off each other, and you want the best for each other. Are any of those things untrue?"

"No," I replied.

"Right. So tell me what part of you and Sam isn't a relationship," he said.

"Why does this matter?" I asked.

"Okay. Let's look at it a different way. What if I told you that Jude and I found someone we'd like to set Sam up on a date with? How would that make you feel?" Derek studied my face for a reaction while I slumped down onto the leather sofa I'd been leaning against and tried not to puke.

"Right," he muttered. "That's what I thought. But have you two spoken about being exclusive?"

I didn't bother opening my mouth since the answer was obvious.

"Right," he repeated. "Is it because you want to keep *your* options open?"

My eyes flew up to his. "Hell no. I don't want to be with anyone else."

"Have you ever told him that?" Derek asked.

"Surely he knows," I said like an idiot.

Derek smiled at me the way wiser people smiled at idiots.

"I've gotta go," I muttered before walking out. I stopped and looked back over my shoulder. "Thanks, Derek."

His wide grin was enough to remind me why my brother had fallen for the guy.

"Griff, one more thing," he said.

"Yeah?"

"Don't think that there's anything else in your life more important than being with your person, because there isn't."

Jude was a lucky bastard. But I wasn't at all jealous, because I was a lucky bastard too.

23

Sam

It was one thing to try and give Griff all the time in the world between just the two of us, but quite another to hear him being such a blatant hypocrite in front of his family. Not to even mention suffering the pitiful glances the entire Marian crew shot my way after Shit For Brains opened his big mouth.

I carefully disposed of my dishes and made my way out the back door, palming my phone to search for an Uber.

After arranging for the ride, I sat near the end of the driveway feeling numb. I'd been ready to claim Griff since practically day one. I wasn't a player. I never wanted a fuck buddy. What I wanted was a relationship. Love. Something real and dependable.

I knew Griff was easily spooked, but I was starting to wonder if maybe he was always going to try holding me at a distance. Maybe this thing was never going to turn into more than a casual hookup.

The Uber driver pulled up and I stood to get in the car. Griff ran out and called for me.

"Sam, wait. I'm sorry," he said as he jogged the remaining distance to grab my hand. "Please don't go."

"I'm not going to be very good company tonight, Griff. Stay here and enjoy trick-or-treating with your nieces. We can talk tomorrow."

"No. If you want to go home, I'll drive you," he said, squeezing my hand. "Just let me grab the keys to the Jeep." He turned around to head back to the house, but I held on to his hand and pulled him back.

"No, Foxy. I'm going home and you're staying here. I promise we're okay. I just need some time to myself tonight, okay? We'll talk later." I leaned forward and kissed his forehead. "Tell your parents I'm sorry for racing out like that."

The look on his face was heartbreaking, so I turned quickly and got in the car. I rode the whole way home in silence, watching trick-or-treaters come out of houses in the neighborhood and thinking about whether I would have kids one day.

When I got back to the apartment, I went straight to Lacey's room and lay down on her bed, grabbing her pillow with the purple pillowcase that smelled like lavender. I really missed my sister. Maybe I had gotten too close to the Marian siblings when I should have been keeping them at arm's length.

With Lacey gone and me mostly estranged from my father, I was left with my two closest friends. Robbie and Jason were fantastic. We'd been close since college. But they also had their own families and lives.

I tried calling my sister but it went straight to voicemail. It was later on the East Coast, so I assumed she was at a loud Halloween party and could only hope she was being careful.

A few minutes after I'd retreated to my room, I heard the apartment door open and several sets of voices talking. I assumed Robbie and Jason had gone out to dinner with friends, and since I was in no mood to be social, I stayed in my room and wasted time on my laptop until finally falling asleep.

Three hours later I wasn't surprised to be awakened by a brain that wouldn't shut the fuck up. After another hour I finally gave up and went to the kitchen, which is how I heard the knocking on the door a little while later.

I looked through the peephole since it was after one in the morning.

Griff.

My heart did a little dance and suddenly I wanted nothing more than to put my hands on him and inhale his scent. I swung open the door and saw the most timid version of Griffin Marian I'd ever seen. He looked awful. Worry lines were etched in his forehead and the scar in his eyebrow I loved so much was pronounced somehow with concern. His jeans were dirty, and I wondered if maybe he'd been walking for a long time.

"Are you okay?" I asked.

He shook his head. "No. Sam. I'm so sorry. I tried to give you space tonight, but I couldn't. I wasn't about to let the night pass without telling you I'm sorry and I need you."

His eyes were so unsure it broke my heart. "I need you too, Griffin."

"Will you...? Uh... God, there's no way of saying this without cheezing it all up, is there? Will you...? Can we... be dating? Or whatever. Not seeing other people. Exclusive, I guess. And then that would make us... ah..." he stammered, his face beet red.

I barked out a loud laugh, causing him to jump.

"Oh my god, you are the cutest damned thing that ever walked the earth. Come here, jackass." I reached for his jacket and yanked him into my arms. I kissed him like crazy, my smile pressing up against his full delicious lips and my tongue licking his.

When I pulled back and cupped his cheeks, I still grinned. "Did you just ask me to go steady?"

He dropped his head onto my shoulder with a groan. "Argh, don't remind me. Is this how it's going to feel every time someone calls you my boyfriend?"

"Nah, only when you say it," I teased.

"Never," he swore. "I'm going to call you my love muffin or my poopsie-woopsie."

I decided to call his bluff and shrugged. "As long as you claim me somehow, I don't care what words you use."

His eyes turned downright evil.

Oh shit.

"I mean, within reason," I stammered.

"Hell no, Lothario. It's on." And then he got a glint in his eye and threw my own damned words back in my face. "Not like, *it's on*, but the stain stuff is *on*. The stain. I got you. I mean, I don't *have* you. What I meant was, I *got* you. You know, the stain."

"Ugh, shut the fuck up, cruel bastard. You broke my tongue that night," I accused.

"How so?" he asked, stepping forward into my personal space in a very, very good way.

"You, like, had tattoos and shit. And skin. I remember accidentally touching the skin." I swallowed.

Griff's nostrils flared and his eyes smoldered. Was smoldering even a thing? Apparently so. "Accidentally, my ass," he said.

"That too," I squeaked. "Stop. You're doing it again. The thing. With the other thing."

His chuckle went straight to my cock, making me realize I could make millions if I invented a magic trick where you could snap your fingers and have someone's clothes go up in smoke.

"Sam Coxwell, how about we do that thing we like to do with the thing and the other thing?" he purred, hot breath against my ear, and I shuddered.

I tried swallowing again. My gorgeous *boyfriend* was plastered to the front of my body wanting to do *all of the things.*

"Lead on, husband," I teased with a giant smile.

He might have fainted.

24

Griff

THE FOLLOWING WEEKEND AT MY PARENTS' HOUSE WENT more smoothly than Halloween. My family was in rare form, and Tilly had a hard time deciding between manhandling Derek or feeling up my own love bug.

Everyone was excited to see Sam back in the mix, and I was secretly grateful it wasn't awkward.

Blue and Tristan gave us all updates on how their surrogacy was going. The baby was due in February and my niece Chloe was convinced she'd need to be named Valentine.

"We can call her 'Val' for short. Come on, Uncle Blue. Uncle Tristan already said it was okay," she said.

Ginger rolled her eyes and got up from the table to head toward the kitchen. Pete laughed into his napkin.

"No, sweetie. But you should ask your mom and dad if you can pick the name of *your* baby," Blue said.

Every time I heard the word "baby" I felt my heart pick up. I couldn't help but think of seeing my mom in the hospital and remembering how badly I'd wanted a sibling growing up. Why couldn't I get over it?

I reached over and grabbed Sam's hand under the table without realizing it. He squeezed back and then leaned over to whisper in my ear.

"Want to take a break and go sit outside for a minute?"

I nodded and stood up, grabbing my dirty dishes to return them to the sink.

When we got to the kitchen we caught Ginger stealing cookies out of a decorative jar on the counter. She was a thousand-months pregnant with a baby boy and was about as big as a double-decker bus. I didn't tell her that of course, but I thought it every single time I saw her these days.

Unfortunately, she wasn't due for a few more weeks and was so uncomfortable she had gone way past pissed off and landed somewhere around homicidal.

"What the fuck are you looking at?" she spat at me as she clutched the cookie jar tighter.

"I was just thinking about how beautiful you look," I lied, before continuing to lie some more. "I can't wait to meet the baby. Any ideas on names yet? I just can't wait to meet him," I repeated like an idiot.

Her eyes narrowed and I swear her fingernails sharpened in front of my eyes. "I don't give a crap what he's called as long as he just gets the hell out. Everyone is in the other room. Feel free to leave me in peace with the Thin Mints."

Sam grabbed my hand and pulled me away from the hormonal spectacle. Instead of leading me outside, however, he pulled me into the mudroom near the door to the garage.

"Griff," Sam said after the door closed behind us. "What's going on with you?"

I tilted my head and studied him, trying to figure out what he was asking me.

"What do you mean?"

"What's the deal with you and babies?" he asked.

My stomach rolled and I felt my heart speed up. "Nothing. What deal?"

He narrowed his eyes at me. "Every time the subject of babies comes up, you get weird. I want to know why."

"I don't get weird. Let's go outside and make out," I said, pasting on a smile and grabbing his hand.

He yanked my hand back toward him, pulling me off balance so I fell against his chest. His arms came around me in a big hug and I instinctively returned it, melting into the familiar embrace of my Sam.

"Griffin, I'm not going anywhere. At some point you're going to have to stop freaking out and talk to me about stuff that matters to you," he said in a gentle voice that seemed to float into my heart.

I knew he was right, but that didn't mean I could make myself behave any differently toward him than before.

"It's fine. There's no stuff, Sam. Really," I lied again. It was something I seemed to be getting better at. Or worse, depending on who you asked. "You're hearing something that isn't there."

He pulled back to study me, reaching up to brush hair off my forehead. The look he gave me was so sweet and empathetic, like his heart knew the truth even though my mouth hadn't shared it.

"It's okay," he murmured before kissing me softly. My chest felt tight and I wanted to pull him back against me and cry straight into his goddamned neck.

But I didn't.

Instead, I smiled again. "Let's go get some air, sunshine." And I walked out of the mudroom away from my family.

* * *

Late that night after we'd been asleep for a few hours, something woke me up. The first thing I noticed was a cold spot next to me where Sam should have been. I got up and visited the bathroom before going to look for him.

It wasn't the first time I'd woken to find him cooking in my kitchen, but it was the first time I made the connection that he cooked when he was upset. Deep furrows creased his forehead and tension pulled his lips together in a frown.

"Hey," I said softly so as not to startle him.

His head snapped up in surprise. "Hey. What are you doing up? Did I wake you?"

"No, but why are you up?" I asked, walking up to him and sliding my arms around his waist to give him a kiss.

"Couldn't sleep. Thought I'd make some cookies for the kids at the shelter."

"That's nice. I'm sure the kids will love them," I said. I walked to the fridge to get out some orange juice.

"I used the last of your vanilla extract," he said as he turned back to the dough he rolled out on the counter.

"I have vanilla extract?" I asked.

"Not anymore," he said.

"Right. Okay. Anything else you want me to stock up on for your midnight therapy sessions?"

Sam looked up at me again in confusion. "What do you mean?"

"Never mind. How can I help?" I asked.

We worked together for the next hour rolling out dough and shaping it into pumpkins, leaves, and footballs before transferring them to cookie sheets to bake.

While we worked, I asked Sam more about his dream job of owning his own restaurant.

"What kind of food were you planning on making in this restaurant?" I asked.

"I'm used to making high-end gourmet fare. You know, froufrou stuff."

I looked over at him while he concentrated on lifting the cookies from the sheet without breaking them.

"I can't picture you making that kind of food," I admitted.

He looked up. "What do you mean? That's practically the only thing I ever cook."

I laughed. "No, you mostly cook comfort food."

His eyebrows furrowed again. "No, I don't. Remember when I made you those filet medallions with a tuber fusion blend?"

"Sunshine, you made me steak and potatoes with carrots," I corrected him.

"Well, I adapted it to make it more like my grandmother used to make. That's probably why it tasted like comfort food to you."

"It was the best thing I've put in my mouth. I love your cooking," I said with a smile. "Wait. On second thought, the *next* best thing of yours I've put in my mouth."

His face finally lit up in a smile. "Haha. But thanks. I've been thinking about asking your parents if I can cook Sunday dinner one of these weeks."

"Wow. They'd love that. Why don't I text them tomorrow and ask?"

"Yeah, let's do it. I can start brainstorming what I want to cook." He smiled. "Sometimes that's the best part."

I was glad his mood seemed to be improving. He slid in the last sheet of cookies and set the timer on his phone before taking a seat next to me on a stool. I'd been toying with an idea for a few days and finally decided to bite the bullet.

"I, ah, have this thing on Friday night," I began.

"What thing?"

"It's a big fundraising party that some of the local print media put on every fall," I explained. "Lots of my journalist friends will be there, and I was wondering if you might want to come with me." My heart beat a little faster than I'd liked because I didn't usually bring a date to work functions.

"Of course I would," Sam said with a smile. "Do I need a tux?"

"No. Just a nice suit is fine. They usually have an open bar and heavy hors d'oeuvres."

"Sounds good. I'll have to find someone to cover my shift at work, but that shouldn't be a problem."

After the final cookies cooled on the rack and the rest were put away to be decorated the following morning, I led Sam to the sofa.

When we settled down beside each other, I turned to face him.

"Now will you tell me why you were upset tonight?" I asked.

He turned so his body was mirroring mine. "What makes you think I was upset?"

"It's four o'clock in the morning, Sam, and you just made over a hundred cookies from scratch."

His forehead had stress lines across it again. I hated to see that.

"Griff, it bothered me earlier when you wouldn't talk to me about why babies are an issue for you," he said.

"What?" I asked. I had no idea that had stuck with him.

"You know exactly what I'm talking about, so don't act stupid," he warned with a sigh. "There's something there that you don't want to talk about, and it just made me feel like you still don't fully trust me. Which I'm trying to accept."

My stomach turned a little at his words. "You had trouble sleeping because of something I said earlier? I'm sorry, Sam."

His hand came out to brush my shoulder. "Griff, I get that you have a hard time letting people in, but it's hard to see you upset by something and not be able to help or even understand what it is you're going through."

I thought about whether or not to open up to him. I'd never talked about this to anyone. It hadn't come up with other people because I was rarely around babies or even in a conversation about them. But honestly, even if it had, I still wouldn't have shared it. It was just too personal.

"I've never told anyone, Sam." My palms felt clammy and my

heart picked up its pace. His face was kind and supportive. How in the world did I get lucky enough to attract the interest of someone like him?

"My parents had a baby when I was seven. A little boy," I said, words I'd never spoken to another human being my entire life.

25

Sam

I FELT MY EYEBROWS RAISE AS MY HEART DROPPED. GRIFF continued to speak, his voice quiet and carrying a vulnerability I'd never heard before.

"The whole time my mom was pregnant, I was so excited because I knew that a pregnant mom meant a new baby sister or brother. I couldn't wait to have someone else to play with in the apartment. Having a sibling seemed like a blast.

"When my little brother was born, they called him Ben. A brother. I couldn't wait to teach him all the cool stuff about being a boy. We were going to have so much fun together. My dad took me to the hospital to see my mom. I visited with her and little Ben for a while until a nurse came to take me to the vending machines. I didn't realize that my parents had planned on putting him up for adoption all along. When I got back to the room, Ben was gone and my mom was crying. I assumed he was in the nursery or maybe one of the nurses had taken him for some reason. No big deal, right?" he said. His eyes were watery and shifted away from me.

I wanted to reach out to him, to pull him toward me and comfort him, but I was afraid to break the spell. Part of me waited for him to clam up again.

"My mom came home from the hospital the next day without the new baby. I asked her where Ben was and she said he'd gone home with his new family."

I finally couldn't stand it anymore and put my arm around him to pull him close. "Oh shit, Griff."

"Yeah. Apparently, they never thought to inform me or prepare me in any way. Or, more likely, they were just too chickenshit."

"God, I can't even imagine what that was like for you," I said, pressing a kiss to his temple.

He let out a watery laugh into my hair. "Honestly, it happened so long ago, I don't know why it's still such a big deal to me."

"It's a big deal because you have a brother out there somewhere in the world who you never had a chance to grow up with," I suggested.

"I guess you're right. But I know he was most likely better off wherever he ended up than with us. So it was for the best, really."

"How did your mom die, Griff?" I asked gently.

"She came home from the hospital with pain pills and just never stopped taking them. She died of a drug overdose the following year."

It all made so much sense. The baby thing, the fear of letting anyone in. The strong hatred of drugs. He continued telling me more about his mom and the good things he remembered about her. When he finally slowed down, I realized how emotionally spent he'd become.

"Fox, let's go to bed," I suggested. I wanted to hold him for a little bit and keep him safe so he could get some rest.

He nodded and let me lead him back to bed, falling asleep quickly in my arms while I stayed awake thinking about this amazing man who'd been dealt a bad hand as a child. Despite his circumstances, he seemed to have a bigger heart than he knew. If only he'd let others care for his heart the way he cared for theirs.

I was of two minds about what happened that night between Griff and me. On the one hand, I was happy he finally opened up to me. On the other, I was devastated to learn more details of the reasons why he didn't trust anyone to stick around. Everyone he'd ever needed had left him. I was thankful to the Marians for loving him and keeping him safe, but my heart was bitter and angry at his biological parents for abandoning the little boy who needed them so desperately.

* * *

That Friday night we went to the media fundraiser. I was looking forward to meeting some of Griff's journalist friends until he began the introductions and I wanted to melt into a puddle of embarrassment.

"Hey, everyone, this is Sam, my shmoopie-woopie," he said with a straight face, putting his arm around my waist possessively. White wine shot out of my nose, and I choked. But not so badly I couldn't shoot him angry eyeballs.

"What?" he asked innocently. "You are. You're my little love flower."

I turned to his friends and proudly proclaimed my revenge lie. "He's kidding. I'm his husband. It's nice to meet you all."

Now it was his turn to choke.

After we settled down, he began to introduce me to his friends and colleagues in earnest. I liked the first woman he introduced me to right off the bat. Lori introduced me to her husband, who turned out to be in high-end wine sales.

We spent fifteen minutes standing by the bar discussing restaurant wine selections and food pairings while Griff greeted a few other colleagues who wandered over to us. When I finished discussing wine with my new friend, I followed Griff to meet another group of journalists he knew.

Everyone seemed fun and friendly, welcoming me immediately with warm smiles and teasing jokes about why I was slumming it with Griff. I could tell he was well liked by the group and that made me happy for him.

"So, what kind of writing do each of you do?" I asked.

There was a mix of news reporting, creative writing, and freelancers like Griff. The most interesting answer was from a quiet man in glasses and a sweater vest drinking a bottle of water.

"I write about naughty priests," he said.

I almost spit my wine across the room again.

"I'm sorry, what?" I asked.

He smiled. "I write erotic gay fiction. Specifically, priest kink and other religious taboos like that. Choir boys, confession booths. You know."

"Uh, no, not really. But that's... cool. Do you, ah, enjoy that? I mean, do you enjoy writing...? Is that a lucrative—?" I needed to be saved, and Griff came through for me in the form of a bark of laughter.

"Ned here is a priest himself, Sam," he said through his laughter. "Just thought you should know that little tidbit in case it helped you ratchet up the awkwardness a little."

I shot him a death glare as I felt the blood rush to my face. "Thanks, Griffin," I growled at my date before turning back to Ned. "What I meant to say was, 'Oh, how interesting. I'm going to need another drink.'"

The people standing with us all laughed by the time I finished stuttering generic apologies at Ned. It wasn't until I finally gave up that Ned winked at me and put his hand on my shoulder.

"I'm just fucking with you. I write technical documentation for a software company here in town. This is my wife, Jen," he said, gesturing to a lovely blonde woman whose eyes were sparkling with humor. "She's a reporter for the *Chronicle*."

"Please excuse him, Sam. That's his favorite bit to pull on

newbies," she said.

"*Ohdeargod*," I breathed with a laugh. "You totally had me. Not that there's anything wrong with a priest writing… religious smut," I finished lamely.

Griff laughed so hard I thought he might bust something, and if he didn't stop soon, then I might have to bust something for him.

Through his laughter he managed to utter a strangled, "Sorry, babe," but it wasn't convincing.

After a few more minutes of conversation, we made our way to stand around a high-top bar table. Just as we were laughing at another one of Ned's dry jokes, I heard a man's voice from behind me.

"Sorry I'm late, everyone. You wouldn't believe the asshole Uber driver I had," the voice rang out. Up walked a strutting peacock of a man with dark hair slicked back and a shiny black suit with an ostentatious purple pocket square jutting out from his chest. The man looked like a character out of a cheesy Italian mafia soap opera.

He took a spot at our table with a flourish.

"Welcome!" Lori gushed at the man. "Monte, this is Griff's date, Sam. Sam, this is Monte Mancini."

My polite smile of anticipation at meeting the new stranger froze in a death grimace as the name sank in.

Monte fucking Mancini. The restaurant reviewer from hell. I felt my jaw tighten as my internal monologue turned horribly bitchy. Someone was going to have to reign that diva in before this night went completely pear-shaped.

"Well, hello there, Sam. It's nice to meet you," Monte said. "Griffin, you're looking stunning as usual."

I felt my entire body vibrate with anger and tension. What had started off as a promising evening with some interesting and friendly people had taken a turn down Shit Street.

Unfortunately, my only saving grace was the unlimited supply of delicious free alcohol, and I proceeded to take advantage of the generous bartenders.

26

Griff

SOMETHING WAS DEFINITELY WRONG WITH SAM. ONE MINUTE he was laughing with Ned and the others about the priest kink joke and the next he was turning fifty shades of hissy fit right in front of my eyes.

I had never seen Sam Coxwell lose his cool. But that night his anger started simmering until it rocketed into a full-on boil. It was so unexpected, I almost didn't notice at first.

We were chatting over little appetizer plates, trying a pear-and-walnut salad I thought for sure Sam would rave about. Instead, he frowned at it, forking it with attitude while throwing down a third glass of wine. I peered over at him with a quirked brow, but he pretended not to notice.

When someone mentioned needing a refill, my friend Monte offered to go get it, and I noticed Sam roll his eyes.

I leaned over and whispered into his ear.

"Is everything okay?"

"Yup," he said. "Why wouldn't it be?"

"I'm not sure exactly, but it seems like something's bothering you."

"I'm fine."

Well, then. What else could I do? We continued chatting across the table with my friends Nick and Guy, who described a Halloween party they'd been to the weekend before and the costumes they'd made. Nick recounted how he'd basically given up and slapped something together at the last minute, which was a surprise because he was usually the one between the two of them who went all out on costumes.

Monte laughed. "Nick, you couldn't be bothered to try harder and make something nice, for god's sake?"

Sam stiffened next to me and cut in. "Sometimes it's not easy to make do with what you have on hand, Monte. Cut the guy some slack."

A few people at the table looked at Sam with questioning glances while Monte glanced over in surprise. I intervened to explain.

"Sam, Monte's giving Nick a hard time because Nick usually goes all out and upstages everyone when he goes to a costume party. His version of phoning it in was probably still spectacular," I explained.

Guy laughed. "Exactly. He did one of those big clear trash bags around his body and filled it with little multicolor balloons like he was a gumball machine. Slick bastard had guys handing him quarters all night."

The table broke into laughter at the image and Ned asked Nick which slot he preferred to take the coins in. I took that opportunity to pull Sam away from the group under the guise of getting us some fresh drinks.

After visiting the men's room and returning to the ballroom for another drink, I asked him again what was wrong.

"Nothing. I told you. Do you want to dance?" he asked. I couldn't figure out if he was trying to distract me.

"Okay. If you'd like."

Sam's face lit up in a grin and I noticed his eyes were glassy from all the wine. He was so fucking cute.

"Lead on, Foxy," he said.

We danced for several songs and I loved seeing him relax and have fun. Saying a silent prayer of thanks to myself for having the courage to bring him as my date, I enjoyed dancing with him until the band took a break.

Once we left the dance floor, Sam offered to get us refills. Because of my low tolerance for alcohol, I had switched to sparkling water after my first glass of wine.

I caught the eye of one of the editors I enjoyed working with and told Sam where to find me after he got our drinks.

While I chatted with the editor, I noticed Sam having words with Monte again. What the hell was his problem with that guy? I excused myself and made my way over to the side of the ballroom where Sam seemed to be taking a moment to himself. He swayed a little on his feet; I wondered if it was time to call it a night. Maybe he'd had too much to drink.

He stood alone, muttering soft curses under his breath, and I could have sworn I even heard him say something about eggplants.

"Babe?" I asked as I approached him. His head snapped up in surprise.

"Fuck," he muttered.

"What the hell's gotten into you?"

"I'll be right back," he said before walking back over to where Monte chatted with some of our friends.

I followed him, stopping only when someone grabbed my shoulder for a quick greeting. By the time I approached Monte's group, I could have sworn I heard Sam yelling something about testicles.

"And what kind of foodie doesn't know a globe artichoke from a Jerusalem artichoke?" he continued, on a roll now. "The fuck is a citrus poof? It was lemon foam, for god's sake!"

I grabbed Sam's elbow and pulled him away, holding up my other hand to the group in a conciliatory gesture. "So sorry, he's not usually like this. He took some pain meds earlier for a migraine and begged me not to make him come tonight," I lied. "Then I encouraged him to drink, thinking it would help him feel better. My fault. See you guys later."

Sam still muttered out nonsense about gelatinous sprouts and eggplants speaking French until I managed to get him out into the fresh air.

I turned on him and pushed him against the exterior wall of the hotel.

Just as I was getting ready to ream him out for being so rude to my friends, his words to Monte sank in and landed in my gut like a cement block.

Testicles. Artichokes. Lemon foam. Eggplant.

Oh fuck.

Holy mother of god, this was a nightmare.

And it was all my fault.

"How can you be friends with that pompous ass?" he accused, the words coming out in a bit of a slur.

"Monte?" I asked, stalling for time while I tried to decide how the hell to handle this.

"Yes, of course. Monte fucking Mancini. Tell me how you can be friends with someone who thinks it's funny to ridicule someone else's hard work and takes pleasure in crushing people's dreams?"

"Sam, we need to talk about this, but not here. Not on the street. Let's go home." I grabbed him by the hand and led him toward the parking deck. Once seated in the Jeep, Sam continued to rant.

"That asshole happened to come in on a day when everything went wrong and eviscerated my kitchen in his review like it was all some big joke. The day after the review came out, the owner fired me."

I ran my hand through my hair and looked out the window. This was even worse than I thought. The review I'd written had gotten Sam fired. How would he ever forgive me for something like that?

He thought about it for a minute and then seemed to deflate a little. "I'm sorry, Griff. I didn't mean to be rude to your friends. I guess it just caught me by surprise before I could talk myself into being the bigger person in there."

I reached my hand out to grasp his as I scrambled for something to say. "Sam, do you wish you were still at your old restaurant working for that guy?"

"Hell no," he said.

"And if you were still there, you wouldn't have been working at Harry Dick's when I came in," I added.

"Which means I would have missed out on meeting my Fox," he said, grabbing the front of my shirt and pulling me toward him so our noses almost touched. "That would have sucked."

I smelled the wine on his breath and wanted to taste it. But I knew better than to kiss him before telling him the truth.

"Exactly. So, really, when you think about it, we owe Monte fucking Mancini a big kiss on the lips," I suggested.

"Let's not go that far, cutie pie," he warned with a wink. He leaned forward to kiss me before I could stop him. God, he felt good. When he pulled back slightly, I moaned my disapproval out of habit.

"These lips are only for my Fox." He smirked before closing his eyes and leaning back in the seat.

I started the car and in a few minutes we were back at my place. I had to wake him up to get him upstairs and into bed. I told him to stay awake because I wanted to talk to him about something, but by the time I came out of the bathroom, he was asleep again.

27

Sam

I WOKE UP FEELING LIKE I HAD A SWEAT SOCK IN MY MOUTH.

"Bleh," I mumbled, trying to spit it out. My tongue bumped into a warm stretch of skin and it took me a minute to realize it wasn't my own.

"Why're you licking me?" a familiar voice asked in a sleepy tone.

"You're my favorite flavor," I replied without thinking.

A deep chuckle rumbled out of Griff's chest as he turned to face me.

"Are you still drunk?" he asked.

"No idea," I confessed. "But my mouth feels like I gargled with city bus exhaust."

"Hang on," Griff said, as if I planned on moving an inch.

He got out of bed, returning with a big glass of ice water and some pain reliever. My hero.

"I'd tell you I love you but then things would just get awkward," I teased, sitting up to take his offering.

Griff laughed. "Yeah, don't do that. I'm not sure my delicate heart could take it in such a romantic situation as this."

"If I said it while dry-heaving, at least it would make a fun memory to last a lifetime," I suggested.

Griff sat cross-legged on the bed next to me. After I took the pills and several sips of water, he reached over for my glass to set it on the bedside table.

"Sam, I have something I need to tell you," he said. His face had turned serious and my stomach truly did threaten to hork up the pills I'd swallowed. As much as I'd love to hear Griff declare his love for me, this wasn't exactly the way I'd imagined it happening.

"I wrote that review."

His words made no sense. I squinted at him, trying to figure out what he was talking about.

"What review?"

"The review of the Willow House," he said.

"No, you didn't," I corrected.

His teeth caught his lip before he let out a sigh. "Yes, I did."

I felt my throat tighten. "No. You. Didn't," I repeated.

"I'm so sorr—" he began, but I cut him off.

"Don't," I spat as his words began to sink in. "Explain to me what you mean when you say you wrote the review."

"Monte was called out of town and needed someone to do the assignment. He begged me to cover for him, so I did."

"But it was published under his name," I pointed out.

"His editor is a hard-ass and would have fired him for ditching the assignment on someone else."

My stomach revolted and my head pounded. I didn't have the mental capacity to understand this right now.

"You're the one who eviscerated my cooking in the magazine?" My voice sounded foreign and desperate to my ears.

I could see the regret in Griff's face, but I didn't care. If what he was saying was true, he could regret all he wanted. It wouldn't change a thing.

"Babe—"

"Don't call me that, goddammit," I bit out, climbing off the bed and reaching for my clothes. I needed some time to think. Some time for my head to stop hammering and my chest to stop squeezing my heart.

"Please, Sam. Let me explain," he said, standing to get his own clothes on.

"What's there to explain? You ridiculed me in front of my peers when you wrote that article. And then, what, you decided not to tell me? We've been together for months, Griff!" I scrambled for my shoes, gaining momentum as the lure of freedom beckoned me from beyond his apartment door.

"No! I didn't know. I didn't know until last night. The name of the chef was never made known to me when I wrote the article. I thought I was reviewing Franklin Willow, for god's sake. You have to believe me. I would have told you. I *am* telling you now. I wanted to tell you last night, but you fell asleep."

I headed to the door but Griff got there first and blocked it.

"Get out of my fucking way," I seethed.

"Don't be ridiculous. We're going to talk about this first."

"Griffin Marian, don't make me remove you from the door."

His eyes couldn't help but sparkle at my threat.

"Try it."

Fuck. He knew I would never lay hands on him in anger.

"I'm so mad at you right now I can't think," I told him.

"I know. And I'm sorry. But please just give me a few minutes to talk to you about it before you leave."

I gave up the fight and threw myself down on his sofa. "Fine. Talk."

He sat down on the other end of the sofa and I said a silent prayer of thanks that he wasn't touching me. I wouldn't be able to resist him touching me.

"Do you remember what I asked you last night about whether or not you wished you were still working at Willow House?" Griff asked.

"Yes."

"And you said you were glad you weren't there anymore."

"Griff, you don't understand. That review crushed me. I was on the verge of signing a lease on my fucking dream, and that review caused me to throw it all away," I explained.

I could see the pain in his eyes as my words hit him, and part of me wanted to take it back. But his face changed from pain to anger as he seemed to have a new thought.

"Bullshit," he growled in a low voice, catching me by surprise.

"What?" I asked.

"Are you telling me that one goddamned review caused you to throw away a lifelong dream? Are you really that fragile? I call bull- shit, Sam."

"Now you're deliberately pissing me off," I barked. "What the hell, Griff?"

"Do you know how unqualified I am to write a review of a gour- met restaurant?"

"Clearly. As evidenced by your bathroom humor in the article," I snapped.

"You know what I'm good at, Sam? Humor. So that's what I fell back on when I wrote it. But what are you good at?"

"What do you mean?" I asked. Clearly he was trying to make a point, but I'd be damned if I could follow it.

"Did you honestly think that gray pile of eggplant was your best work?"

"Shit went wrong, Griffin. What were supposed to be high-end cuts of meat showed up as goddamned vegetables. I did the best I could with what I had."

"Right. And did it make you happy? Even if you'd had the meat, would you have been happy that night in Willow's kitchen?"

As I opened my mouth to respond, I realized I couldn't lie to him. No. I hated working there.

"There's a difference between being happy in your job and taking pride in your work, Griff. I may not have been happy there, but I was still proud of making do with a bad set of circumstances that night," I explained.

"And if I'd known the circumstances, I would have written a different review. But I didn't. As it was, I was a bull in a china shop. There's always going to be one idiot out there criticizing you, even at your best. Are you really going to let that idiot get in the way of pursuing your dream of owning your own restaurant?"

"Christ, Griff! That idiot was you. And who the hell are you to say all of this to me anyway? You're so scared of following your own dream, you can't even define it to yourself." Gone were the semi-polite boundaries of not offending each other.

"What do you mean by that?" he asked.

"What's your career dream? Because floating around writing freelance shit for others can't be what you really want to do long term."

"Don't make this about me."

"If you're going to talk about being strong enough to follow your dream, then I want to hear about yours," I countered.

"I'm living mine," he lied.

"Bullshit," I said, standing up and going to his bookshelf. I pulled out the notebook I'd found a few weeks before when I was looking for something to read.

Returning to the sofa, I dropped the notebook on the cushion next to him.

Deafening silence fell as I resumed my seat. We both sat there looking down at the notebook.

Finally Griff stood up, carefully returned the notebook to its spot on the shelf, and began walking toward his bedroom.

"You can go," he said in a quiet voice.

28

Griff

I CRAWLED BACK INTO MY BED, MY HEAD SPINNING WITH THE implications of Sam having seen my illustrated stories. They were just doodles, really. Warm-up exercises for when I had trouble getting into the groove of writing for an assignment.

When I was little, I fell in love with drawing. My mom brought home used crayons from the restaurant where she worked and I covered every scrap paper I could find with color. Over time I began to draw figures—animals, people, situations.

When I hit the streets, the drawing turned to graffiti. I was so angry and felt utterly helpless. Creating a piece helped me escape into alternate world where life was normal for a gay kid or a kid in the foster system. Where everything I did wasn't about my sexuality or being an orphan. God, how I wished foster kids and LGBTQ kids could just *be*. Not be defined by that one part of them, but by who they were as a whole person. Who they were inside.

I felt the bed dip behind me as Sam crawled under the covers and moved in to wrap his arms around me, pulling my back in close to his front and resting his nose behind one of my ears.

"They're amazing, Fox," he said in a quiet, kind voice. He was so fucking sweet. "You're very talented. And the world needs your stories. Please tell me about them."

I shook my head, feeling my eyes fill.

Warm lips pressed into the tender skin of my neck before I heard him whisper, "Please."

I turned to face him, burying my face in the warm familiar skin of his neck and letting out a deep breath. His lips dropped small kisses in my hair and his hands came around to smooth up and down my back.

"I'm so sorry about that review, sunshine," I whispered against his skin.

"I know," he said.

"I wish I could take back time and do it all over again. It's killing me knowing I'm the one who fucked things up for you," I confessed in a raw voice. "That my words caused you pain."

"I know."

"But we wouldn't have met if you'd stayed there. And I… I just can't wish for that, you know?"

"I know," Sam said for the third time. "I feel the same way. And you're right. I let one jackass reviewer push me off course."

I pulled back to glare at him for calling me a jackass, but his eyes twinkled with mischief. I pressed my face back into his neck. He smelled like Sam—all warm and familiar and wholly *mine*.

"I've been creating graphic novels about kids living in the system," I explained after a few moments, wiping my eyes. "Like something I would have wanted to read when I was a teen and felt like my sexuality or not having parents was all anyone ever knew about me. I want kids to know no one thing has to be what defines them. If I can somehow normalize those two things in my stories, maybe some kids like me can relate and not feel so alone."

Sam pulled back and cupped my face. "Why haven't you published them?"

I shrugged. "Don't know."

"You're scared."

"Maybe," I admitted.

"What if we encouraged each other to get real about following our dreams, Griff?"

"You mean you'd consider opening a restaurant again?" I asked.

"If you start making a plan to publish your books."

Suddenly I remembered one of those cheesy lines about finding someone who brought out the best in yourself. I wondered if this was what it meant. Someone who recognized what was really in your heart and encouraged you to be strong enough to let it manifest itself in the world.

When I looked into his eyes, I thought, just maybe, Sam might be that person.

"Okay, then. Let's do it."

His lips landed on mine in a caress, soft brushes of tender skin against tender skin. His hands snaked back to my face and held me to him. My own fingers found the buttons of his shirt and began to work them out of their tiny holes until I lost patience and began to yank.

Sam must have sensed my desperation because he took a hand away from my face to fling the covers off us and grapple for my waistband. Our moves turned from soft and sweet to frantic and fevered as we raced to undress each other.

Fingers grabbed at skin and teeth nipped. Breathing sped up and my heart rocketed around my chest like a pinball. I couldn't get enough of him—his taste, his touch, his skin.

"Fox," he breathed in between gasps of breath. "Jesus, *fuck*, I want you so badly."

He palmed my cock as his teeth sank into the skin of my neck. My hands squeezed his ass cheeks before I slid a finger down between them. I wanted to taste him, so I slid down his body and took his cock in my mouth.

Sam hissed, sliding fingers into my hair. "Oh god, Griff," he groaned.

My wet tongue slid over his silky shaft until his voice pled and he was close to coming. I ran my hand up to his chest, enjoying the feel of the coarse chest hair sprinkled there. His hand landed on mine and squeezed it as I continued to work his shaft with my mouth.

He grabbed me under the arms and yanked me up, crushing his lips on mine in a bruising kiss. I felt my erection slide against his and let out a moan into his mouth, reaching a hand down to grasp both of our cocks together and pull.

"So good, Sam," I breathed. "*Fuck*, that feels incredible."

He leaned over and grabbed the lube from the table and slicked us both up, our hands bumping against each other as we searched frantically for that perfect friction.

As our cocks thrust together in an erotic slide, Sam's hands reached around to fondle my ass. I held our shafts together as we moved against one another faster and harder. Finally we found a rhythm that drove us both over the edge, causing us to cry out within moments of each other and shoot wildly all over Sam's chest.

When we were finished, we lay there sweaty and sticky, chests heaving with labored breaths. The man was so damned sexy that a part of me wanted to do it all over again right away.

As we lay on our backs next to each other, he turned his head to meet my eyes.

"You turn me on more than anyone, Griff. God. All you have to do is look at me like that and I want to jump you again."

I couldn't help but laugh. "I was just thinking the same about you."

"Why don't we get up and I'll take you out for breakfast?" Sam suggested.

* * *

When we were seated at the little French cafe with our coffees, Sam laughed. I looked up from my warm mug with a raised brow.

"I was just trying to picture you sitting at Willow House with that fancy food. I can't even imagine what was going through your mind," Sam said with a grin.

"I thought it was ridiculously pompous, honestly. I have as hard a time picturing you there making it as me there eating it."

"But that's the kind of food I've always made. It's what high-end chefs create."

"No. It isn't. You make incredible food for me, and it almost never has foam and frothy shit," I corrected.

"That's different. It's not the same when I'm at home with you."

"Why not?"

"Because when I'm cooking for you, I just make my favorites. My old family recipes and stuff," he explained.

"So, when you're left alone to cook what you really want to cook, you cook your favorites?" I asked, pinning him with a stare.

"Right," he said, before realizing I'd been making a point. "Wait. That's not the same thing as cooking for culinary success," he amended.

"What the fuck is culinary success?" I asked.

"You know, the *right* way to cook. What the critics expect, not what the people want," he said.

I smiled at him. "Sam, are you listening to yourself?"

29

Sam

DAMMIT.

I was dating a know-it-all.

"Fine, maybe you're right," I admitted.

"Babe, I'm not trying to be right. I'm trying to help you discover what will truly make you happy. Do you want to cook for eaters or reviewers?"

It was a fair question. One I hadn't really put any thought into.

"Eaters," I decided.

"Okay. Good. Then what kind of food would you like to cook to make eaters happy?" Griff asked.

"Well, I do like high-end versions of traditional comfort food. I don't exactly want to cook at a diner. Plus, I'm interested in wine pairings. So I would want to be able to offer a wine list as well."

"Why don't you come with me to the vineyard for Thanksgiving so you can talk to Tristan more about it?" Griff asked.

"Fox, are you inviting me to spend Thanksgiving with your

family?" I teased. "That's an awfully big step."

His face bloomed dark pink. "Shut up. You've been with my family a million times. You met most of them before we even got together."

"I'd love to come to the vineyard with you for Thanksgiving, if you're sure. But will you tell me if you freak out and change your mind?"

"What makes you think I'll freak out?" he asked.

"You're terrified of commitment," I said, stating what I thought was the obvious.

"Thanksgiving in Napa is hardly a commitment," he replied.

It struck me he didn't disagree with my accusation about his reticence, only disagreed the Marian clan gathering was a big deal. What was it going to take to convince him he could trust me?

For the rest of that day, my mind kept rolling that thought around until I had an idea. I'd invite him to spend Christmas with Lacey and me. Introduce him to *my* family.

But a couple of weeks later, a different situation brought the issue to a head.

* * *

Griff had been spending more and more time at my apartment so I could cook in my own kitchen. With Jason and Robbie there, I also had a larger audience to test my recipes. Griff had convinced me to work on creating a menu of dishes I'd like to serve at my dream restaurant, and it was fun experimenting with my three closest friends.

Usually, Griff showed up with a couple of bottles of wine for us to try, and I wondered if he secretly asked Tristan's advice on what to get. I used a phone app I had to keep notes about the wines and the dishes so I could create a database to help me remember.

That night I made a beef burgundy stew. Robbie had offered to pick up some bread at a local bakery, and Jason showed up with some fudge for dessert.

Griff sat on a stool next to the counter in my kitchen while I cooked. We each had a glass of wine and Griff was telling me about the art store he'd visited earlier that day when my phone rang. I grabbed it with my free hand.

"Sam Coxwell," I answered while stirring the stew with my other hand.

"Hey, Sam, it's your father," the familiar voice said over the line.

I felt the blood drain from my face and dropped the spoon onto the counter before looking over at Griff. His eyes met mine with a questioning glance, and I held out my hand for him without thinking.

He took it and squeezed, pulling me against him so that his face was against my chest and I stood between his legs.

"Hi," I said to my father. We hadn't spoken in almost a year.

"I'm coming out there for a game next Monday and was hoping we could meet up," he said.

"Why?"

"I want to catch up with you and find out how you're doing. I can get you tickets for the game if you want."

"No, thanks," I replied. He knew I wasn't a big fan.

"Why don't you just come by the hotel, and we can get a cup of coffee together."

I thought about why I was so opposed to seeing him. He was my father, after all. And he was reaching out. Would a cup of coffee kill me?

"Okay. Just tell me when and where," I said. I brought my free hand up to Griff's hair and twisted a curl around my finger. Maybe I could get him to come with me for moral support. It would be the perfect opportunity to introduce him to part of my family. Maybe if he met my dad, it would help him understand more about my past.

At the very least, it would force me to tell him the truth about who my father was. And maybe that would show him how much I trusted him to stick around through the challenging shit.

"Sounds great, Sam," my father said. "It'll probably be Tuesday morning, but I'll text you when I finalize my plans."

"Okay, bye," I finished before disconnecting the call and setting my phone on the counter. Before I could lean down to hug Griff, he stood up and embraced me instead. I felt a big sigh escape and buried my face in his shirt over his shoulder.

"What was that about?" he asked.

"My dad," I said. "He's coming next week and wants to see me."

"When was the last time you saw him?" Griff asked, pulling back and holding my jaw in his warm palms. His green eyes with the bisected eyebrow never failed to make my heart race.

"Five years ago when he showed up at my college graduation."

"Wow, five years is a long time. He didn't come for Lacey's high school graduation?" he asked.

"No. We didn't tell him about it," I explained. "When he showed up at mine, it turned into a big thing. I'd forgotten he didn't know I was gay."

The timer went off on my phone and I realized dinner was going to be ruined if I didn't get my head back in the game.

I cleared my throat. "I need to fix the salad, and you need to set the table," I said before leaning in to kiss Griff on the lips. "Keep those green eyes away from me or we'll all starve to death, Foxy."

He smiled and swatted my ass as I turned to check the stew.

* * *

Later that night when we were getting undressed, I tried to decide how to ask Griff to come with me to meet my dad. I realized asking him before explaining who my dad really was might be construed as a bait-and-switch deal. I kept going back and forth in my head about how to bring it up, but Griff beat me to the punch.

"You haven't been yourself since your dad called. What are you thinking?" he asked.

I took in a deep breath. "My father is Ray VanBuren," I stated.

Griff looked at me with a tilted head. "Your last name is Coxwell."

"Coxwell is my mother's maiden name. Lacey and I took it when we moved in with my grandmother Coxwell."

"Your father is Ray VanBuren?" Griff exclaimed. "Really?"

I nodded, watching him for his reaction.

"Holy shit, Sam. Ray VanBuren, the quarterback for the Dallas Cowboys?"

"Yes. Now he owns the Oklahoma City Steers. That's what he's coming to town for. A game against the 49ers."

"Isn't he the one who—?"

"Yes," I interrupted. "He slept with his coach's daughter and the whole world saw the video. That's why my mom left. Now she supposedly travels the world on the divorce settlement and could have settled down with another rich idiot for all I know."

Griff followed me into the bathroom to brush our teeth.

"All I can think to say is I'm sorry. I can't imagine going through all of that media crap when you were in middle school. That must have sucked."

"It did. But it wasn't nearly as bad as what you went through at that age, so let's just forget about it," I said. "I was wondering if you'd come with me next week, though, to meet him."

Griff was quiet for a while before answering. "I don't know if that's such a good idea."

"Even though we aren't close, I really want him to meet you. To see how great you are."

I could see his jaw tick under his evening scruff of beard. "Okay, sunshine. I'll go."

Relief washed over me, causing me to realize he'd passed a test I'd never meant to give.

We climbed into bed and turned out the lights, finding each

other and sliding closer until Griff's curly mop rested on my chest. I leaned up to kiss the top of his head.

"You're a good egg, Griffin Marian." I said.

Griff chuckled, blowing warm breath against my skin and following with his lips until we were tangled together.

30

Griff

I<small>T WAS THE</small> M<small>ONDAY BEFORE</small> T<small>HANKSGIVING, AND</small> I'<small>D STAYED</small> over at Sam's place the night before. We'd had fun staying up late hanging out with his roommates. During the evening, I'd gotten the sense that Robbie and Jason were treating Sam with kid gloves, though, so I pulled Robbie aside to ask him about it.

"Why are you guys acting so weird around Sam?" I asked as we grabbed more beers from the fridge. I didn't think Sam had told them about meeting up with his dad the following day.

"It's his first Thanksgiving without Lacey," he said. "We're just trying to keep him distracted, that's all."

"But he said she's going home with her roommate's family to DC," I said. "She'll be fine."

"It's not her we're worried about," Robbie said, looking at me with a gentle smile.

"Ah, I see. Good point."

"When you guys go to Napa, just keep an eye on him, okay,

Griff?" he asked.

"Of course I will. No problem." I tried to reassure him I had it covered, but my gut coiled uneasily. I wasn't sure I'd be any good at looking out for someone else's feelings like that. How did you even go about taking care of someone else's heart?

When we finally retired to Sam's room for the night, I was still thinking about it. I watched him take off his clothes and had a familiar jolt of lust when he exposed his muscular chest.

His lips curved up in a shit-eating grin. "Enjoying the show, Foxy?"

"Fuck, you're one hot piece of ass," I admitted.

He burst out laughing. "You're acting like you haven't been sleeping with me for the past few months."

I walked over to him and placed my hands on his bare chest, fingers roaming over chest hair and nipples, down to the ridges of his abdominal muscles.

"How do you stay this fit when you're around food and alcohol all day?" I wondered out loud.

"I have lots of sex. Pounding ass is good for the abs." His hands came up to fiddle with the fly of my jeans.

I snorted before leaning in to kiss his soft lips. "I think I read that on a billboard somewhere."

His lips curved up in a smile while I teased them with my tongue. "You taste like beer and potato chips," I mumbled against his mouth.

"Mmm, so do you," he said, lowering my zipper and pushing a hand down into my briefs. God, it felt so good when he touched me. I wanted to purr like a cat whenever Sam gave me physical affection. I craved it. Craved him. Couldn't get enough of him.

"Love it when you touch me," I whispered into his ear.

"Love touching you," he whispered right back as he pulled and stroked my cock with one hand and held the back of my neck with his other.

He pushed me back to sit on the edge of the bed after yanking my jeans and briefs down to my knees. I sat and kicked them off, letting go of Sam only long enough to free myself of the rest of my clothes.

He leaned over me, pressing kisses to my jaw, my neck, my shoulder. I struggled to get his clothes off while he distracted me with his mouth. My breathing sped up until I practically panted.

"Get these fucking clothes off," I growled through sharp breaths.

He chuckled and I felt the vibrations through the skin over my ribs where his mouth was busy sucking.

"Griffin, lie back," he demanded, and I was on my back before the words even broke through my conscious thought. I'd do anything for him. *Anything.*

He finished removing his clothes and leaned back over me, grasping my stiff erection and lowering his mouth over it. The fucker looked up at me with mischief in his eyes and I wondered what was going through his head.

My hands came out to run fingers through his hair, and his tongue hit a good spot on my cock, sending shivers through my stomach and causing me to gulp. He alternated sucking me in deep, satisfying strokes with pulling off to drop light kisses on my thighs until I barked at him to stop fucking around.

Hot, wet licks teased me through a grinning mouth, and I began to figure out what his game was. Tease the fuck out of Griff until he cries the ugly cry and begs on his hands and knees. Well, two could play that game.

I sat up and pulled his face up to kiss me, deepening the kiss for a minute before making my way over to bite his earlobe and grasp his cock in my fist at the same time.

"If you don't fuck me in the next five minutes, Mr. *Cocks Swell,* I'm going to hold you down and fuck that lonely hole of yours until you apologize for making me beg," I warned in a low grumble straight into his ear. He'd never bottomed with me, but I was sure as hell willing to give it a go if he didn't stop dicking around.

A whimper escaped his mouth as his erection hardened even more in my hand, releasing a thick bead of precum to slide down over the head.

"Well, well, well," I purred. "What have we here, sunshine? Someone wants to play the catcher tonight, hmm? Just say the word, Sam, and your tight ass is all mine."

My words were like thick blood being pumped straight to his cock, making me feel powerful and so goddamned turned on. His face leaned more firmly against mine, and his body seemed to follow.

"Griff," he implored, voice dragging over gravel. "Dammit, Griff. I don't... I... I can't even think straight when you're touching me."

I opened my mouth to tell him it was okay, that we would proceed as usual, but he spoke again before I had a chance.

"Yes. Please." It was a plaintive whisper, full of want and desperation. The sound went straight to my heart, and I wanted to give him the entire fucking world. I'd have to settle for mind-blowing physical pleasure.

I knew he'd bottomed before, so it wasn't going to be anything new for him. We had just fallen into our preferred roles and not gotten versatile with each other yet.

My mouth moved back over to his and attacked. The man had lit a fire under me and I was hot for him. The kiss was predatory, full of possession and claiming until I flipped him around, dropping him on his back on the bed below me.

I crawled up his body with my mouth, licking and nipping at his golden skin until the noises he made forced me to do something with my own throbbing cock. I stroked myself while I lowered my mouth to his shaft and sucked him, sliding a wet finger into him and searching around for that tight bundle of nerves.

Hands and mouths were everywhere.

Sam twisted and grabbed the lube from the table, shoving it into my hand before reaching his own back to grasp the headboard.

I put it down and moved my mouth to his entrance instead.

When my tongue landed on his tender skin, he clenched instinctively, which only turned me on more. I licked and probed until he was complete putty in my hands.

Only then did I grab the lube to begin stretching him wider with slick fingers. His channel was so warm; I couldn't wait to be inside it. For a brief moment I was struck by how strange it was we hadn't reversed roles up till now, but I honestly didn't care what came before. All I cared about was getting into Sam's hot body.

After I felt like he was as ready as he'd ever be, I gave his cock some more attention before traveling up his body to kiss his neck and double-check we were on the same page.

"You good?" I asked him.

"Huh?" he asked with glazed eyes. I felt my mouth turn up in a smirk.

"What do you want, Sam?" I teased.

"Wha—?"

"Do you want me to slide my cock inside of you and fuck you into this bed?"

His eyes rolled back in his head. "*Hngh*. Stop talking."

I laughed as I crushed his body into the bed, reaching for the condom. Within moments I knelt between his legs, ready to go. Pushing his knees up toward his chest, I pressed myself against him and began to push.

31

Sam

IF THAT BASTARD DIDN'T SHUT THE FUCK UP AND GET ON WITH it, I was going to jack off and be done.

Not really. But still.

The foreplay had my entire body buzzing. When Griff began to push in, I remembered to push out. The sharp burn made me wince, but Griff's mouth dropped onto my shoulder and bit down hard on my skin, diverting my attention and confusing my body for a brief moment.

Before I knew it, the pain had become a good kind of stretch, and I pulled Griff closer with my hands under his firm ass. I bent forward enough to kiss his mouth, and one of my hands came up to grip his curls and hold his face to mine.

His hips pulsed shallowly while we kissed, and I felt his hot breath against my face. He pulled back to gaze at me, green eyes dark with intensity.

"You okay?" he asked.

I nodded, struck by his thoughtfulness. And damned if that isn't when it hit me, the thought pummeling me the way Griff's hips did.

This was *it*. Griff was the guy.

The guy.

My stomach flipped over and started tumbling. I felt my heart stutter in my chest and my eyes begin to smart. No.

No, no, *no*.

It was too soon. He wasn't ready. I couldn't fall for him now, like this. I'd scare him off. It wouldn't work. Somehow I'd fuck it up.

Griff's thrusts began to strike repeatedly over my prostate as his hand stroked me expertly. My mind spiraled, and my gut jackknifed. The sweet, sexy man above me overloaded my senses in every possible way, and when I came, it was like the shearing off of the part of my life that was pre-Griff, leaving only the part that was Griff. The sob that came out of my mouth seemed to take us both by surprise.

I fought for breath and shuddered as I came down off the high, my hands clutching at sheets, at Griff, at anything I could reach. He disappeared for a second and then was back, lying on top of me, face pressed into the side of mine and arms wrapped around me.

Either he was trembling or I was. Or we both were. I stared up at the dark ceiling of my room as my thoughts bounced around like spilled ping-pong balls. My legs wrapped around the back of his and my hands roamed up and down his back.

Despite my mental disquiet, I knew I was right where I wanted to be.

We didn't speak. I wasn't about to tell him what I was thinking, and I was just as sure he didn't want to know.

As usual though, our bodies spoke for us even when our brains were too stubborn to say a word.

That night we spent wrapped as tightly around each other as we could possibly get. When one of us rolled away, the other followed. I awoke the next morning with Griff's nose practically inside my ear and my hands in his hair, thick curls wrapped around my fingers.

Sweet mother of god, I loved him.

"Your heart is pounding so hard I can see the pulse in your neck," Griff mumbled against my neck. "Should I call a doctor?"

"I just… it's just… nerves," I stuttered, trying to think of something, anything, to explain it away.

He shifted, propping himself on an elbow so he could see me. "About seeing your dad?"

His hair stuck up everywhere and he looked so adorable. Sleepy and naked in my bed. There went my heart rate again. *Dammit.*

I shrugged before bringing my hands behind my head in a fake relaxed pose. "Dunno. Thanksgiving with your family maybe. Or not having Lacey here. It's probably nothing," I lied.

"Surely you're not stressed about being with my family. You've been to family dinner a million times."

"No, you're right. Maybe it's the Lacey thing. Sometimes she gets emotional around the holidays, and I'm not with her to comfort her this time."

Griff ran a hand over my chest. "Why don't you call her? It's a decent hour on the East Coast, so you can call and catch up while I fix us some breakfast. Then I have to go in to the magazine office for that meeting with the editor before joining you at the coffee shop."

"Okay, but first will you please give me a pity blow job in the shower? I'm feeling very sorry for myself." I looked up at him with puppy eyes, and he barked out a laugh.

"Yes, but not because of that ridiculous face. I'll do it because I need some protein to tide me over until your phone call is done." He winked at me before getting up and heading to my bathroom. His tight, rounded ass was magnificent, and I drooled after it while he walked away.

"The nutritional value isn't as high as people think," I called out after him without thinking. "Less protein than one egg white and only one measly calorie. Plenty of zinc though."

Griff laughed and looked back over his shoulder. "Never mind then. You talked me out of it. I'll just wait and have breakfast."

Fuck, I thought, climbing off the bed to follow him.

"I was kidding. That shit is a superfood. 'Nutrient dense' I think is the term they use. I was getting it confused with water. Totally not the same thing."

After breakfast we were sitting around the table drinking another cup of coffee with Jason when the phone rang. We must have been thinking about each other because it was my sister. I greeted her happily and asked if she was all set for her trip with her roommate.

"Yeah, Sam. Her parents are actually coming to pick us up, so it's all good. Listen, I got a call from Ray, and he said he's there in the city with you," she said.

Well, hell. I wasn't expecting to talk to her about it until after I'd met him for coffee and seen how it went.

"Yes. I'm meeting him in a few hours for coffee before he heads back to OKC," I said.

"He and our mother are getting back together," she said. My brain whirred, trying to check and recheck if my ears heard right.

"What? That can't be right. What exactly did he say?" I demanded.

"He called to tell me he met back up with her recently on a trip somewhere and they decided to try again. They are planning a big family Christmas and want us to all be together in Oklahoma."

My stomach fell as I realized my father had been planning on blindsiding me at the coffee meeting.

"Holy shit, Lace. Thanks for the heads up. What do you think about all of this? What did you say to him?"

"I told him I had to go to class and couldn't talk, and then I called you. I don't know what I think, Sam. I just need some time to process, I guess. What about you?"

"No idea. Maybe I'll get some better insight after I meet with him," I said.

"Sam, you aren't going to take Griff, are you?" she asked.

I caught Griff's eye and saw concern. His brows knit together in confusion so I held up a finger for him to wait.

"Yes. Why?" I asked her.

"You know how he feels about you being gay. Maybe you should just meet with him on your own this time," she suggested.

"Screw that, Lacey. If he doesn't like me the way I am, he can fuck off," I said, walking out of the room and into the privacy of my bedroom before continuing.

"If he doesn't want to meet Griff, then I don't want to see him. Griff's very important to me and hopefully he's going to be around for many more family events in the future. I'll be damned if I'm going to pretend not to have a boyfriend to fit into some macho role dear old Dad wished I'd been born into," I seethed.

"Calm down, Sam. I was just trying to suggest starting off slowly with him. Think of poor Griff, for god's sake. Do you think Ray's going to be nice to him?"

"I *am* thinking of Griff. I want him to know he's important enough to introduce to my family. I care about him, Lacey. A lot."

"I can tell. Then do what you think is best for the two of you. You know I support you no matter what," she soothed.

"I'll call you afterward, okay?"

"Okay, Sam. Good luck," she said before hanging up.

I walked back into the main room and looked at Griff again as I felt the information about my mom sink in. "That was Lacey. Apparently my father has gone off the deep end and reconnected with my mother."

Griff's concerned brow grew even deeper and he looked almost nervous. "Is your mom going to be there today?"

Nerves slithered into my gut. I hated that feeling. "How should I know? I wouldn't put it past him to spring something like that on me, I guess. That's the kind of messed up shit this family seems to thrive on," I said through clenched teeth. Fear began to grip me and I second-guessed agreeing to meet him at all.

"How long has it been since you've seen her?" he asked.

"A long time," I breathed. My entire body vibrated, and I felt like I might lose the contents of my stomach.

"How long is long?" Griff pushed.

"Twelve fucking years," I said, not thinking about my tone of voice or what Griffin might be thinking.

"It sounds like there's a lot you're dealing with right now. Sorry I have to head out to my meeting," he said as he made his way to the door.

As Griff walked out of the apartment, I was so deep inside my head I didn't notice the fact he looked even more terrified than I was.

* * *

As I stood in the lobby of the hotel waiting on Griff a couple of hours later, I was surprised he hadn't beaten me there. I figured his meeting would have let out in plenty of time for him to get to the hotel early and be waiting for me. I texted him.

Sam: *Are you almost here or should I go in without you?*

There was no answer, so I tried calling him. The call went straight to voicemail. Maybe his phone was still turned off. After a few more minutes, I decided the meeting must have run over and he was going to be late. I texted him again to let him know I would be inside the coffee place and to come find us or text me when he arrived.

The meeting with my father was excruciating. I was relieved to discover my mom wasn't there but my father did, indeed, tell me they were reconciling. He made a pretty speech about reuniting the family over Christmas. I told him I had no intention of going to Oklahoma for the holidays and was more than happy to spend it with my boyfriend's family instead (not that Griff had invited me yet). Ray wasn't happy, and I could sense he wasn't going to let the subject go.

By the time we'd been speaking for an hour, my disappointment at Griff's delay had turned into fear that something bad had happened to him.

Finally I left my father and went straight to Griff's apartment. There was no answer when I banged on the door. Still no answer on the phone, and no responses to texts, so I headed home.

After thirty minutes of pacing in my apartment, my phone pinged where I gripped it hard in my fist.

Griff: *I'm sorry I couldn't make it.*

My stomach dropped with relief as I dialed the phone as fast as I could.

"Hey," he said, sounding hesitant.

"Thank god you're okay. What the hell happened?" I said in a rush.

"Something came up at the magazine and they needed someone to cover an event for an article. I went straight there."

That lying asshole. I could hear it in his voice. I didn't know what bothered me more—that he'd ditched me or that he'd lied to me about it.

"Bullshit," I snapped. "What was the assignment, Griff?"

"An event at a children's museum that needed—"

"Don't fucking lie to me. Do you really think I'm buying the fact you couldn't call or text me to tell me you were going to a goddamned children's museum? You bailed. You got scared and bailed."

Silence for a beat.

"You're right. I bailed," he blurted. "Might as well get used to it now, Sam, because that's what I do. I bail."

"Well, that's awfully convenient now, isn't it? The going gets tough so you get going? How nice for you. You know what, Griff? I fucking needed you today. I needed you and you weren't there. Where are you? Still at the imaginary museum?"

"No. I'm almost to the vineyard," he admitted.

My jaw dropped.

"So you weren't just bailing on coffee with my dad. You were bailing on taking me to Marian Thanksgiving too? *Jesusfuckingchrist*, Griffin. I should have seen this coming. Go to hell," I spat before disconnecting and powering down my phone.

I heard a sound in the kitchen and turned to see Jason standing there. He must have heard everything, and the look of pity in his eyes was untenable.

"Don't say a word, Jason," I warned.

"Well, you know I'm not going to take that advice, but nice try," he said with a slight smile. "You need to go find him, Sam," he said.

"No way," I scoffed. "Clearly he didn't give enough of a shit about me to even talk about it before he stood me up." My breathing had sped up until I felt like I couldn't get enough air with each breath. Jason sat me down on a chair and tilted my head down between my knees, which only made it harder to breathe. I swatted him away and sat up straight, mentally chastising myself for falling for Griffin fucking Marian in the first place. Should have known he would pull this shit at some point.

But what the hell did it matter now? Clearly I'd been much more invested than Griff ever was. My heart was fucked, and I got up to take my sorry ass back to bed. I'd just hide under my comforter through Thanksgiving and then start fresh the following Monday. Pretend none of this relationship crap ever happened.

Jason had other plans.

"If you think for one goddamned minute that you're going to stay here and wallow in self-pity, then you're mistaken. You're going to go get him and tell him you love him."

"Jason, you don't understand," I began.

"Fuck that. I don't need to understand. Each of you is dancing around the fact that you've found something special together, and you're both so terrified of screwing it up that you're screwing it up.

Just go. One of you needs to take a chance and swallow his pride, Sam. Is he brave enough to do it? Are you?"

I wasn't sure I was, and I sure as shit knew he wasn't. It was all I could do to get into my bedroom and close the door before collapsing on the bed like I'd planned.

32

Griff

WELL, THAT WAS THAT, I GUESSED. SAM HAD TOLD ME TO go to hell, and who could blame him?

Families scared me during the best of times, but a family with drama and the power to hurt someone I cared about? That was the scariest kind of all. What if I went to the coffee place and saw Sam hurting? What if his dad said something awful to one of us? What if he disappointed Sam yet again? Or worse, abandoned him?

I wouldn't be able to take it.

It was easier if I didn't go. Just didn't see any of it happen. Then maybe I could pretend it hadn't. Caring for someone hurt like hell.

After volunteering to cover the kids' museum event, I had powered down my phone and focused on the writing assignment. Once I'd finished, I'd headed by my apartment to pack a bag for Thanksgiving and left for the vineyard early. Without Sam.

I felt like the asshole I was, but I couldn't make myself do the right thing for him. It was too much.

When Sam had taken his phone call with his sister to his bedroom, I'd still been able to hear him. Words about wanting me to be around and caring about me a lot. Words that implied permanence and promises.

No, thanks.

My heart thundered in my chest just remembering how I'd felt while listening to him. Part of me loved hearing it. Of course I wanted Sam to care about me and want to be with me. But another part of me curled up into a scared little ball wanting to run and hide.

That part won.

I'd decided to walk away. Just leave him to find someone better. Someone who could play happy family with him and be counted on to be there when it mattered. Not someone broken and unreliable and fucked up. He deserved better.

I hadn't known how I would explain myself to him, but it turned out I didn't need to. When I'd texted to tell him I was sorry I didn't make it, he'd called and handed me my ass.

When I arrived at the vineyard, I felt wrung out. Almost two hours in holiday traffic had added anger to my self-pity and given me way too much time to think.

I was fucking heartbroken. The strength of my feelings came out of the blue and hit me head-on. I'd known I was falling for Sam but didn't quite realize how vital he was to my happiness. That is, until I started thinking about the possibility of walking away from him.

And now I didn't know how I would live a life without him in it.

What I did know was I was heartsick and bone tired with a pounding headache, which was why, when I saw Mom standing in the lobby of the vineyard lodge, I burst into tears like a jackass.

My brother Blue must have been standing nearby because he had a room key for me and my duffel bag in hand by the time I finished hugging Mom.

"I'm okay," I lied, wiping my eyes. "Just really tired. I think I'm going to lie down for a little while."

Mom knew I was lying since I'd arrived earlier than expected and there was an obvious lack of Sam with me, but she also knew when not to push. She'd spent years learning that pushing Griffin Fox made him run.

I stripped down to boxers and slid into the bed in my hotel room in the familiar lodge. The vineyard had become like a secondary family headquarters for us. We spent most holidays there together because there were enough bedrooms for everyone in the lodge and the main dining room in the estate house was big enough for our crew to spread out. Blue and Tristan loved hosting everyone, and it gave us all a chance to get away from the city and the distractions of work or school.

I hadn't noticed Blue's dog Piper in the room with me until I heard her yawn. Peering over the edge of the bed, I saw her curled up in an afternoon sun patch coming through the window. She normally stuck to Blue like a cheap price tag on a picture frame, but she was a sucker for the brokenhearted.

"C'mere, girl," I said, patting the bed next to me. She perked up and took a flying leap, landing on the high four-poster bed and curling into a ball against me. I turned to spoon her and fell asleep feeling a little less lonely than when I'd arrived.

* * *

I awoke several hours later to a knock on my door and slid on my pants before answering it. It was Dante. Apparently Mom could only take so much worrying before sending in the troops.

After a quick trip to the bathroom, I put on the rest of my clothes and silently followed him to the lobby to join the others. Everyone who'd arrived that day sat on overstuffed chairs and sofas in front of a blazing fire in the enormous stone fireplace that dominated the center of the lobby.

As I looked around to choose where to sit, one face in particular stood out.

Sam.

I stopped in my tracks as Dante continued past me to take a seat on a sofa. Sam stood up to walk toward me.

"Hey," I said like a dumbass.

"Hey," he replied before grabbing me into a tight hug. I sank into him and felt my eyes overflow again, only this time it was with relief.

"You're an idiot," he said into my ear.

"I know," I breathed. "I'm sorry."

"Can we talk?" he asked.

I nodded and pulled away, taking his hand and surreptitiously wiping my cheeks with the other.

We went back to my room and closed the door behind us.

"Griff, I'm so mad at you right now I don't even know where to begin," he said.

"I shouldn't have stood you up," I admitted.

"No, you shouldn't have," he said.

"I should have been there for you," I added.

"No shit, Sherlock. What were you thinking?"

"I wasn't thinking," I said.

"Liar." The word was accusing, but the delivery was softened by a watery smile.

I took a deep breath.

"I love you, Sam," I said, feeling the tears escape again. "And it scares me. When I get scared, I run."

A bigger smile broke over his beautiful face as he walked toward me. "It's okay, Griffin. I'm not going to let you run away from me. Actually, that's not quite true. You want to run? Fine. Go for it. I'll just follow you."

My heart resumed its crazy Sam staccato. "But I'm not good for you. I'll hurt you. You deserve someone better."

"What if I said the same thing to you? That I wasn't good for you and you deserved someone better," he asked.

"I wouldn't believe you. You're one of the best things that's ever happened to me," I confessed.

"Likewise," he said with a sweet smile.

I couldn't believe my ears.

"I'm not good at this, Sam. There's shit about me you don't know yet."

"I know there is. We've got time to deal with it later. Right now I want to kiss your face until you don't look like a terrified animal getting ready to bolt."

"I'm not going to bolt," I said, surprised to hear its truth coming out of my mouth. "Tonight anyway," I added, because after all, this was me we were talking about.

He smiled. "Good. Because I have plans for you tonight." The promise sent shivers up my spine and made me consider how much shit my family would give me for not showing up in the lobby again until morning.

"Don't even think about it, Fox." Sam laughed, reaching up to cup my cheeks. "You may be able to withstand their teasing and sexual innuendo, but I can't."

"Sam, it's been a million hours since we last fondled anything," I complained, leaning my forehead against his and inhaling his delicious scent. "I was hoping we could at least sneak in a quickie before we went back out there."

"Kiss me, gorgeous," he breathed. Goosebumps tickled every inch of my skin as I brushed my lips against his. His mouth tasted like every reach-for-the-stars dream I'd ever had and never gotten.

"I love you too, Griffin," Sam finally said after we were naked in my bed a few minutes later and building up steam for some truly epic makeup sex. His hands drove me nuts while I did my best to lick every inch of him.

I lifted my head up to stare at him, tongue still hanging out.

"Huh?" I asked. Because, as a writer, I was very good with words.

"I love you." He laughed. "Dammit, I know you're just making me say it again because you want to hear it."

I grinned right back at him. "It worked, didn't it?"

"Fucker," he muttered before tackling me back down onto the sheets.

The display that greeted my family a good forty-five minutes later must have been a sight to behold. There were beard burns and swollen lips, messed-up hair, wrinkled clothes, and possibly even some hickeys. Unfortunately, there was no hiding it as we sheepishly made our way back to the lobby.

It was pretty bad.

Because it had been *So. Very. Good.*

Wolf whistles rang out across the cavernous space, and Sam's face turned cranberry red. Our hands were laced together, and he squeezed mine in a death grip until we took seats next to each other on the sofa.

Of course it was Aunt Tilly who broke the awkward silence.

"Griff, it's a good thing Sam showed up or you would have had to invite your buddy Jack."

I looked at her, wondering if she had the beginnings of dementia. "Jack who?" And hell if I shouldn't have known better.

"Jack Soffalot," she said, erupting in giggles. "Oh shit, I think I peed."

At that, everyone laughed and talked over each other as if Sam and I had been there all along. Thankfully, Tristan brought us some wine and I was able to relax against Sam's side while everyone took turns coming up with dirtier and dirtier fake names.

Sam put his arm behind me on the back of the sofa and began running his fingers through my hair, lulling me into a serious state of relaxation. By the time Blue and Tristan told everyone to head over to the estate house for dinner, I had melted against Sam with my head on his shoulder and one arm tucked behind his waist.

"Can't move," I murmured. "Send food."

Sam turned to press a kiss to my head before gently sitting me up. "Let's go, Foxy. I'm starving. Haven't eaten since breakfast."

"Me neither. Good thing I had that pre-breakfast, or I wouldn't have made it this long," I said as he stood and reached out a hand to help me up.

"Do you need a little something similar to tide you over right now?" he asked. "I'm happy to give it to you."

"I'll take it!" Granny said from somewhere behind us.

33

Sam

BY THEN I'D SPENT MANY MEALS WITH THE MARIAN CLAN, BUT it wasn't until Thanksgiving Day that I began to truly feel like a member of the family. Maybe it was due to Griff's admission of his feelings for me or maybe it was just all starting to come together. I began to see a future with them, and it almost felt too good to be true.

Thomas and Rebecca had treated me like another Marian kid from the moment we met at the shelter. By Thanksgiving, the siblings and spouses were doing the same, teasing me and grilling me the same way they would any of the other brothers. When I called Lacey on Thanksgiving night, I told her about them.

She already knew Griff and I were together and that I was spending the holiday in Napa with the whole family, but she didn't know I was in love with him.

We sat around the lodge fireplace again after stuffing ourselves earlier with turkey. Half the Marians were in their rooms sleeping off the big holiday meal while a handful of us preferred dozing by the fire. I was lying on a sofa with my head in Griff's lap while he read something on his iPad, his free hand sneaking under my shirt to do naughty things to the skin below my rib cage.

"Sounds like you've been shot with Cupid's arrow, big brother," Lacey teased through the phone.

"Yep, he got me right in the ass," I agreed. "And it felt so good."

The wandering fingers stilled and Griff stared down at me with wide eyes.

"What?" I asked him.

"What exactly are you telling your sister about us?" he asked.

I rewound the conversation in my head and felt heat climb up my neck. "Your mind is just as dirty as Tilly's."

"I heard that," Tilly's voice sounded from somewhere off to my right.

My sister laughed on the other end of the phone. "Can I talk to Griff?" she asked.

I looked up at the man with a smile. Green eyes met mine with a questioning look.

"Sure, Lace. Hang on. Here he is." I handed the phone to him. "She wants to talk to you."

He took the phone and greeted her with a big smile that included the dimples.

Those motherfucking dimples. *Jesus.*

I adjusted my jeans with a wiggle of my hips. Griff shot an eyebrow at me. Fucker.

"Hi, Lacey, it's nice to kind of meet you."

They spoke for a few minutes, but I could only hear one side of the conversation. I ran a hand up Griff's inner thigh until I felt his thigh muscles squeeze together to stop my progress. Buzzkill.

Finally he gave back my phone, and I continued the conversation with my sister. She seemed happy and was having a nice time in DC with her roommate's family. Before we wrapped up the call, however, she dropped a bomb on me.

"Mom and Dad are getting married again, and they're asking for our support."

My stomach fell, and I knew my smile faded away.

"What?" I asked, sitting up. "How do you know?"

"He sent me an email."

"Fuck that, Lacey. I'm out. Not interested. He can go to—"

"Sam, I know this is not what you wanted to hear, but I want to see them. I'm going to Oklahoma for Christmas," she said. She'd known I wouldn't accept the news easily. "I'm going to meet with them no matter what. The only question is whether or not you come with me."

I let out a breath. "I can't stop you."

"No, you can't. But I'd rather not meet with them by myself. Will you please consider coming with me?"

She sounded so young and vulnerable. Nothing like the the strong young woman I dropped off in Charlottesville several months before.

"Dammit, Lacey. All I can do is promise to think about it, okay?"

"Thanks, Sam."

"Happy Thanksgiving. And tell Sarina's family the same. I assume you've thanked them properly for the visit, yeah?"

"Of course. I also bought them a cookbook I thought they'd like. Don't worry."

When I disconnected the call, Griff looked at me with furrowed brows. "Everything okay?"

"No. She wants to go to Oklahoma to meet our parents over Christmas." I closed my eyes and leaned against him until my face was buried in Griff's shirtfront and I could get both my arms around his waist. His hands came down to rub my back and he curled down to drop a kiss on my head.

"Do you want to go somewhere and talk about it?" he asked. I loved the rumbling feel of the sound through his chest.

"No."

"Do you want to go somewhere and *not* talk about it?" he asked in a playful voice.

"Hell yes," I answered as I stood. "You have the best ideas."

"We can play pilgrims' first feast," he snickered. "I'll even let you be the turkey."

As we turned to speed walk to our room, I heard Tristan's granny call after us from her spot in a chair by the fire. "Irene makes the best Pocahontas. Want me to loan her to you boys for an hour? I think she even brought her buckskins."

I froze mid-stride and turned to look back at the woman. Griff grabbed my hand and pulled. "Don't listen to her. Irene's buckskins caught fire during the summer solstice ritual."

We continued to our room, trying desperately to unthink the images injected into our unsuspecting brains. Griff finally resorted to drastic measures by describing in great detail a dirty scene of two wayward pilgrim boys lost in the woods with only each other's hot bodies for warmth. They were naughty, naughty pilgrims, but boy, did they know what to do with those big belt buckles. I'd never been more grateful to date a creative writer in all my life.

After I was heated up, basted, and eaten until nothing was left but a spent pile of bones, Griff asked me again what Lacey had said.

We lay next to each other on the bed with our legs intertwined, upper bodies leaning apart in an attempt to cool off after the delicious sex feast. A forgotten white droplet was caught in his happy trail, and I leaned forward to lick it off him. Ab muscles contracted under my tongue, and I noticed Griff's cock wake back up.

I moved my tongue slowly from his abs to the barbells, causing him to hiss. It wasn't until after I'd rolled on top of him again and really went to town on the barbells that he grabbed my hair and pulled my head up.

"Nice try, Satan. Stop avoiding my question," Griff asked. His green eyes flashed, and I could tell he was this close to letting me tempt him away from the conversation.

I moved up to nibble on his neck and heard him groan. His long fingers raked through my hair until he pulled my face up to his again, kissing me deeply.

"Mmm," I moaned into the kiss, chasing his tongue with mine and enjoying the feel of his strong hands on my head and five o'clock shadow scratching against my nose. His masculinity was intoxicating.

"Tell me," Griff said, lips still moving along my skin.

"Anything," I breathed through a dizzy haze.

The crocodile grin erupted into all teeth and victory. "Tell me what Lacey said."

My sister's name popped the lust bubble, and I fell back onto the bed, deflated. "Cocktease."

"Sam, I could tell it upset you. Talk to me."

"She wants me to go with her to Oklahoma. Apparently dear old Dad and Mommy dearest are getting hitched," I told him.

Griff shifted up on an elbow to peer down at me. "Fuck. And?"

"And I really don't want to witness it. I sure as hell don't want *her* to go. They're just going to upset her, and then I'll have to send her back to school with a broken heart or at least under a pall of disillusionment."

"Babe, I'm pretty sure she's not expecting to meet Mother and Father of the Year. She probably just wants to see them again now that she's an adult. You can hardly blame her, can you?"

"No. I don't blame her. I just know she's going to be upset by it. I wish I could save her from that, you know?" I asked. My arms were crossed over my eyes until Griff pulled them away.

"You're projecting your own feelings and experience onto her. Give her a chance to have her own interaction with them and learn her own life lessons, Sam. Dealing with this is part of growing up, and she needs to do it her own way. But she does need you there to catch her if she falls."

I looked at him and saw the same familiar face I slept next to every night. The curly hair and playful good looks punctuated by mesmerizing green eyes. It occurred to me he was the only person who didn't know how attractive he was, and I didn't mean just physically. He was thoughtful and kind. Caring. I blew out a breath.

"What about me?" I asked, my voice coming out whinier than I expected. I was starting to lose hold of my equilibrium the more I thought about my parents. "That means I have to be there, Griff. I have to see them too. I don't want to open up all that old shit again. It's buried in the past for a reason. How will I be able to stand watching them interact with Lacey when I'm the one who's been her parent for twelve years? How will I even sit there without spewing out all of the words I've been shoving down? How will I—?"

He stopped me with a kiss. I inhaled through my nose as I let his tongue take over my mouth.

"Slow down, sunshine. It's okay," he reassured. "I'm coming with you. She'll have you, and you'll have me."

I latched on to him, wondering if I could believe him. "Griffin," I breathed against his neck. It was gratitude, a wish, a question.

"Yes."

34

Griff

I SPENT THE NEXT TWENTY MINUTES DISTRACTING HIM WITH MY mouth, trailing kisses along his chest, arms, and back. We talked on and off between my explorations but not about anything important.

By the time my mouth moved past his lower back to his ass cheek, he was done talking. I continued the slow pace but amped up the use of my teeth. Sharp nips here and there until I could make out a definite growling sound coming from Sam's chest.

I rolled him back over and climbed up to kiss him on the mouth.

"Lambchop, because you have me so hot and bothered, the sex menu for round two is a smorgasbord. Anything you want. What sounds good to you?"

Sam put a finger to his chin as if he was in deep thought.

"Hmm, I'm trying to decide between a golden shower and—"

"Jesus *fuck*, I was lying about the smorgasbord. The sex menu is simple meat 'n potatoes fare. I was confusing it with something else before when I said smorgasbord. That was a mistake. What I said. Earlier."

He laughed before I even finished talking. "Enjoying your meat and potatoes sounds just about right to me, Foxy."

I rolled my eyes but didn't discourage him. In fact, I swiveled around so we could both enjoy the meal at the same time.

* * *

That night around the fireplace I noticed Sam and Tristan deep in conversation about the vineyard. Sam explained some of the things about wine he'd learned in school and Tristan suggested some of the wine specialty courses at the CIA campus not too far from the vineyard.

"One of my professors kept suggesting I attend the CIA for some advanced coursework," Sam explained. "So I've been thinking about taking some courses there to prepare for the certified wine professional exam."

"That's a great idea. I've taken several good ones at the Napa Valley Wine Academy also," Tristan said. "In fact, I'm trying to get Blue to take one of their intensive courses just so he can answer guests' basic questions." He laughed at the evil eye Blue shot his way.

"I can answer basic questions," Blue corrected. "It's when people start talking about peppery notes and chewy tannins that I start to zone out. No offense, Tris, but wine snobs are unbearable. One woman told me she found our Cabernet to be 'fleshy' and 'intellectually satisfying.' I mean, Jesus Christ. Who gives a shit? Does it taste good going down? Great, then swallow it."

Tristan's eyes lit up in a way that seemed to promise Blue he'd show him "fleshy" and "satisfying" in private as long as Blue agreed to "swallow it." And sure enough, not fifteen minutes later, neither man could be found.

Simone pestered Jude to break out his guitar and sing while

Derek argued against it.

"What's your problem, Wolfe?" Simone asked the beefy guy. "Don't you like to hear him play?"

"Of course I like to hear him play. It's one of my favorite things, but in order for him to play his guitar, I'd have to let him get up, and right now I'm enjoying lying here like a slug and using his body as a blanket."

Jude smiled and snuggled even closer to Derek if that was possible.

Simone rolled her eyes. "I'd ask Blue to play if he hadn't just disappeared for a booty call."

"What about some Cards Against Humanity?" I asked.

"I'm in," Granny yelled from where she'd been dead sleep in an armchair. Irene's head snapped up from her own snooze, brows furrowing in confusion.

"Me too," Tilly called out from where she worked on a puzzle at a nearby table.

"What's Cards Against Humanity?" Dante asked, pulling his nose out of the schoolbook he read.

Jamie snorted and Teddy smacked him on the chest. "Shut up, Jamie. Dante, it's only the funniest damned game ever. And playing it with Granny and Aunt Tilly makes it about a thousand times better. People would probably pay money to see it. I'm in. We're all playing," Teddy said with a big grin.

"That's the spirit," I said, getting up to find the game box.

By the time we'd pushed some tables together and gotten the game set up, Tristan and Blue came sauntering back into the lobby looking significantly happier than they had thirty minutes before.

I locked eyes with Maverick and we both wolf-whistled as loudly as we could across the lobby. Blue blushed all the way to his ears, and Tristan barked out a laugh. Surely he was grateful his parents weren't there and Mom and Dad had retired an hour earlier.

We played several rounds of the game, each one significantly raunchier than the last until even Teddy blushed a deep red and my stomach muscles hurt from laughing.

Sam offered to help Tristan clean up while Blue asked if anyone wanted a drink. Maverick and I touched base about the happenings at the shelter, and I found out Demarcus, one of the boys I'd been worried about, had been seen back out on the streets.

"Frankie also asked about you, Griff. Said he hasn't seen you around the shelter much," Mav said.

"Sam and I have been up there at least once a week, but I always seem to miss them. I think it's because I'm coming at a different time of day than I used to," I said, beginning to worry. "What do they think Demarcus is into?"

"Londa said she thinks he might be considering working with Lou or Eduardo."

"Shit, Mav. Did you talk to him?" I asked.

"I tried, but I could tell he wasn't going to listen to it from me. It would be way better coming from you since you've been there."

I ran my hand through my hair and let out a sigh. If he was tricking for Lou or running drugs for Eduardo, he was going to end up dead or in jail.

"Where is he now?" I asked.

"Don't know. Hopefully at the shelter," Mav said. "I told Londa to call or text if she needs help."

"Good. Thanks for letting me know. I'll go find him when we get back to the city."

That night as I fell asleep against Sam, I couldn't help but worry about Demarcus and hope that Londa really would reach out if he went missing. She couldn't force him to stay at the shelter, but she could ask one of us to track him down.

I tossed and turned so much that Sam finally sat up and turned on the lamp.

"Okay, what's going on with you?" he asked.

"Sorry. Want me to find another room?"

He reached out a hand to smooth a wayward curl off my forehead. "No, Griff. I want to know what's stressing you out."

"Remember that kid at the shelter named Demarcus? He reminds me a lot of myself, and he's been seen back out on the streets lately. I'm just worried about him."

"Why? What do you think might happen?" he asked.

I shrugged. "Lots of things, really. He could get in with bad people, get taken advantage of, or get hurt."

"Maybe we could leave in the morning and go home to check on him," Sam suggested.

I looked into his brown eyes and saw the sincerity directed at me. He was so freaking kind.

"I'd like that, Sam. Thanks," I said.

He twisted to turn off the lamp and then leaned into me, his warmth drawing me toward him like a bonfire on a cold night.

"Come here," he murmured, moving his arm so I could lay my head on his shoulder. I pressed closer to him, resting an arm and leg on top of his warm skin. He brought a hand up to smooth across my forehead before placing a kiss there.

"Get some sleep, Fox."

I love you so much, I thought.

But it was still too new to say it again so soon. To make it even more real. To put myself out there again to be hurt or left. Because even wonderful, loving partners left each other when you least expected it.

I didn't know what I'd do if he ever abandoned me. But maybe if I held a little piece of myself back from him, it wouldn't completely destroy me if he did.

As if holding myself back from him was even possible.

35

Sam

THE NEXT DAY WE LEFT THE VINEYARD BEFORE MOST PEOPLE made it to breakfast in the lobby. We grabbed some coffee and muffins to go and Griff spent a few minutes talking to his parents before we headed out.

I'd gotten a ride to the vineyard with Dante and Maverick so I was able to ride home with Griff. Just as I was climbing into his Jeep, I saw a familiar old lady getting out of a sedan I didn't recognize.

Tilly walked around from the passenger side to the driver door and leaned in the window to speak to the driver. I recognized her outfit from the night before and her normally impeccable hair was flat on top and tangled in the back. Holy shit, the woman was doing a walk of shame.

"Fox," I hissed. His head came up at my tone and he looked at me across the roof of the SUV.

"What?" he asked.

I jerked my head in the direction of the scene, and Griff's eyes turned to see what I was gesturing to.

He saw Tilly just as she turned to catch us standing there.

A smug grin spread across her face as she met my eye.

"Hi, Sam. Would you like to meet Mike Hunt?" she asked with a saucy wink.

Oh. Dear. God.

"Uh," I stammered. "No, ma'am. Never. No, thank you."

Griff snorted and made a sound that could only be described as giggling. Or maybe desperate braying, bordering on hyperventilation.

I threw myself into the vehicle with a weak backward wave in the direction of the old woman and looked around the car for a paper bag in case either one of us needed something to breathe into.

* * *

When we returned to the city, we drove straight to the shelter. Griff seemed more and more on edge the closer we got to the city and didn't settle until we were inside the shelter looking for Demarcus.

A man I'd never met manned the front desk. "May I help you guys?" he asked when we walked up.

"We were hoping to find Demarcus. Do you know if he's here?" Griff asked.

The man looked at him before answering. "I'm not allowed to divulge who's at the shelter at any given time."

"Right," Griff said. "I should have introduced myself first. I'm Griff Marian, a regular volunteer. And this is Sam Coxwell, who also volunteers."

"Are you scheduled to work today?" he asked.

"No. We just stopped by to check on Demarcus," Griff said. I could hear frustration building in his voice. "Look, man, I just want to make sure he's okay."

I put my hand on his arm and leaned in.

"Are you new?" I asked the man. He was attractive enough that I would have remembered him had we met before.

"Sort of. I'm Londa's nephew, AJ," he said. "I'm just in town for the holiday."

"Nice to meet you, AJ," I said, holding out a hand for a shake. "Is Londa around? She was hoping Griff here could talk to Demarcus for a few minutes. Apparently he's been having a hard time, and she thinks Griff can help."

AJ called her on the phone and spoke to her quietly for a moment before handing the phone to Griff. When the conversation was over, Griff grabbed my hand.

"Let's go."

"Thanks, AJ," I called out over my shoulder.

"No problem. Good luck," he called out.

Griff turned back. "Sorry. Thanks for your help, AJ. Hopefully we'll get to meet you properly next time. Happy Thanksgiving," he said.

Once we were loaded back up in Griff's car, he began driving toward the Tenderloin, one of the roughest parts of San Francisco.

"Do you know where he is?" I asked.

"I have an idea. You need to drop me off and take the car home, okay? No one will talk to me if you're with me, and I don't want you mixed up in this."

"You sound like a made-for-TV movie, Griff," I said.

He turned to look at me with a serious expression on his face. "Don't argue with me, Sam. Just let me do this my way. I know what I'm doing."

"Fine, but now you're spooking me," I confessed.

"I'll be okay. Just slide over to the driver's side when I get out and go home. I'll meet you at your place later."

"Do you have your phone and your wallet?" I asked. It sounded stupid, but I didn't know what else I could think of to ensure he had options if he got into trouble.

His lips turned up as his face broke into a smile. "Yes, dear."

I grabbed his hand and kissed the back of it. "Please call me if you need me, okay? And don't try to be a hero. This area is no joke."

"I know this area from when I lived on the street, and it's broad daylight, Sam. But I get what you're saying. I'll call you if I need you."

When he stopped the car at the mouth of an alley, I did as he asked and drove the car home, stopping by a food market to pick up some groceries since we'd been away. It was only after I returned home that I began to think more about Griff wandering the streets in a rough part of town in search of Demarcus. Griff had never felt comfortable opening up to me about his time as a teenager.

It occurred to me I'd avoided thinking too much about it, but there, in the quiet solitude of my kitchen, the reality of what Griff must have experienced hit me hard. Where did he sleep? What did he eat? How did he handle basic challenges like needing medicine or a shower or shoes?

My heart began to hurt and I threw myself into making a nutmeg cinnamon bread I'd been thinking about recently. While I punched out the dough, I couldn't help thinking of a teenaged Griff, cold and alone. And how that experience shaped the man he was now.

Those thoughts led me to worry about Demarcus and hope like hell Griff could find him and get him back to Londa and the shelter.

36

Griff

I COULDN'T FIND DEMARCUS ANYWHERE. AFTER HOURS OF checking all the regular places I thought he could be, I ran into a low-level dealer I recognized named Mo.

"Hey, Mo. You seen a kid named Demarcus around lately?" I asked.

He clapped me on the shoulder and gave me a grin. "Hey, Griff, how you doing these days? Haven't seen you in forever."

"I'm good. Just looking for a friend of mine. You know him?"

He looked up and down the street before locking eyes with me. "Don't worry about it, G. Go on home."

I stared back at him, feeling the familiar helpless anger in my gut begin to stir. "Nah. I just need to ask him a quick question. No big deal."

Mo's lips pursed and his nostrils flared. "Not kidding, Griff. Leave it alone."

"Just tell me: Lou or Eddie," I said as quietly as I could, not knowing which to hope for between the two.

"Eddie," he said just as softly. Part of me was relieved, although I wasn't sure dealing was much better than prostitution.

"Where?" I asked.

"Probably laying low right now, but later tonight, I'd say the Chip," he said, referring to a sleazy hotel I knew.

"Thanks, Mo. I owe you one," I said. I grabbed a twenty out of my pocket and passed it to him in a handshake.

"For what? Saying hello to an old friend? Look out for yourself, Griff. That shit's no joke."

"Will do," I answered before heading back down the street and finding my way to Sam's.

When I got to Sam's place, I found him elbow deep in savory ingredients in the kitchen.

"Hey, sunshine, this place smells amazing. What are you making?" I asked.

He looked up in surprise and I saw relief in his eyes. Before I knew it, I was engulfed in a tight hug and Sam's nose was buried in the crook of my neck.

"Fox," he whispered.

"What's wrong?" I asked. "Did something happen?"

"No, nothing. I'm just really glad you're here," he said. He stepped back and cupped my face in his large palms. Warm brown eyes peered at me as his thumbs caressed my cheeks. "I was worried about you."

Stupid butterflies took off in my chest as I registered the utter sincerity in his words.

"I'm fine, Sam. But are you sure *you're* okay?" My hands came up to smooth over his rib cage and around to his shoulder blades when Sam pulled me into another hug.

"Yeah, I'm good. I promise."

We stayed like that for a few moments, relaxing into each other's bodies and enjoying the quiet moment of being there together. I had the familiar sensation I always got with Sam of feeling like a jigsaw piece that had just found its perfect fit in the puzzle.

"What are you cooking?" I asked, breaking the spell before I started blabbing about silly stuff like freaking puzzle-piece love crap.

He stepped back and looked over to the stove. "Oh. It's a chicken risotto dish I've been mulling over. Thought we could have an early dinner," he explained. There was a sheepish look on his face. "Well, that's not entirely true. I was worried about you out there, and before I knew it, I was halfway through making risotto even though it was only four in the afternoon."

I laughed. "It's a good thing I missed lunch then, snickerdoodle. I'm starving. What can I do to help?"

Sam's face lit up in a grin. "Why don't you pour us some wine, sweet cheeks?"

While I poured the wine, I told Sam about my afternoon search and what Mo had told me.

"Who's Eddie?" Sam asked.

"A dealer," I said. My eyes flicked up to gauge his reaction.

"Ah, shit, Griff," he said.

"I know. That's why I'm worried," I said.

"Did you ever get caught up in that when you were on the street?"

"No. After what happened with my mom, I stayed well away from drugs," I explained.

"Did you...? Did you ever...?" Sam began.

"No," I cut in, knowing he was trying to ask about the other profession homeless teens got sucked into on the streets. "Not really."

"What do you mean, 'Not really'?"

And suddenly we were there. Having the conversation I'd put off for so long with him, and struggling to come to terms with the fact he was going to learn some ugly things about me.

"I never took money for sex, but sometimes I picked up men so I could have a warm, safe place to stay. And food. And a shower.

Things like that," I admitted. My heart raced, and I realized I was scared of him judging me. Or being disgusted by me.

The look in Sam's eyes wasn't pity like I feared, but understanding. I let out a breath.

"And I stole things from them. But only when I was really desperate. Like a coat once and a pair of running shoes. Those were probably the worst things I took. But I also nicked little things— toothbrush, deodorant, socks. The only time I took money was when this asshole was a complete dick to me and then left a bunch of singles sitting on his dresser. I swiped them before I left and ended up feeling dirty and guilty later. It was only twelve bucks, but to me it was a lot."

"Griff, how did you live for a year on the streets without getting messed up with drugs or prostitution?" he asked.

"I kind of fell into this group of other homeless people who looked out for each other. That's how I met Nico. I'm not from the Bay Area. When my dad kicked me out, we lived in Bakersfield. So that's where I went into the foster system."

Sam had finished the risotto dish and served up two plates, so we moved to the table and sat down to eat.

"The first family I was placed with was rough. There were two other foster boys there, and one of them thought I was a tasty treat," I said.

Sam's jaw tightened. "Did he touch you, Griff? Jesus."

"No, but I was pretty sure it was just a matter of time. That's when I decided it wasn't a good situation. I told the mom and she just put us in separate rooms. Then I tried to tell the social worker, but she seemed a little out of it. I got the feeling he'd done shit like that before and she was running out of options. Finally, I took money out of the foster dad's wallet and bolted."

"How'd you get from Bakersfield to San Francisco?" he asked.

"I hitchhiked like an idiot," I admitted. "But I got lucky and made it here in one piece. When I arrived, I went to a shelter because it was really cold that night. The volunteers kept asking me how old I was and told me they would need to move me to a special shelter if I didn't have a parent with me. This older homeless lady pulled me aside and said if they knew I was a minor on my own, they'd have to turn me over to social services. She helped me lay low that night and then took me to a place the next day where she introduced me to the group."

I ate some of the risotto dish and moaned my appreciation. It was delicious and by far one of my favorite meals Sam had cooked.

"God, this is good," I mumbled through a mouthful.

"Glad you like it. There's cinnamon bread for dessert later," he said with a big smile. "So this group stuck together and watched out for each other?"

"Yeah, pretty much. I mean, it's not easy to help others when you can't really even help yourself. But if you can find a handful of people you trust, then at least you don't feel like you'll get rolled in your sleep.

"I panhandled and did stupid shit for money like helping people carry heavy things if I saw someone struggling on the streets or offering to watch someone's car if they were parked in a dangerous area. Shit like that. I'd get a few bucks here and there, but that's all I really needed to cover me on the days I couldn't get to a food kitchen to eat. The people I hung out with taught me lots of tricks and things, like how to get the most food for the least amount of money and how to find things when I needed them."

"How did you get into graffiti?" Sam asked.

"Nico. He'd done some in the past wherever he'd come from. One day we saw some taggers getting run off by the cops, and they left all their gear behind. After they'd been gone for a while, we snuck in and grabbed the spray cans they'd left. There wasn't much in them, but Nico let me have it all and took me to a place to practice. God, I loved it. It was the first time I felt like myself again since I'd left home, you know?"

"Tell me more about it. Did you ever get caught?"

I laughed. "Hell yes. All the time. But one of the cops in the area had a crush on me and always let me off with a warning. Then he'd offer to take me to the nearest food place and ask if I needed any-thing. If he wasn't the one who caught me, I had to sweet-talk my ass off to get out of it. But usually it worked. They had bigger fish to fry, honestly."

Sam's eyes narrowed. "A cop had a crush on a homeless kid? That's gross."

"He was a very young cop. Most foot patrol guys are. Plus, I was sixteen by then and didn't look so much like a kid. He's the one who actually brought me to the Marians in the end."

"Really?" Sam asked. "How did that come about?"

"I was in a rough part of the Tenderloin, running an errand for someone for some cash." I saw the look on Sam's face. "Not that kind of errand. I was delivering a cell phone to someone who'd left it across town. When I dropped it off to the owner, it turned out to be a guy who worked for this pimp, Lou. Everyone knew who Lou was, and I knew to stay well away from him. If he saw an attractive boy, he'd do whatever it took to get him on the payroll. As soon as I realized who I was delivering to, I freaked out. My plan was to get the cash and bolt. But that's not what happened."

37

Sam

Listening to Griff describe his life on the streets was like watching a dark and depressing documentary with one huge exception. The documentary was about your best friend, and it was heartbreaking.

I didn't know how much more I could handle, but I also knew I couldn't stop listening. If I was going to be with Griff, love Griff, then I was going to know the whole story. The good and the bad. All of it was what had come together to make the man in front of me the person he was.

"What happened at Lou's?" I asked, reaching for his hand and pulling him up to move to the sofa. I sat down and pulled him in close to me, lacing our fingers together and kissing the back of his hand before holding it against my chest. He looked at me with gratitude, and I took a moment to lean in and kiss him softly on the lips.

"I love you so much," I whispered against his mouth. "I'm in awe of you."

His eyes filled and I reached a thumb up to run under one of his eyelids.

"Thank you. For listening and understanding. For not judging me," he said just as quietly.

"Never. Please tell me more. I want to know what led you to the Marians so I can know what led you to me," I said.

He rested his head on my shoulder for a few minutes before continuing.

"So that guy Lou started in on his recruitment pitch, explaining how he'd look out for me and take care of me if I worked for him. I'd be under his protection—blah, blah. I told him no as politely as I could and tried to leave. His guys blocked the door so he could keep trying to convince me. Finally I told him I'd think about it, just to get him off my back and let me go, you know?"

I nodded against his head and ran my hand up and down his arm.

"Once I got to the end of the block, his guys caught up with me and beat me up. Told me they wanted to make sure I had plenty to think about when making my decision. Once they left, I just lay there for a while feeling sorry for myself. And that's when Officer Brady showed up.

"I'd never been so happy to see a cop in my life. I was a mess. It's not that I was injured that badly physically as much as I was terrified. I'd hit my breaking point. It was all just too much. Being on my own, finding my own food, clothes, shelter. Keeping myself safe. It was exhausting. I broke down and sobbed like a baby. I think I scared the poor guy. He gave me a choice: the youth shelter or back into foster care."

"What happened when you got to the shelter?" I asked.

"Londa mothered me to death." He laughed. "She made me stay in bed for two days while my black eyes turned yellow and my nose stopped bleeding. She fed me to within an inch of my life and then made me get a haircut. After a week of all the attention, I freaked out and left. But when I found Nico, he said Lou had been looking for me. That time when I went back to the shelter, I convinced Nico to come with me."

"And the rest was history?" I joked.

Griff laughed and sat up straight to look at me. "Not quite. The rest was choppy as hell. Just when I began to trust someone, I'd freak out and bolt."

"You don't say," I said with a big grin.

He tweaked a nipple through my shirt. "Shut up."

I grabbed his face and kissed him silly. Emotion flooded the space between us and it was a heady concoction of relief, sadness, loss, and joy. We were there, together. And it was so easy.

Griff straddled my lap on the sofa and kissed me deeper. His hands crept to the hem of my shirt and lifted it off. My own hands snaked under his shirt to toy with his nipple rings. Favorite fucking things in the world.

His lips left my mouth and traveled to my neck, igniting my blood and thickening my cock. I pressed my hips up into him and heard him groan in response.

"Bedroom," he grumbled against my Adam's apple.

"Mm-hm," I agreed. But he didn't move. Just kept driving me up the fucking wall with his mouth and hands.

I slid my fingers over his ass, beneath his waistband to the bare cheeks below. God, he had such a nice, tight ass. My middle finger slid up and down the crease, and I heard his breath catch.

"Bedroom, dammit," Griff repeated against my collarbone before sucking the skin in and making my eyes roll back.

"Want you so fucking badly," I breathed. As if that was big news.

Our breathing was hot and heavy and we ground our erections together like horny teenagers making out in their parents' basement. It was painful.

I reached for his fly and began unfastening the button and zipper. My fingers weren't working well enough and I cursed. He laughed and took over, undoing his before moving to mine. Within moments, our hands were in each other's pants, and groans of relief filled the room. I took a moment to strip off his shirt so I could put my mouth on his chest. He hissed as my mouth grabbed on to a nipple and tugged.

Griff stood up to shuck down his jeans when we heard a rattling sound at the front door.

"Oh shit, Jason's home," I said with a laugh. We scrambled to my room, Griff duck-walking in his lowered jeans. We barely made it before I saw the apartment door swing open. I slammed my bedroom door and grabbed my boyfriend, slinging him up against the door face-first and pressing my entire body against his back.

My mouth found his ear and my hands found his. I threaded our fingers together and stretched his hands high above us on the door before grinding my hard cock against his ass.

"I'll do anything you want, Fox. Anything," I murmured into his ear. "Just tell me."

"Jesus, fuck," he whimpered. "Take off my clothes. Hell, take off your clothes," he demanded through labored breaths. "Do away with all the fucking clothes."

I laughed as I stripped us, taking my time with it and drawing wet lines down his back with my tongue. I nuzzled my nose into his armpit, smelling the scent of my favorite man and the body that drove me most wild. He groaned and kept his arms outstretched. My hands ran from his hips all the way back up his sides and arms to his hands above.

This time when I pressed myself against him, the full body contact was all skin on skin. Hard cock against naked ass. He felt amazing, and my head spun.

Griff shivered with anticipation, and I knew what I wanted to do to him. I wanted to tease the hell out of him until he couldn't remember a single feeling on earth that wasn't desperate longing for me.

I reached the tip of my tongue out to taste his shoulder before moving it to his ear and his neck and his shoulder blade. Tiny touches and swipes. Just enough to make him shiver and wonder where it would land next.

"Sam," he gasped when I barely landed my tongue on the back of one arm. "*Sam.*"

I reached my hand around to stroke him lightly. His shaft was hard and straight against his belly, leaking precum. My mouth returned to his ear.

"You are so fucking hot right now. I want to put my mouth on you *everywhere.*"

More whimpers escaped him as I moved my hands to his hips and pulled his lower body away from the door, bending him forward before kicking his feet farther apart.

I knelt down and put my tongue at the top of his crease. "God, this ass, Fox," I mumbled. My mouth roamed up and down the crevice and my teeth nipped at the rounded full cheeks. I'd never been so obsessed with an ass before. But Griff's was perfection. And it was all mine.

My mouth found the most sensitive parts of him, teasing and licking and wetting until even I couldn't stand it anymore. I stood back up and kissed between his shoulder blades, sliding my finger into his wet hole, making him suck in a breath.

"Going to make you beg, Foxy," I promised, wrapping my free hand around the front of his throat to hold his ear against my mouth. "Want me to make you beg?"

"Oh god, *yes*," he said before his entire body shuddered.

"Do you want me to bend you over my bed and fuck this ass, or do you want me to lie you down on your back and go slow and sweet? Because I want to do both. I want to take turns fucking you and loving you all night until neither one of us can move again."

I slid my finger out of him and wrapped that arm around his front, pulling him against me. One hand stayed wrapped around his throat and the other stroked his cock rhythmically. My mouth never stopped whispering dirty promises into his ear until finally his legs buckled and I had to keep him from collapsing in a puddle on the ground.

I moved him over to the bed and laid him in the center so he was on his back with his legs and arms outstretched.

Then I started over from the beginning.

38

Griff

SAM DROVE ME ABSOLUTELY INSANE. MY BRAIN WHIRRED LIKE a washing machine in a jacked-up spin cycle. I couldn't think, couldn't speak, couldn't remember my own fucking name.

"Guhh," I said as a hot, wet mouth moved from my inner thigh to my cock. Finally. Finally his mouth was in the right place. After he'd been making me dizzy with it.

Just as I was about to let out a sigh of grateful relief, the mouth was gone.

What? No!

"Aghh," I cried. I heard the deep rumble of a familiar chuckle as beard scruff scratched along my hip.

Aha, he was within reach. I grabbed his hair and pulled his head up until he was nose to nose with me.

"Find some combination of dick and hot, wet something and make it happen before I lose my goddamned mind, sunshine," I threatened. And I was super serious too.

Sam's face erupted into a giant laugh, brown eyes dancing and cheeks flushed from all the licking of things.

Oh, fuck this.

I grabbed him and flipped him until he was on his back and I was straddling him. Our erections slid together, and I couldn't help but let out a groan.

Don't even think about frottage right now, Marian. Your options are already too plentiful as it is.

I leaned in to kiss him while I debated whose dick and what hot, wet something I would choose. Dammit, I couldn't think straight.

Sam's arm came around to hold my back as his other arm reached for the bedside table. Before I knew what he was doing, I was on my back again with lubed fingers in my ass. *Ohdeargod*, he was so much better at deciding than I was.

"Mmm-hmm," I encouraged. It was the best I could do under the circumstances.

His wide grin shined down on me and I was so gone. So goofy gone for the man getting ready to own me.

"Please, Sam," I begged. And that was it. That's what he'd been waiting for.

He suited up and pushed into me while holding my legs in his firm grasp. My head arched back and my entire body seemed to sing with relief. He was there. My Sam was there with me, pressing into my body where he belonged.

He thrust into me with furrowed brows of concentration as if he wanted to get it just right. When he sensed he was hitting the perfect spot, he kept at it until drool was probably coming out of my mouth the way precum was surely coming out of my cock.

He stroked me expertly while I clutched at his face to draw him in for more kisses. My breathing was rapid and unsteady so I ended up pressing my cheek against his instead.

"Love you," I gasped. "*Sofuckingmuch.*"

"Love you too, baby," he said into my ear. "Want you to come.

Want you to feel good."

My climax rose up out of me from my toes to my brain like a tsunami of nerve endings all firing at once. My fingers dug into his skin and I slammed my eyes closed. I felt the heat of my release and registered Sam's final thrusts into me before I let myself drift off into brainless relaxation.

What that man promised, he delivered.

* * *

I awoke to the last remaining voices of my dreams. Unfortunately I recognized those voices as belonging to a trio of old ladies I'd rather not appear in my dreams. I rolled my eyes and was just getting ready to tell Sam about it when his bedroom door slammed open and the aforementioned trio waltzed into the room.

I scrambled to cover our naked, cum-soaked bodies as I heard Sam shriek like a little girl.

"What the fu—?" I stammered.

"Get some clothes on, lover boy, Ginger's having the baby and we need a ride to the hospital," Aunt Tilly commanded.

"Aunt Tilly, *Jesus*," I cried. "Give us a minute, will you? You could have at least knocked."

"Oh, for the love of god, Griffin. You boys don't have anything we haven't seen before. Although yours is a bit more impressive than most. Well, maybe not Sam's…" She trailed off as she tried to manifest X-ray vision at the bedsheets.

My bed partner sat in shocked horror with a ghostly white face and the sheet clutched in a death grip under his chin. I couldn't help but laugh, which promptly earned me a glare.

"Right," I muttered. "Tilly, Granny, Irene, *out*. I'll take you to the hospital, but I'm not giving you a Magic Mike show in the meantime."

"Dammit," Granny huffed. "Then what's the point?"

They left the door wide open, and I had to make a break for it to slam it closed behind them. In the process, I caught sight of Jason laughing his ass off outside the bedroom door.

"Jackass," I called out.

"Like I could have stopped them," he countered.

I turned back to Sam, who still sat immobile on the bed.

"Sorry about that. Yet another reason why family sometimes makes me bolt," I joked.

He blinked and seemed to regain some of his color. "What the fuck just happened?" he stammered.

"We just got Tillied," I explained with a shrug. "It happens."

"How did she even know where I live?" he wondered.

"Who the hell knows? I have to go. If I take too long getting dressed, they'll barge in again."

Sam seemed to shake himself out of it and jump up, still clutching the sheet to his body in a protective shield.

"I'm coming with you," he said. "But we have to take a quick shower. I smell like ass. And before you say anything, please refrain from making a smart aleck comment about whose ass I'm referring to."

"You said it, not me." I grinned, pinching Sam's own delectable tush.

After we showered in record time, we took turns barring the bedroom door while the other one dressed. Finally we joined the anxious trio in the living room, and I gave Aunt Tilly the stare-down.

"You'll never win a staring contest with someone who has cataracts, Griffin," she said. "Now, move your ass or we'll miss the main event. Ginger's been in labor for a few hours now, and I want a front-row seat to the shitshow."

Granny clutched her huge purse and gave me the evil eye. "Do you have any idea how filthy that girl's mouth is when she really gets going? If we miss Ginger's delivery because you had to clean man juice off your boyfriend, then I'm gonna be pissed."

I felt Sam's hand clutch the back of my shirt, and I reached back to grab it and give him a reassuring squeeze. "Okay, let's go then. What are you guys even doing here? Why didn't you take a cab?"

As we made our way to where my Jeep was parked, Tilly explained that they'd been dropping some old clothes off at the shelter when they got the call from my mom about Ginger. Londa told them where to find me and they figured I'd give them a ride for free instead of them having to shell out for cab fare. It always cracked me up when Tilly acted stingy. As if she didn't have gobs of money. She even had a driver, for god's sake. No telling where he was right now.

I turned to Sam as we got into the vehicle. "That reminds me. I need to go out tonight and try and find Demarcus again. I think I know where he's going to be. There's a place called the Chip, and—"

"I'm coming with you," Sam interrupted.

"No, Sam. It'll be better for everyone if you don't. I'll be fine."

He glared at me. "I wasn't asking your permission, Fox."

I rolled my eyes but decided not to make it into a big thing in front of the ladies in the backseat.

When we got to the hospital, a woman at the reception counter pointed us in the direction of the maternity wing, but she needn't have bothered. We could hear Ginger's screams from a mile away.

"Get this motherfucking jackass off of me," she screeched. I could only hope she was referring to Pete and not the new baby.

39

Sam

YOU'D THINK I'D BE USED TO THE MARIAN CHAOS BY THEN. But they still managed to surprise me. When we rounded the corner to the room where Ginger was obviously in great pain, we saw a thousand Marians hovering outside the large door.

Tristan held Blue in a protective embrace, Jamie had his hand over Teddy's mouth, probably trying to stop him from saying something inappropriate, and Thad leaned casually against the wall thumbing his iPhone. Thomas Marian paced in front of the nurses' station.

The crazy ladies shoved all of us aside and waltzed straight into Ginger's room. Those women had balls of steel. I wouldn't have gone within throwing distance of Ginger right now, even if the survival of the universe demanded it.

I reached out for Griff's hand without thinking, and he looked over at me. Lines of stress etched his forehead, and the story of his baby brother came flooding back to me.

"C'mere," I murmured, pulling him in for a hug. "You okay?"

I could feel a slight tremble in his body and I kissed the side of his face.

"We don't need to be here for the screaming part. Why don't we go get a cup of coffee in the cafeteria?" I suggested.

"Yes, please," he said into my hair.

I led him away from the crew after asking if anyone wanted us to bring anything back.

We took our time getting coffee and relied on text updates from Simone, who was in the thick of things. Apparently Ginger was fine with Rebecca, Simone, and the grannies in the delivery room, but she was increasingly *not* fine with Pete in there. Her own parents had elected to stay back at the house with the twins, who I was sure were waiting with nervous giggles to hear news about their baby brother.

Finally, when the texts stopped coming, we decided that meant it was go time. We returned to the corridor outside of her room in time to see Pete step out with a blue-wrapped bundle in his arms.

His face was flushed, cheeks covered with tear tracks and a goofy grin stretched from ear to ear. Everyone tittered excitedly around him, dying to see the newest Marian.

"Everyone, meet my son. We picked a name that honors our Biblical tradition as well as our musical heritage. I'm proud to introduce Nimrod Nickelback Marian," he said with complete conviction and excitement.

Everyone went silent as the ridiculous name bounced around the hallway.

"Like hell it is," shouted Ginger from inside the room behind Pete. "It's Thomas Andrew Marian, Tommy for short. Stop fucking around."

Everyone's eyes flew up to Thomas Marian Senior's face as the news sank in. His cheeks were already wet with tears of joy for the new arrival, but now fresh tears brimmed as he made his way forward to peer down at his tiny namesake.

"Are you serious, Pete?" he asked.

Pete held the baby out for Thomas to hold. "Yes, Dad. If he turns out to be even a fraction of the man you are, we'll be grateful. We love you."

It was such a sweet moment between father and son. My heart was torn between being full of love and happiness for them and being bitter about my own failed relationship with my father. I knew if I was feeling torn, Griff sure as hell would be.

I turned to find him, to grab his hand again or put my arm around his shoulders, but he wasn't there.

I looked around the corridor where we all stood and even peeked inside Ginger's room. No Griff.

My heart pounded as I realized he'd ducked out. It wasn't like I blamed him for being overwhelmed. I just wanted to be there with him. Let him know he wasn't alone.

Just then I heard a commotion coming from one end of the hallway. It was Derek and Jude, but they were swarmed by a gaggle of teens who'd seen them come in. Finally Derek nudged Jude toward us before turning back and escorting the teens out of the maternity wing.

I walked up to him and asked if he'd seen Griff.

"Yeah, he was racing out the front doors of the hospital. I called to him, but he must not have heard me. What's going on?" he asked, concern etched into his face.

"He freaked. I'm going to look for him," I said.

"Sam, do you want me or Derek to come with you?" Jude asked.

"No. Pete named the baby after your dad, and everyone is celebrating. Go be with them."

He reached out to grab my arm. "Text me when you find him, okay?"

Jude gave me his cell number and I entered it into my phone. "Okay. I gotta go."

I tried calling Griff, but of course he didn't answer. Next I tried

221

texting him as I headed to where he'd parked his Jeep.

Sam: *Where are you? I'm coming to find you.*

Griff: *Don't want to talk right now, Sam. I'll come by your place later.*

Sam: *Dammit, Fox. Just tell me where you are. I don't want you to be alone right now. You headed to your place?*

Griff: *No. I'm going to find Demarcus.*

Oh shit.

Sam: *Are you deliberately trying to piss me off? You know I don't want you going to the Tenderloin by yourself in the middle of the night.*

Griff: *The keys to the Jeep are in the passenger side wheel well. You can drive it home if you want or I can get it tomorrow. Gotta go, Sam.*

There were no more answers to my texts. I found the keys to the Jeep and hopped in the driver's seat before having an idea.

He'd said he was going to a place called the Chip. I looked up what that could be but didn't find anything that seemed right. I wondered who would know what it meant.

I used my phone to find the address for Nico's tattoo shop. I remembered Griff telling me he lived above the shop in an apartment. After finding a parking spot a block away, I made my way to the front door of the shop and tried it first. The door was locked, but there were still lights on inside. I knocked as loudly as I could.

Finally a figure emerged from a back room and I recognized

Nico. I waved to him and gestured to the door. As he got closer, I could see him look beside me, expecting to find Griff. When he didn't find him, his face etched with worry.

"I need your help," I said when he opened the door to let me in.

"Where is he?" he asked.

"Do you know of a place called the Chip?"

His face fell and he turned to grab a jacket from behind a counter. "Shit. Yeah. Let's go."

* * *

On our way to the rough area of town, Nico filled me in on what the Chip was. A seedy rent-by-the-hour flophouse where the pimp named Lou congregated with his crew and a drug dealer named Eduardo targeted both the prostitutes and the johns. The idea of Griff trying to rescue Demarcus by himself in a place like that made me irate. Did he think he was some kind of hero? Hadn't he learned his lesson years before when Lou's punks beat him up?

We parked several blocks away from the Chip in a lot with some security measures in it. Before I got out of the vehicle, Nico grabbed my arm to stop me.

"Hold on there, Richie Rich," he said as he climbed into the backseat to search for something. He came back up to the front and handed me Griff's old swim team hoodie. "Take off the Abercrombie and put this on."

I glared at him but did as he said. The sweatshirt smelled like Griff, and I couldn't help but suck in a deep lungful. Unfortunately, I wasn't stealthy enough to evade notice.

"God, you must really like him if you can smell his old sweats and not want to puke," he teased.

"I love him, Nico. Now help me find him."

"I will, but first we need to call someone for help."

40

Griff

THE SCENE AT THE HOSPITAL HAD BEEN TOO MUCH. AT FIRST, I thought I'd take a step outside to get some fresh air and regain my composure. But when I got outside I remembered Demarcus, and I knew I could do more good helping him get out of trouble than by being one of a million Marians overwhelming the new baby.

I deposited the keys at the Jeep so Sam could get home. Then I took off in the direction of a nearby hotel that had a taxi stand away from the hospital.

The cab dropped me off a few blocks from the Chip, and I began walking. The night was cold and the streets were darker the deeper I got into the rough area. People checked me out from the corners of their eyes, and I did my best to walk strong and proud without making eye contact with anyone. Old instincts came back like riding a bike as I made my way to the hotel.

Before I got there, my phone rang, and I pulled it out of my pocket to silence it. The call was from the shelter, so I raced to answer it.

"Hello?"

"Griff, he's here," Londa said. "Frankie found him and convinced him to come in for dinner."

I let out a breath. "I'm on my way. Don't let him leave."

When I finally made my way to the shelter, Frankie was waiting for me by the front door. "They're in Londa's office."

Londa's office was really a tiny storage room with a desk and old sofa in addition to rows of old dented filing cabinets and shelves full of canned goods.

Demarcus sat hunched on one end of the sofa while Londa played solitaire on her ancient desktop computer. When I entered the room, they both turned to me. One with a smile of relief, the other with a dramatic eye roll.

"Londa, can you please give us a minute?" I asked, eyes only on Demarcus.

"Sure, Griff. Glad you're here," she said before scooting out and closing the door.

Demarcus rolled his eyes again, making sure he had my attention first.

"What the hell are you thinking?" I began.

"Dammit," he huffed. "You don't understand, Griff. You don't—"

I cut him off with a bark. "Don't you fucking tell me I don't understand. I understand more than you know. I lived this shit, Demarcus. For over a year. And that's why I'm standing here trying to look out for you. You start dealing with Eduardo and your life is over. Do you know how many people who worked for Eddie when I was on the streets are still around?"

He shook his head and maintained eye contact with me, jutting his chin out in defiance.

"Zero. None. They are all dead. Not gone. Dead. So quit trying to front, and talk to me instead. Why are you taking your chance at a decent life and screwing it up?"

"Decent life? That's a hoax, G," he shot back. "Not everyone gets the magical family you did. Some of us have to make our own way out there, and there aren't exactly a ton of options for kids like me without all the chances you got."

A familiar feeling of guilt and unworthiness coiled in my gut at his mention of the Marian family. He was right, after all. I'd gotten extremely lucky. But I'd also worked my fucking ass off for what I had.

"You're right in some ways, Demarcus. I did get a magical family. But you know what chances I really got? The chance to swim my ass off to earn a scholarship to college, which gave me the chance to study my ass off to earn a good-paying job, which gave me the chance to work my ass off to prove to people like you that people like us can make something of ourselves despite out circumstances. The only things the Marians handed to me on a silver platter were shelter, food, clothes, and love. And you have all of those things right here if you'd only get your head out of your ass long enough to see it."

He rubbed his hands over his face. I could see the wheels turning in his head and knew my words might take some time to sink in.

"Promise you'll stay here tonight and let me come back tomorrow to talk some more," I said quietly.

"Eddie's expecting me. He'll send someone looking for me if I don't show up. It's too late, Griff."

"Bullshit. It's never too late," I muttered. "Hang tight and let me see what I can come up with."

I squeezed his shoulder as I walked past him out of the tiny room. After grabbing a cup of water from the kitchen, I found Londa sitting with her nephew at a cafeteria table, and reached out my hand to shake.

"Griff Marian," I said. "I'm sorry, I forgot your name."

Londa smiled proudly. "This is my nephew, Angel."

The man smiled back at her before turning to me. "Actually, I go by AJ. Nice to properly meet you, Griff."

I returned his smile and turned to Londa to brainstorm options when she beat me to the punch.

"AJ has an idea," she said.

Before I could ask what it was, I heard Nico's voice ring out in the large space.

"Griffin Marian, why the hell didn't you tell me you'd gotten hitched? Sam here tells me you begged him to make it official."

Turning to Nico in surprise, I saw Sam and a familiar police officer standing next to him.

I felt a grin stretch my cheeks as my heart flipped at the sight of Sam.

"Not true. Although I'm starting to wonder why not," I admitted with a wink. I wasn't sure who was more surprised at the words—Sam, Nico, or me.

I stood up and walked into Sam's embrace, inhaling his familiar scent.

"What are you doing here?" I asked before remembering Pete's new baby. "The baby," I blurted. "How's the baby?"

"He's perfectly fine, Griff. Beautiful, healthy, and already spoiled rotten by your father," he said with a lovely smile.

"Good." I sighed before turning to greet Officer Brady and Nico. After they walked over to grab a cup of coffee, I turned back to Sam. "His name's not really Nincompoop, is it?"

"Nimrod," Sam corrected. "Nimrod Nickelback, and I don't think Teddy will ever let the kid forget it. He's having a field day. He's even trying to get Blue to make T-shirts. But no. He's named after your dad, and they're calling him Tommy."

"Ginger okay?" I asked.

"As far as I know. But I left soon after you did," he said with a cross between a glare and a smirk. "Had to save your sorry ass."

"Thanks, sunshine. But you didn't need to come looking for me," I said. "I'm tough."

"Oh," he said, losing the teasing smile and turning around to head for the door. "I guess you want me out of here then. I'll just—"

I grabbed the back of his shirt. "Don't you dare," I growled.

He turned back to me, laughing, and I realized he'd been calling my bluff. "Asshole," I muttered as I turned to gesture to his companions. Nico and Officer Brady had helped themselves to some coffee and were seated at the table with Londa and AJ.

"What's with those two?" I asked.

"My posse, apparently." He said. "I didn't know where to find you, so I went to get Nico. When we got to the Tenderloin, he called Officer Friendly over there for help."

"Officer Brady," I corrected. Sam narrowed his eyes at me.

"Officer Pedophile," he said under his breath.

"Continue." I smirked, reaching for his hand. I kind of liked jealous Sam.

"Before we got very far, I got a text from Jude telling me that Londa had called someone in your family to report you were at the shelter. Jude knew I was looking for you, so he contacted me."

"Thanks, Sam. I'm really glad you're here."

I walked him over to the group to thank Officer Brady and Nico for helping Sam during his protective routine. As we chatted, I realized Nico was being awfully friendly with the local PD and decided it was a good time to sneak out.

There was a baby I needed to meet and a boyfriend I needed to reassure.

41

Sam

LATER THAT NIGHT GRIFF AND I RETURNED TO THE HOSPITAL to meet the new baby. After the obligatory cooing and congratulating, we took a break on a sofa in a small waiting room. I pulled his head onto my shoulder and put my arm around him to hold him close.

He explained in more detail the plan that AJ had come up with to take Demarcus and Frankie from the shelter back to the Chicago area with him to a similar program he helped run there. The boys were understandably nervous but also thrilled for the opportunity for a chance to start over in a new place.

Griff's fingers played with mine, and I loved the way it felt. But I still had something I needed to get off my chest.

I shifted to face him.

"Why didn't you ask me to come with you, Griff?"

He looked up at me. "When?"

"When Pete came out of the delivery room with the baby," I said.

"I know it freaked you out, but you could have asked me to step outside with you."

"I didn't want to make a big deal about leaving, so I just snuck out. I'm sorry."

No shit, I thought.

"Griff, at some point you're going to have to realize you're not alone anymore. I'm here now too. And I love you. Do you have any idea how I felt knowing you were dealing with that shit alone?" I locked eyes with him.

"I'm sorry," he said again.

"Dammit, Griff. Stop being sorry and start trusting me. What's it going to take to convince you I'm not leaving?" I asked.

"Just give me some time, Sam. This isn't easy for me, okay?"

I saw pain in his eyes and I wondered if it was heart pain or head pain. Either way, I didn't want him to be in any kind of pain.

"Okay. I'm sorry too. I was just really scared, Fox," I admitted.

Griff leaned in to kiss me. "We should get out of here before everyone else finds us."

"What do you mean?"

Just then about a hundred Marians entered the small space all chattering at once about baby Tommy.

Griff reached for my hand and gave me a small smile and a shrug.

I laughed. Sometimes you just got hit with the Marian clan whether you liked it or not.

Simone sidled up to me with a sinister grin on her face.

"So, lover boy, I heard through the grapevine that your bedsheets have big juicy hot dogs in them," she teased. "I mean, *on* them."

Blood rushed to my face as I shot lasers at Aunt Tilly and Granny across the room. They caught me staring and giggled. *Those loose-lipped busybodies.*

"Dachshunds, Simone. Little dogs," I corrected.

Griff snorted beside me before catching Simone's eyes and

dissolving into full-on laughter.

Maybe Griff was right and family was nothing but a giant pain in the ass.

* * *

I took Griff back to my place for the next few days to pamper him and make sure he felt loved. I knew his head spun with thoughts of his past, his lost brother, his parents. Every few hours I forced home-made food on him and wouldn't listen to any complaints. He dozed on and off while I sat beside him on the sofa or in bed with my lap-top, browsing commercial real estate listings for potential restaurant space. Nothing I saw seemed to excite me.

One night we were sitting down to dinner with Jason and Robbie when Griff asked me about it.

"What did you make tonight?" he asked.

"Jambalaya. Hope you like it," I said, refilling my wineglass and offering more to anyone who wanted it.

Griff took a bite and I saw his eyes roll back in his head. "Oh my god, Sam." He moaned after he swallowed. "That is amazing." The other two guys nodded their enthusiastic agreement with mouths too full to speak.

"Thanks. My other grandmother taught me this one. She grew up in New Orleans, and there are a ton of restaurants there that make it."

I took a bite and savored my twist on an old favorite. The dish re-minded me so much of happier times, memories of my grandmother and the sound of jazz music playing when I visited her as a little boy.

We ate some more in comfortable silence, everyone taking their time to enjoy the tastes of the dish. Finally, Griff asked the question I'd been dreading.

"Why haven't you found any restaurant space you want to go look at?" He took a sip of his wine and wiped his mouth with a napkin.

Jason and Robbie watched me for an answer.

I shrugged. "Nothing feels right yet. It'll happen in time."

"What do you think it is? Location, space? Money?" he asked.

"Yes," I agreed. "All of the above."

"What's your ideal environment?" Robbie asked.

I took a minute to organize my thoughts. "I guess I'd like a place where people plan to linger. Settle in and enjoy the experience of good food and wine without feeling pressured to make room for the next people in line. I want it to be large enough to have big comfortable chairs so people don't get antsy to leave. But if I get those things, then it's an issue of money."

"What kind of clientele do you envision coming to your restaurant?" Jason asked.

"Well, they'd have to have money. Which means being in a nice part of town. Which means expensive real estate." I sighed. "But mostly, I just want them to be ready to indulge. Or be ready to relax and enjoy themselves. No racing off to the theater, you know?"

"It sounds like a nice experience, Sam," Robbie said with a smile. "I can't wait to eat there."

I returned his smile before offering everyone seconds on the dish. For the rest of the meal, I mulled over what really held me back. Fear. Well, that and money. I refused to use the money my dad had given me for anything other than education, and I wasn't sure I'd qualify for a business loan with my spotty employment history.

I needed to spend some more time thinking about it, but the conversation reminded me I hadn't asked Griff about his plans lately.

"Griff, have you heard back from any publishers about your books?" I asked.

"What books?" Jason asked with sincere interest.

"He's created these amazing graphic novels. He's done both the writing and the illustrations. They're fantastic," I explained. "He's really talented. Tell them about it, Griff."

When he looked over at me, I could see the guilt on his face.

42

Griff

I SHOULD HAVE SEEN IT COMING. IT'S NOT LIKE I COULD ASK HIM about his restaurant without him turning the tables to ask me the status of publishing my books. We'd agreed to follow our dreams together, and then I'd gone ahead and gotten a sum total of diddly-squat accomplished.

"They still need some polishing before they'll be ready to pitch to publishers," I hedged.

Sam trapped me with his stare. "Is that right?" he said in an overly calm voice.

"Yep."

"Well, then. I guess it's a good thing you have the weekend to work on them, isn't it?" His lips delivered the lines, but it was his eyes that claimed checkmate.

"Sure is," I replied. "If only I had my stuff here."

"That's not a problem. I forgot to tell you I thought we'd head over to your place after dinner for a change of scenery," Sam informed me.

Bossy jackass.

"Perfect," I muttered. "Can't wait."

On the walk over to my place, Sam asked me about it again. This time Jason and Robbie weren't around to hear the conversation.

"What are you so afraid of, Griff? Your work is really good," he said. He carried a backpack on his shoulder with some of our stuff in it and a reusable shopping bag dangled from his hand with some leftovers and groceries in it.

"They won't like it, they'll reject it, and then what? That's it. That's the end of the dream," I explained. "It's just easier not to send it and I can still hold on to the dream, Sam. Maybe the dream is more important to me than the reality."

"Fear," Sam said softly. "I know fear. I get it."

"Right. So here we are right back where we started. Too afraid to reach for the dream."

He looked over at me in the cold December night and gripped the back of my neck with his free hand.

"Have you ever wanted something so much in your life that you were willing to go all in?" Sam asked.

Yes, I thought. *You.*

The realization rocked me to the core. Because it was true.

"Fox?" he prompted. "Have you?"

"Yes," I snapped. "I fucking want everything. All the things I've always dreamed about but never even hoped for."

"Then at some point, you'll have to take the risk," he said before pulling my lips to his in a kiss.

* * *

He was right. And I spent the following few days mulling over his words. What was I willing to do to get what I wanted? And what would it take for Sam to get what he wanted too?

The Oklahoma trip was coming up and we'd booked our flights.

I knew full well he expected me to pull a Griff and bail on him. But I was determined to prove to him I was committed. I would be on that plane next to him no matter what.

After those few days of thinking it over, it was time for action. I threw myself into polishing my books and uploading them into a digital format for submission. I sent query letters and tried hard not to think too much about what I was doing. I looked into an idea I had for Sam's restaurant and started putting together a plan.

It was time for me to go all in, just like Sam had implied.

The day of the Oklahoma trip arrived and I was excited to have several days together with Sam without either of us having to work. Sam had been busting his ass at Harry Dick's lately in an effort to save up some money for the restaurant. I had spent the previous night at my parents' house helping watch my nieces while Pete and Ginger tried to get some quiet time at home with the new baby. When the girls finally fell asleep, I texted Sam to tell him I was going to crash on my parents' sofa instead of heading home.

The next morning, after staying over at Mom and Dad's house, I hopped in the car to head home. On the drive back to the city, my phone rang. I answered it without looking. "Griffin Marian."

"Hi, Griffin, this is Shonda Maxwell with Panko Press. I was hoping to talk to you for a few minutes about your graphic novel submission," the woman's voice on the other end of the line said.

Holy shit. Panko Press was the holy grail of young adult graphic novel publishers.

"Hi, Shonda. Thank you for your call," I answered as professionally as I could.

"Do you have a few minutes to talk?"

"Sure," I said, looking around for a place to pull my car over. I found a parking lot and pulled in.

"Great. We love your work and wanted to talk to you in person. Our offices are in Chicago, but our CEO will be in San Francisco today for a layover on his way back from Tokyo. He was hoping you'd have a chance to meet with him while he's there. Sorry for the short notice, but we just put two and two together realizing where you were based."

"Well, I'm flying out myself today and will be at the airport around mid-afternoon. I can get there early if that will work for him," I suggested. "I'm assuming he's flying through SFO?"

"He is, and that might work. His flight is scheduled to land at SFO at 2 p.m. I'll send him your phone number so he can text you as soon as he lands. I'll also send you his flight information so you can know where to go."

"That sounds great. Thank you so much for the opportunity to meet with him," I said.

"Sounds like it was meant to be," she said with a laugh. "Good luck, Mr. Marian."

I hung up the phone with a big grin on my face. I couldn't wait to tell Sam about my interview.

* * *

Unfortunately, Sam was in a mood. The stress of his parental visit was turning him into a monster, and I wasn't quite sure how to snap him out of it. When I asked if he could leave for the airport early with me, he freaked out.

"Never mind, babe," I said quickly. "I need to go early though. There's a publishing house executive on a layover, and he's agreed to meet with me for a chat before our flight."

"Fine, whatever," he muttered as he went through the shirts hanging in his closet. Hangers snapped against each other and billows of freshly pressed shirts wafted from one side of the rail to the other as they were each rejected.

"You sure you're okay with me meeting you at the gate?" I asked.

He looked up at me with a glare, but I couldn't decide if he was miffed I was bothering him while he was packing or if he was anticipating me running off again. It didn't really matter, I would prove to him I was there for him when I showed up at the gate.

"Okay, then I'm going to go ahead and leave so I have plenty of time," I said before walking into the closet and kissing him goodbye.

"See you in a few, sunshine," I said over my shoulder as I turned to leave.

"Goodbye, Griffin," he replied.

A pain shot into my heart at his tone, and I knew then which fear he was fighting. There was no way in hell he expected me to show up for that flight.

43

Sam

I WAS TIRED OF WONDERING WHAT GRIFF WAS THINKING OR IF HE was going to bail. I'd had enough emotional turmoil as it was with the visit to see my family. My stomach was in knots and my brain was working a hundred miles an hour replaying the vague, choppy memories I had of my mother.

Earlier that day I'd spoken to Lacey for the tenth time that week, going over our plans to meet up and present a united front when we saw our parents. I was sure Lacey was more nervous than I was since she had fewer memories, thus less idea of what to expect.

When I arrived at the gate for our flight, there was no sign of Griff. No big surprise. I let out a breath and took a seat, putting in earbuds to distract me from scanning the crowd of faces every ten seconds to look for him.

Boarding was called and he still wasn't there. I waited until the last possible moment to board and took my seat on the plane, eyes stinging and heart heavy. So that was it.

I slid into my aisle seat beside an empty window seat and began looking for my seatbelt when a familiar voice spoke above me.

"Excuse me, sir, is this seat taken?" Griff smiled.

I stood up and grabbed him in a fierce hug, whispering into his ear what a jackass he was. He agreed and hugged me back just as tightly.

When we were both settled in our seats, I asked him what had happened.

He shrugged. "The guy's plane from Tokyo was late. There was nothing I could do."

"So how did the meeting go?" I asked.

"I didn't meet with him," he said.

"What do you mean?"

"I told you. His plane was late. There wasn't enough time. I waited as long as I possibly could and then hauled ass to make this flight."

I stared at him. "Griff, you could have taken another flight. That meeting was important."

He chuckled. "Sunshine, nothing was as important to me as making this flight with you. There was no contest. If they like my work, they'll fly me to Chicago or contact me over the phone."

I felt a warmth spread through my chest as I realized he'd made showing up for me and this family trip a priority. Griffin Marian had made a promise to me and followed through on it.

"Thank you, Griff."

His smile grew even wider. "Plus, I couldn't miss our first shot at making the Mile High Club, now could I?" he said with a wink.

We didn't end up joining that exclusive club, but we did get a little handsy under the airline blankets.

When we landed and exited the plane into the terminal, I spotted Lacey right away. She'd landed before us and was waiting at our gate.

I caught her up in a huge hug and inhaled the familiar scent of peppermint gum. She looked as good as I could hope for, happy and healthy. UVA must have agreed with her.

"Lacey, this is Griff Marian. Griff, this is my sister, Lacey." I beamed as my two favorite people finally met in person. Griff gave Lacey a hug and they laughed through their greetings, having talked a few times already on the phone. As soon as Griff's back was turned, Lacey did one of those big comical deals, dropping her jaw and mouthing, *He's so cute!*

I mouthed back just as big, *I know, right?*

After collecting our bags, we looked around for the driver our father would have sent. I couldn't find a sign with my name on it but after just a few moments I heard a woman call my name with a gasp.

My head snapped around as a whisper of memory blew through me. My mother.

I reached for Griff's hand, starting to feel complete and utter panic.

"No," I whispered under my breath. I wasn't ready. I didn't want to do this.

Griff squeezed my hand and pulled me back, stopping our forward motion. He came around in front of me and cupped my cheeks with his palms.

"It's okay. She's just a human being. Think of her as an asshole reviewer who doesn't know his ass from an aubergine. Just because she's trying to fill the role of your mother doesn't mean she's qualified or knows what the hell she's doing. She's flying by the seat of her pants."

My hands shook as my eyes locked on his. Green eyes searched mine to anchor me.

"Sam, remember what we talked about? You can be an incredible chef and still get a bad review by an idiot. You are an incredible human being, no matter what they think. You are who you are today despite your parents' influence. Not because of it."

"Thanks," I mumbled, leaning in to kiss his cheek.

When my lips brushed his skin I heard him whisper, "And if that pep talk didn't help, then consider this. If you can make it through the next several hours without losing your shit, I'll make you come later tonight using nothing but my tongue."

That dirty motherfucker.

"Great," I grumbled only loud enough for him to hear. "Now I get to greet my family with a hard-on."

"Remember that day you came to my parents' house for the first time when Mom invited you to family dinner?"

"Yes?"

"I was sporting wood the whole day. Now you know how it feels." He winked and faced forward, preparing to meet my parents. As we found them in the crowd already greeting Lacey, Griff's hand grasped mine and never let go.

Those few days in OKC were excruciating. The only way I survived was by listening to Griff's words replay in my head over and over and by crawling into his arms at night. He did his best to charm my parents while I sat in a haze made up of half memories and worry about how Lacey was holding up.

My mother might as well have been a stranger. I recognized her, sure, but she was so shallow and materialistic I wasn't sure there was a real woman left underneath the facade.

The tipping point came on the third day, which was the day before Christmas Eve. We were all set to spend Christmas there until Lacey pulled me aside and burst into tears.

"I want to go home," she said through sniffles. "I hate it here. I hate them. This was a huge mistake, Sam. I'm so sorry."

I held her and soothed her as best I could. "Then let's go," I said.

She lifted her head up to look at me. "What? We can't. Not really. We said we'd stay through Christmas."

"We don't owe them anything, Lacey. Pack your things and let's go."

So we did.

When we returned to San Francisco, we had just enough time

to stop off and buy a little scraggly tree and some lights at a home store on the way back to the apartment. Jason was home and he was thrilled to see what we'd picked up.

The four of us turned on Christmas music and decorated the tree in our pajamas, taking turns refilling wine glasses and fetching snacks from the kitchen. I couldn't imagine a happier night in all my life.

Until Griffin Fox Marian took my hand and went down on one knee.

44

Griff

I NEVER EXPECTED TO GET MARRIED, MUCH LESS BE THE ONE proposing. But I knew for damned sure I wasn't going to let Sam Coxwell get away. He was mine. And I wanted him to stay with me forever.

I grabbed his hand and knelt down on one knee right by the Christmas tree. Jason saw what was happening and turned down the music. Lacey squealed and got out her phone to take pictures.

"Sam, I was all set to take you out to Lake Hefner Lighthouse in OKC and propose at sunset, but this is a thousand times better. I've never been as happy in my life as I am right this minute."

I reached into the pocket of my pants and pulled out the ring I'd gotten him the week before. Sam's free hand flew to his mouth when he saw I meant business. I couldn't help but laugh.

"You bring out the best in me. You see the good in people and make them feel like they can do anything. It's time for me to show you that I'm one hundred percent committed to you. Because I am.

"Being with you has taught me to trust and believe in someone. To hand over a part of myself for safekeeping and know that the person I've chosen will take good care of it. You're my person, Sam. You make everything in my life brighter and warmer and just... better. Do you think you might want to keep doing that, like, forever?"

I grinned up at him and saw his answer before it manifested itself into words.

"Well, when you put it that way," he said with a wink before pulling me up and into his arms. When his mouth landed next to my ear he continued. "I definitely want to keep doing that, like, forever, Foxy. I love you so much."

I exhaled into his hair and let the feel of his embrace surround me. "Thank god," I sighed.

The rumble of his laugh vibrated through me before he pulled back to land a big kiss on me. Jason and Lacey were busy cheering and high-fiving, and I could tell my cheeks were going to be permanently stuck in a giant grin.

I remembered to slip the ring on his finger and enjoyed watching him smile at it on and off for the rest of the evening.

Later that night in bed, I caught him staring at it again with a goofy grin.

"Did that really just happen?" he asked. "Do you really want to marry me?"

"It did and I do." I put my hand over his cock under the sheets. "Do you need me to pinch something to prove to you this isn't a dream?"

His large hand landed on top of mine. "Don't you dare. You'd just be shooting yourself in the foot. But while you're there, maybe you can do something about this problem I seem to have."

He pressed my hand into his cock, and I felt him getting hard beneath it.

"Mmm," I teased, fondling and squeezing. "Seems like a personal problem to me."

"Foxy, I'm pretty sure it's a *husband's* duty to take care of his man's boner. You want to be a good *husband* to me, don't you?"

I smiled at him and got right in his face, our noses almost touching.

"Sunshine, if you think that word is scaring me, you're mistaken. I can't wait to be your husband. You may not realize this, but when I make up my mind about something, that's it. You asked me if I'd ever wanted something so much in my life that I was willing to go all in. Well, I have. You."

His warm brown eyes were shining up at me and he brought a hand up to run a finger over my bottom lip.

I reached my tongue out and swirled it around his finger, drawing it into my mouth and caressing it. The only sound in the room was the combined hush of our breathing. My body shifted until I was lying on top of him fully, warm skin on warm skin.

Sam smelled so good. Like cookies and Christmas trees. His hands moved around to run lazy fingers up and down my back as he leaned up to kiss me. The kiss was light at first, gentle and teasing. Flirty.

I moved down his body, dropping kisses along the way, detouring to suck in a pebbled nipple and then to dip my tongue down into his navel. His stomach muscles were rippling as his cock continued to harden and pulse against my breastbone.

When I finally arrived at the junction of his thighs, I placed small kisses above the nest of curls there and around to the inside of his shaking legs. Sam's hands were in my hair and I felt him idly tugging a curl with his fingers.

I grinned up at him and caught him squeezing his eyes closed, his teeth raking over his top lip as if trying to keep himself together.

"Baby, do you want me to—"

I couldn't finish the sentence without laughing. His eyes snapped open and he looked down at me with a cocked eyebrow.

"What?" he asked. "Want you to what?"

"I was going to ask if you wanted me to suck your dick but then the look on your face just…" I laughed again, crawling up his body to kiss his lips before moving back down to resume my ministrations. "You looked so desperate," I finished with a grin.

"Fuck you, Griffin," he muttered. "I am desperate. And, yes, suck my dick goddammit."

I kept eye contact while I stuck my tongue out to draw a line up his shaft and then sucked his foreskin between my lips, tugging gently. I fucking loved toying with it. Rolling it up and down with my hands, my lips, my tongue. Couldn't get enough.

Now it was his turn to laugh. "What's your fascination with foreskin?"

"Complaining?" I asked.

"Oh Christ, no," he breathed. "Never mind. Continue."

Between licks and sucks I mumbled words about how maybe it was the novelty of something I didn't have, or maybe it was just part of my complete obsession of all things Sam.

When he was rock hard and gasping, I moved up to kiss him on the mouth again before reaching for the lube in the nightstand. We had already shared test results in an effort to forgo condoms, and it struck me that I'd never have to use condoms again.

I sat up, straddling his thighs and slicking him up before moving forward to seat myself on his length. His forehead was crinkled in a mixture of concentration and anticipation and he looked stunning. My heart was slamming in my chest with the knowledge that he was mine forever. Fuck, I'd won the lottery.

"Griffin," he growled. "You feel so good, you're so tight, *god.*" His hips arched up into me, sliding his cock deeper into my body, eliciting a groan of pleasure from me.

The feeling of fullness, of Sam's bare body inside of mine, was overwhelming. We moved together, pulsing in and out with an increasing tempo. My fingernails dug into his shoulders as his own hands grabbed my hips with almost bruising pressure.

"Jesus, Sam, *gnnhhh*," I gasped as his cock stroked along my prostate, sending sparks of nerves firing deliciously in my entire lower body. Part of me wanted him to feel this kind of pleasure too.

Suddenly, I pulled off him, grabbing his shoulder and shoving him over onto his belly. He scrambled onto his knees, knowing full-well what I had in mind, while I grabbed the bottle of lube and slicked myself up. Even that business-like touch was enough to make me want to come. I clutched the base of my cock to stave off the feeling and lined up with his entrance.

"Yes," Sam said between fevered breaths. "Fox, *Please*."

When I slid into him, carefully making sure not to hurt him, it felt like I could breathe again. Sam and I were together. Our bodies locked tightly and moving in rhythm. I thrust in and out of him with my entire body draped along his back.

My mouth whispered words into his ear as he whimpered underneath me. I had one arm wrapped around his middle and the other stretched out to intertwine my fingers with his on the bed.

He reached his other arm back to grab my hair and hold my head against his.

"Fuck, *fuck*," he panted. "Feels so good. Just like that."

The arm I had wrapped around his middle moved down so I could grasp his erection and stroke him in time with the movement of my hips.

Precum coated the head of his dick, and my hand slicked up and down his length.

"That's it, baby," I breathed into his ear. "Want to feel you lose it." My voice sounded strangled as I held on to my control as well as I possibly could.

Finally he let out a muffled scream into the pillow and shot into my hand, his entire body convulsing, triggering my own climax with a tight pull. I emptied deep inside of him, feeling the connection to him in a way I hadn't quite felt before.

With other people in the apartment, I knew I couldn't cry out like I wanted to, so I bit down on his shoulder instead, feeling tingles upon tingles of pleasure zinging along my spine.

When I felt completely empty and a little dazed, I pressed soft kisses onto the spot on his shoulder I'd annihilated with my teeth.

"I'm sorry," I murmured against his skin. "I didn't mean to hurt you."

He turned around to face me. When I saw the blissed-out grin on his face, I didn't feel as guilty about the bite.

"It's okay. I kind of thought it was hot," Sam admitted. He reached out a hand to grab my neck, pulling my face in for a kiss. "My turn to clean us up. Stay here."

After we were settled and wrapped around each other again in bed, Sam idly twisted some of my curls in his fingers. Whenever his hands were in my hair like that, I felt like I was melting into a puddle of relaxation, and this time was no exception.

Just before I drifted off to sleep, I remembered something.

"Oh, I meant to tell you I have news about the restaurant." I yawned and snuggled deeper into the pillow.

I heard him shift in bed and prop himself up on his elbow.

"What?" he asked.

"It's a long story. Remind me to tell you tomorrow," I explained. "They want it to open in about six weeks though, so don't let me forget."

Sam swiveled in bed to turn on the lamp. I hissed and shielded my eyes.

"Jesus, Sam. What's with the interrogation lights?" I grumbled.

"Wake up and tell me what the hell you're talking about," he demanded.

I tried to shake off the delicious half-sleep feeling I'd been falling into when the conversation started.

"Well, you have the final say, of course, but Tristan and Blue begged me to convince you to come open a restaurant at the vineyard. They want it to be somewhat gourmet to fit in with the expectations of a winery, but laid back to match their own relaxed style. The baby is coming in February, so they need someone they can trust to handle it all without expecting them to do anything. They'll be moving into their new house in two weeks, which leaves their cabin available for us to move into. I can write from anywhere, so it's up to you. You can think about it and talk to them if you want. Maybe Lacey would want to head up there tomorrow and spend Christmas with the crazies."

I yawned again and closed my eyes.

A heavy naked body landed on top of mine and the tip of a nose pressed against the tip of my own.

"Holy fucking shit, Griff. Are you serious?" he asked my crossed eyeballs.

"Mm-hm," I responded, feeling my cock wake back up under his.

"And you'd be willing to move out of the city?" he asked.

"We can still come back in regularly to volunteer and see our friends, but yeah. I love it at the vineyard. You already know that," I replied.

"Let's wake Lacey up early and get on the road. She'll love your family, and your parents will be thrilled if we surprise everyone."

"Mm-hm," I agreed, feeling myself drift again. "If we're getting up early, we should get some sleep though."

"And we can announce our engagement to everyone too," Sam said. "Your family will go apeshit. Just think, they get to plan another Marian wedding."

My eyes shot open and I sat bolt upright, almost knocking him over.

Sam saw the look on my face and started laughing so hard he snorted.

Jesusfuckingchrist.

Another Marian wedding.

45

Sam

I TRIED TO WARN MY SISTER ABOUT THE MARIAN IDIOSYNCRASIES before we arrived at the vineyard, but there was really no way to adequately describe the unique, ah, dynamic of their particular clan. So it ended up being more of a trial by fire.

As soon as we entered the lobby on Christmas Eve, huge cheers rang out.

"They're here!" Simone cried.

Rebecca came forward to wrap Griff in a tight hug, and Thomas stepped forward to give me a hug and welcome Lacey to the family gathering.

"We're so glad you got back to town in time to join us," he said with a friendly smile. Everyone was gathered around the huge stone fireplace as usual. Pete and Ginger's girls sat at a table playing domi-noes with Irene, but I didn't see Tilly or Granny anywhere. I assumed they were off looking for some wine.

Ginger breastfed the baby under some kind of modesty cover

that looked like a backward cape, while Pete lay fast asleep on the floor with his head on a sofa pillow.

There was a woman I didn't recognize sitting with Thad, and I suspected she was Tristan's cousin, Sarah. Thad was looking at her with the goofy grin of a lovesick puppy. I knew that grin because I sometimes felt it on my face when I looked at Griff.

"Come on in, guys," Tristan said, standing up from his spot on the sofa where Blue had been leaning against him. "I have room keys for you over here."

I pointed Lacey in the obvious direction of the tree so she could put the few presents we brought under the tree with all the others.

Griff was busy greeting all his family members, so I grabbed the room keys from Tristan and walked back over toward the group to hand one to Lacey.

Aunt Tilly walked up from the direction of the ladies' room just in time to catch sight of the ring on my finger. Her eyes lit up with excitement.

"Called it!" she proclaimed to the crowd.

"Called what?" Blue asked.

As Tilly took a seat in a comfortable chair, she pointed back over her shoulder toward me and said, "Griff put a cock ring on Sam."

The entire room went silent while everyone tried to work out what was wrong with that sentence.

Griff looked over at me in horror, as if I'd had something to do with his great-aunt going off the rails. I widened my eyes back at him. *Do something.*

Teddy barked out a laugh and asked Tilly to repeat what she'd said. Before she had a chance to open her mouth, Griff finally found his voice.

"*Engagement* ring," he corrected. "I proposed to Sam last night and he accepted."

The room erupted into chaos—sighs of relief, cries of

excitement, and hugs offered in congratulations. Simone begged us to tell everyone the story of how Griff proposed, which somehow led to the story of how Granny and Irene got engaged.

"Oh shit. Tell them what happened later that night, Reenie," Granny said.

Irene blushed a deep red and looked away with a secret smile. "Let's just say we lost the ring in an overly lubricated situation."

Granny laughed so hard she slapped her knee. "You'll never guess where it turned up."

Everyone groaned and tried to stop her from telling us.

Maverick saved the day as usual. "So, Derek and Jude, what about you two? Are you ever going to make it official?"

All eyes swiveled to the men curled up together in the corner of one of the sofas. Derek's eyes sparkled while Jude ducked his head in embarrassment.

"What do you say, Bluebell? Should we tell them?" Derek said with a wink.

"They're going to kill me," he muttered.

"Don't worry, babe. I'll protect you."

"Okay, fine," he sighed. "We snuck off to Hawaii over Labor Day and have been married for months. We didn't want to tell anyone and have the media go nuts. Sorry we didn't say anything earlier," Jude said sheepishly.

The group erupted again and everyone mobbed the two men to give them congratulations.

At one point I heard someone ask why Hawaii and Jude said something about their previous trip there being less than romantic.

That's when I saw Tristan's cousin Sarah approach Maverick where he'd been busy texting someone.

"You're Maverick, right?" she asked. "We met at Simone's almost-wedding."

"Yes," he said, looking up from his phone to give her his trade-mark friendly smile. "Nice to see you again, Sarah. How's Boston?"

"Well, cold, if you want to know the truth." She laughed. "But I moved here a few weeks ago to work at at St. Vincent's."

"Oh, really? My boyfriend works there," he said. "What will you be doing?"

"A fellowship in surgery. I'm excited. So far everyone has been really nice and welcoming, and it's great to finally be in the same city as Thad."

"Oh good, I know you guys have been doing the long distance thing for a while. It's hard starting over in a new place, though, so I'll have to invite you over for dinner one night and introduce you to Dave," Maverick said.

She laughed. "As long as it's not Dave Lassiter since he's apparently the one sleeping with all of the nurses." She saw Maverick's eyes widen and take in a breath as her words hit home. "Oh, but he's married I think," she said, backpedaling desperately. "To a woman. He's not gay… I don't think…"

Maverick smiled politely at her. "No. It's not Dave Lassiter," he lied.

Mav's nostrils flared as his phone buzzed and he looked down at the screen. "Sorry, Sarah. Gotta go."

As he walked away to find some privacy, Sarah blew out a breath and caught me eavesdropping.

"It's Dave Lassiter isn't it?" she asked.

"Yup," I said with a sympathetic smile before walking her over to introduce to my sister, who was busy talking to Griff's brother Jamie by a table with snacks and drinks set out on it.

Lacey looked like a kid in a candy store with all the personalities in the room, and I was reminded of the first time I'd been among this crew. I'd been in awe of how open and accepting they all were. How loving and devoted. The idea that I was going to be a part of this family made my eyes sting.

Griff came close enough for me to grab him and pull him into a desperate hug.

"Thank you for loving me, Fox. For trusting me," I whispered in his ear, lips brushing against his warm skin. "And for sharing your amazing family with me. I'm so lucky."

"Thank you for staying, Sam," he responded. "And for never giving up on me. I'm the lucky one."

Epilogue

Sam

Four Months Later

I CAME OUT OF THE KITCHEN INTO THE MAIN DINING ROOM OF the restaurant just in time to thank the last of our customers for the evening. They were a young couple who were spending the weekend at the vineyard for their first anniversary, and my pastry chef had enjoyed making a special dessert to help them celebrate.

After locking the door behind them and saying goodnight to everyone else, I exited out of the kitchen door into the fresh spring night. It was only half past ten and I was looking forward to seeing Griff at home.

He'd been in the city for a meeting with his agent, and I was dying to know how it went.

As I walked the quarter mile to our cabin I thought about how much quieter it was in the country. Even though it was taking some getting used to, I loved the peace and quiet of the vineyard. We could actually see stars in the night sky and smell the earthy smells of soil and pine trees. Tristan had joined me for a cup of coffee that morning and shared his idea for planting a kitchen garden. He said he had several workers who could help me put it together. My head spun with ideas even though I knew better than to tackle it right away.

After taking the final steps to the front door of the cabin, I opened the door and stopped in my tracks.

There in the living room was my gorgeous fiancé holding a baby in his arms and singing a lullaby as he swayed from foot to foot with the rhythm of his song.

"Hey," I whispered.

Griff's head snapped up and his face lit up with a dimpled smile. "Hey, sunshine."

"How is the lovely Miss Ella tonight?" I asked, still maintaining a whisper in case our guest had succumbed to the melody. Griff had formed an unlikely bond with Blue and Tristan's new baby and was their go-to baby whisperer when they needed a break.

"She's great. I think Blue and Tristan were hoping to catch a nap. At least that was their word for it," he said with a wink before leaning over to kiss me.

He set her down in the small car seat we all called the baby bucket and fastened the straps loosely around her before standing back up and gesturing for me to join him on the sofa.

"I told Blue I'd bring her back over there in another hour or so," he said. "How was work?"

"It was fun. I made that scallop appetizer I had you try last week and it sold out," I said, kicking off my shoes and leaning into him. "Told you so."

"No, I told *you* it was probably my own natural aversion to putting giant squishy things in my mouth and not your cooking," he retorted.

I sat back up and grinned at him, words about squishy things going into his mouth right on the tip of my tongue.

"Shut up." He laughed, clapping a hand over my lips.

I pulled his hand away and kissed it before entwining our fingers and pulling him over to straddle my lap.

"Tell me about your meeting," I said.

"Everything is on schedule for the June release of the first book and the November release of the second. But that's not what she wanted to talk to me about. Scholastic wants to put them in their school book fairs, Sam," he said with sparkling eyes. "Imagine how many kids they can reach that way."

"Holy shit, Griff. That's incredible. Congratulations." I grabbed his face and kissed him. "I'm so proud of you. How do you feel?"

He chuckled. "Like it's too good to be true. While I was in the city, I met with my friend Jen at the *Chronicle*. Remember Ned's wife from that media party?"

I nodded, hoping we could skip past any further mention of that night.

"Her sister freelances for *Out* magazine and said they'd probably agree to do a feature on the book series around the time it's scheduled to release. Can you believe it?"

"Yes," I said, leaning in to kiss him. "Of course I can. Your graphic novels are important, Griff. They're going to make a difference in someone's life."

"Thanks. I never would have gotten up the nerve without your encouragement."

"Yes, you would have, but I'm happy to be along for the ride. Plus, when you're a rich and famous author, I can retire early and live a life of luxury being spoiled by my sugar daddy."

"No, but it occurred to me that with you working so close to home and me setting my own hours, we could think about having children one day," Griff said.

I was floored.

"Do you want children, Fox?" I asked.

Green eyes peered down at me. "I do. Do you?"

I couldn't help but laugh. "Little curly-haired Griff babies? Yes, please. Sign me up."

He grinned. "They don't have to be mine. I wouldn't mind them having your height and movie-star good looks. But you have to admit, I'm the better swimmer. We'd want them to be able to swim the 50-yard freestyle in under twenty seconds, right?"

I poked a finger in his ribs. "We'd want them to be able to cook for us in our old age, right?" I teased.

"Good point. You win." Griff laughed.

"I can't believe you just told me you want to have a baby," I admitted. "That's huge."

"Well, not right now," he said. "I'd like to get married first. If someone would just get off his ass and choose a menu, for god's sake, maybe we could actually have a wedding. I'm starting to feel like we might just have to sneak off to Hawaii like my brothers did.

"You know as well as I do the invitations already went out. June first, Foxy. Be there or be square. I promise there will be food. I'm more concerned about one of the grooms failing to show up," I teased.

"You'd better show up. I changed my tattoo for you and everything."

He knew I wasn't referring to myself, so I didn't correct him.

"What do you mean changed your tattoo?" I asked, nerves swirling in my gut. I loved his tattoos.

"Nico had some time to fit me in, so I had him tweak it just a little."

He climbed off my lap and stripped off his shirt, turning so I could see his dragon. As usual my eyes jumped to its glowing heart.

Only this time there was no cage around it.

Letter from Lucy

Dear Reader,

Thank you so much for reading *Grounding Griffin*, the fourth book in the Made Marian series! I can't wait to help more of the Marian brothers find love in future Made Marian novels.

Be sure to follow me on Amazon to be notified of new releases, and look for me on Facebook for sneak peeks of upcoming stories.

Please take a moment to write a review of *Grounding Griffin* on Amazon and Goodreads. Reviews can make all the difference in helping a book show up in Amazon searches.

Feel free to sign up for my newsletter, stop by www.LucyLennox. com or visit me on social media to stay in touch. To see fun inspiration photos for all of my novels, visit my Pinterest boards.

Happy reading!

Lucy

About the Author

Lucy Lennox is a mother of three sarcastic kids. Born and raised in the southeast, she now resides outside of Atlanta finally putting good use to that English Lit degree.

Lucy enjoys naps, pizza, and procrastinating. She is married to someone who is better at math than romance but who makes her laugh every single day and is the best dancer in the history of ever.

She stays up way too late each night reading M/M romance because that shit is hot.

For more information and to stay updated about future releases, please sign up for Lucy's author newsletter on her website.

Also by Lucy Lennox

Made Marian Series

Borrowing Blue, Book 1
Taming Teddy, Book 2
Jumping Jude, Book 3
Grounding Griffin, Book 4—in your hot little hands.
Made Marian #5 - Maverick's story—coming early March 2017.
Made Marian #6 - Dante's story—coming April 2017.
Keller—A Made Marian Short Story - available for free here (http://bit.ly/5fabfree).

Be sure to sign up for the newsletter for release news!
www.LucyLennox.com

Read an Excerpt from *Borrowing Blue*
Book One in the Made Marian Series

About *Borrowing Blue*

Blue: When my ex walks into the resort bar with his new husband on his arm, I want nothing more than to prove to him that I've moved on. Thankfully, the sexy stranger sitting next to me is more than willing to share a few kisses in the name of revenge. It gets even better when those scorching kisses turn into a night of fiery passion. The only problem? Turns out the stranger's brother is marrying my sister later this week.

Tristan: I have one rule: no messing with the guests at my vineyard resort. Of course the one exception I make turns out to be the brother of the woman my brother's about to marry. Now we're stuck together for a week of wedding activities, and there's no avoiding the heat burning between us. So fine, we make a deal: one week. One week to enjoy each other's bodies and get it out of our system. Once the bride and groom say I do and we become family, it'll all be over between us. Right?

Blue

I didn't sit down at that bar intending to tell a perfect stranger my sorry-ass breakup story, and I sure as hell didn't expect to tongue-fuck said stranger before the night was over. But when my ex came into the bar all lovey-dovey with a damned twink, I couldn't help it. Three beers already sloshed in my empty stomach and I was feeling maudlin. There Jeremy sat, holding hands and staring moon-eyed at a young man who can only be described as a Gap model. One of those exotic red-haired ones with freckles that demanded to be highlighted in black-and-white photography. Jeremy himself was as handsome as ever and had a definite sparkle in his eye for the kid who was practically sitting on his lap. Fuck it. Whatever.

I had just arrived at the Alexander Vineyard for my sister's wedding. A full week of activities that seemed hell-bent on torturing my still-tender heart with romancey shit. After getting my room key, I had made a beeline to the bar to get a buzz on. It was no secret Jeremy would be there since he had been family friends of ours for years even before we started dating. I hadn't been prepared for him to bring a plus-one though, and when I saw them enter the bar two hours later, I was caught off guard.

Shortly after finishing my first beer, a man sat next to me and ordered a glass of wine. Caught up in my own pity party, I didn't notice him at first. But when I heard him call the bartender by name, I was intrigued. Who knows a bartender by his first name out here in the middle of the California wine country where the only thing for miles is the winery and attached lodge?

The man next to me was stunning. Probably in his early thirties like I was, maybe a few years older. He had dark hair and a dark shadow of a beard. He had almond-shaped eyes that were a striking light gray, contrasting against his dark coloring in a way that made him look otherworldly. My heart skipped a beat when he turned those eyes on me and raised an eyebrow.

When he opened his mouth to speak, a husky tone came out. "Enjoying yourself?" he asked.

It was so strange to have those light gray laser beams pointed at me that I almost, for a brief moment, turned to see if he could be talking to someone behind me.

"Not really," I answered, surprising myself with rude honesty.

The man barked out a laugh and the smoky sound surrounded me, plucking at all my tender spots and leaving them vibrating with a feeling I couldn't quite describe. I looked at my beer glass as if maybe it contained a stimulant instead of the local IPA I'd ordered.

"If you keep frowning like that, beer is going to start dribbling out of your mouth. Want to talk about it?" the stranger asked in a low voice. He looked a little bit like Stuart Reardon, an English fitness model I knew from work.

I sighed. "I just spotted my ex in the parking lot, so I came in here to drown my sorrows. Typical, pathetic, crying-into-my-beer scenario."

"Ah. I see. Sorry, man. That sucks."

"Yes, well, I'm mostly over it, but I just wish we didn't have to be under the same roof."

"That makes sense. I've been divorced for a few years but any time I run into my ex-wife around my family, I feel everyone's eyes on us. Even when you're over it, there are still plenty of shared memories that will always have a hold on you. How long were you together?"

"Three years. Been apart for six months now. I think it'll be fine, but who knows, really? We haven't seen each other since the break-up." I shrugged. "The stupid, immature side of me wishes I'd brought someone so I didn't feel so lame. I've dated a little but haven't met anyone I liked enough to bring around family." *And now I'm even more depressed because the sexy man at the bar is straight. It figures.*

"You wish you could make her squirm a little then? See what she's been missing?" he said.

"He's a he, not a she. And I don't know about squirming. I guess maybe a little. But it's more I want him to know I'm okay without him. That I'm not pining away and crying in my soup, you know? I get it. My family worries about me being alone. They want me to be happy. But it's not like I can just produce a life partner out of thin air to make them feel better. I need to get through this week and then I'll be out of the country for a while with a new job." I had been given a huge promotion at work that necessitated me moving to London for a few years. My flight was scheduled to leave San Francisco the following Monday.

"I know exactly what you mean. After Sheila and I divorced, my family looked at me for a long time with those pity eyes. Can't fucking stand that. My brother is the worst. He still keeps trying to set me up on dates. As if I won't be happy or complete until I find someone like he has."

I widened my eyes at him. "Exactly. God, your brother and my sister sound like the same person."

He laughed that smoky laugh. "And my mother still actually tries to get me to reconcile with my ex-wife. As if that would ever happen. No matter how many times I explain to her things were never that great with Sheila to begin with, my mom just tsks and tells me there's no such thing as a perfect woman. At this point, I really think she'd be happy to see me settle down with anyone. Just so she can stop thinking about it."

We smiled at each other in understanding.

The stranger reached out a hand to shake mine. "I'm Tristan."

"Blue. It's nice to meet you, Tristan," I said, shaking his hand. At the touch of his rough palm against mine, I felt that crazy fictional zing that people describe in novels. Was that shit for real? Nope, I'd probably been reading too much lately. Clearly it didn't work since it happened to me with a straight guy.

"Blue? That's an interesting name. Mind me asking how you came by it?" Tristan asked.

"Well, my name is Bartholomew but my oldest brother couldn't pronounce it properly when he was little. He ended up calling me Blue. It stuck."

"I like it. This sounds crazy, but it seems to fit you. Maybe it's your eyes," he said, studying my face. He shook his head and smiled. "Anyway, it's nice to meet you, Blue. Can I get you another beer?"

"Sure. I should probably eat something though. I came straight here from a crazy day at work in the city and haven't eaten yet," I said.

Tristan turned to the bartender. "Hey, Frank, would you get my friend here another beer and order us a couple of burgers with some of those homemade potato chips I like? Thanks," he said before turning his attention back to me.

"You work in San Francisco?" he asked.

"Yes, I'm in charge of graphic design for some fitness magazines."

"That sounds interesting. Do you like it?" he asked, looking interested in what I had to say.

"It's okay. I've been feeling a little jaded about it lately, so my boss gave me a huge promotion. I move to London in a week. Not sure if it will get my creative juices flowing again, but I appreciate the fresh start." Man, that sounded depressing. I tried to mitigate it with a smile, but it didn't seem to work.

Tristan's eyebrows came together in apparent interest. "What usually gets your creative juices flowing?"

I knew the answer immediately but I hadn't spoken the words out loud in years. Why not tell this guy? He was a stranger in a bar for god's sake.

"Sculpture," I said. One word. One word that might as well have been "heart."

Tristan's eyes turned warm and the sides of his lips began to turn up. "Tell me more. What kind of sculpture?"

"Metal mostly. But I like all of it. Wood carving, glassblowing, stone chiseling. I'd probably try ice sculpture if I wasn't deathly afraid of chainsaws."

"Are you able to sculpt in the city?" he asked.

"Not really. I sculpted in high school and college but gave it up after Jeremy and I got together. I've been thinking about picking it back up and trying again. Not sure there will be space enough when I move to London though," I confessed.

"Why did you give it up?"

I blew out a breath. "I listened to discouraging words from others. Unfortunately, I was young enough to take them to heart. It's only been in recent weeks that I've looked at the situation through an adult lens. Why in the hell did I let anyone discourage me from expressing a passion?" I shook my head in frustration at the kid I had been ten years earlier.

"We all do that at some point, don't we?" Tristan supplied, sounding as if he had specific knowledge. I wanted to ask him what passion he had that someone had tried to snuff out in him. Before I had a chance to get the words out, though, I saw Jeremy enter the bar with the twink on his arm.

Jeremy smiled and leaned over to kiss the young man on the mouth. After the kiss, the kid reached up to wipe Jeremy's lips, and that was when I noticed the wedding ring on his finger. My entire body went cold.

77779438R00168

Made in the USA
Columbia, SC
05 October 2017